ARVAH

We must each forge our own path through life

KEVIN F. BARBER

For Ba and Pa,

Guess what …

Time, you thief …

Leigh Hunt

Published by Kevin F. Barber

Cover painting by Johannes van Hest, 1912

ISBN: 978-0-6458709-0-9 (paperback)
ISBN: 978-0-6458709-1-6 (hardcover)

First edition, 2023

For book orders and enquiries,
email: kevinfbarber@outlook.com

A catalogue record for this
book is available from the
National Library of Australia

Contents

Prologue   1

Part I   3

   1   Welcome   5

   2   Childhood   9

   3   Madeleine   13

Part II   19

   4   ARVAH   21

   5   Maria   35

   6   Windows   51

   7   Jo   69

Part III   91

   8   Married   93

   9   Birth   103

  10   Couples   112

11 War   127

12 Family   138

13 Death   151

14 Dispute   157

Interchapter   163

Part IV   205

15 Return   208

16 Widowed   226

17 Chocolate   234

18 Expansion   239

19 Grandchildren   247

20 Together   252

21 Mass   256

22 Change   274

Part V   291

23 Time   295

Epilogue   299

Prologue

Vlijmen, 1912

A shy mid-morning sun cast silvery light on the town. Arthur was with his parents at the markets. While Wilhelmus and Hendrika van Hessel browsed, their five-year-old son grew bored. A rowdy group of older boys ran by, cheering and screeching, kicking and chasing after a tattered old ball. Arthur raced after them. The boys knew his brothers, so they were happy to include him and Arthur did his best to play along.

A strip of dazzling sunlight swept over his face. Arthur stopped and sought the source of the glare through squinting eyes. A man was fitting a sheet of glass into the face of a nearby building. The man worked swiftly, deftly, and Arthur stared in awe. The boys and their game were forgotten.

The glazier wiped the pane with a yellow cloth, then stood back to appraise his work. The window beamed back at him from the shadow of the building to which it now belonged. Satisfied, he shoved his tools into his satchel, slung the strap across his shoulder and disappeared down the street. Arthur, too, felt a sense of fulfilment – as if that transparent shield had patched a hole in him that he never knew existed. But his reverie was brief, for he heard his parents calling his name. His fascination was tucked away to ripen in the breast pocket of his growing ambition.

Part I

January 1988

Two gold rings gleamed upon his finger.

At his feet, shavings of glass and steel formed a fine, sparkling powder that was furrowed in dusty streaks across the factory floor like trails of salt. Hands clasped firmly around the timber handle of his broom, he steadily scratched at the sandy surface, sweeping the powder into thin lines and pyramid piles. He pushed it forwards and scraped it softly backwards. Forward, forward, forward, backward. Thrust, thrust, thrust, drag. Dust rose from the concrete like shimmering steam before settling again. He paused and rested. He stared at his reflection in the window. Had his clothes always sat so loosely? Didn't he once stand a little taller? Had his eyes always been so grey – so deeply hidden behind his glasses? He stared harder. Deeper. His white hair and white tie were lost – transparent in the slick morning sun shining through the glass. And yet the wrinkles ironed from his face by the dullness of the reflection almost fooled him into believing that time had been reversed, and the youthful, ambitious Arthur van Hessel had returned.

Arthur was the founder of ARVAH, the largest glass factory in the south of the Netherlands. The building itself was all squares and rectangles – brick, glass and steel. At one end there were two levels – offices and a breakroom on the upper, administration on the lower. The other end was all one level – the workshop. That's where Arthur was. Sweeping. Sweeping for the sake of sweeping. It was early morning and he was all his own company.

The room had fallen silent after the rhythmic echo of his sweeping ceased. A sudden shortness of breath had forced him to pause, and in that moment he thought several curious thoughts – the thoughts of an old man, he supposed. First a name. Then a face. He shifted them aside and drifted deep into the coffers, as far back as he could, to when and where it all began. Memories played through his mind like a series of silent films, flickering through dust and chattering with incoherent static. He fixed his grip around the broom and swept time and place and mess away. The answer lay somewhere among the rubble of the past, and he had to find it before the pillars of his mortality collapsed upon it forever. He had to dig and sweep. Rend. Churn. Sift. Search. And so, he surrendered to his whim and let his mind wander into the past, lulled by the almighty pull of nostalgia and contentment.

1

Welcome

Andre and Bauke bounced from their beds, met in the hall and burst together through Arthur's bedroom door. He was already awake, sitting up in bed by the light of his candle.

'What was that?' said Andre.

'I don't know,' answered Bauke.

'Did you hear it too?' asked Arthur. His brothers' rooms were on the front side of the house, overlooking the street, but Arthur's was at the back and had a view of the garden and the acres of farmland beyond it. Andre quietly guided the door shut with the handle held down, then shuffled over to Bauke. The pair were soon crouched either side of the window.

'Come on, Arthur,' Bauke said. 'Come and look with us.'

Arthur was reluctant, but he climbed from the covers, fumbled with his glasses and took up a position between his brothers on the floor. They tucked themselves up behind the drapes and peeped, one, two, three, over the sill and into the black, black glass. Suddenly, the door groaned open behind them. In a panic, the boys slid their backs to the wall and drew their knees tight to their chests. Arthur held his breath. But his brothers kept breathing, softly, and he found a slight comfort in the sound of it. An inky outline filled the void and creaked its way across the room towards them. Then their mother's voice whispered, 'Boys, get away from the window! Soldiers!' The obedient boys crawled from behind the drapes. In the candlelight, Hendrika's face was creased with fear.

'Sorry, Mother,' Andre began. 'We heard a noise and—'

'Yes, yes, I know, dear. Now hush . . . I know,' she replied. 'Your father is aware. He has Wolf with him. Everything will be fine, but hush, we need to be quiet now.'

'Let me go, I could take them,' announced Andre.

'Me too!' said Bauke. 'I could help! Let us both go.'

'And me,' said Arthur.

'No way!' said Andre. 'You're way too small.'

'You're all too small,' their mother told them. 'Now hush, boys. I'll look and tell you if I see anything.' Hendrika crept to the window. She pressed her back to the wall and slowly gathered the fabric in, fold by fold, until she could feel the coolness of the black glass breathe upon her face.

'Sorry, boys, there's nothing to see, I'm afraid. Perhaps we should just—'

But she didn't finish. The backdoor crashed shut and there was a clamour of hasty voices below them. Hendrika hurried to the bedroom door and stood guard. The boys were tense and stone-faced.

'Mevrouw van Hessel! Hendrika! Are you there?' a dusty male voice called as it climbed the stairs. Arthur immediately knew that it was his family's gardener, Wolf, a scruffy man who always smelled of the earth. His presence reassured Arthur.

'Ja, Wolf! Yes!' Hendrika replied. 'Is it safe to come out?'

'Yes, Mevrouw, there is no danger. Bring the boys. Their father has requested it.'

It was 1914. Arthur was eight, and war had broken out in Europe. Like all children, he was too young to understand it. And on that night, he found himself, with his brothers, parents, gardener and maid, all packed into the parlour with a family none of them had ever seen before.

'Everyone, please allow me to make the introductions,' announced Wilhelmus, the head of the household. He was usually a man of very few words, but when he spoke, he did so to great effect. He smelled of his shop – of cigars and coffee and wine. 'For our guests, this is my wife, Hendrika. And these are our sons: Andre is the eldest, followed by our second born, Bauke, and our youngest, Arthur. We also have Marinus, who you have met—'

'But we call him Wolf!' called Andre, earning his father's scowl and Wolf's crooked grin.

'—and our maid, Anneke.' Wilhelmus paused a moment to change the focus of his address. 'And this is the van Essen family. They have fled their home in Mol, and having heard of the van Hessel family on their travels, have sought refuge here with us. Boys, you will address this gentleman as Mr van Essen and this lady, his wife, you shall know as Mrs van Essen. And these are their daughters, Anna, Alice, Irma and little Maria. We will share with them what we have. Now . . . Hendrika, could you take the boys back to their beds? I'll have Anneke prepare our guests a light supper before showing them to their rooms.'

Before securing Andre and Bauke into their own beds, Hendrika tended to Arthur.

'Getting the three of you to sleep at the same time has never been easy,' she said. 'Even at the best of times.' To Arthur, his mother smelled of books and liquorice, and her scent alone brought him a sense of safety and calm.

'Do you think the van Lessons will be with us for long, mother?'

'I believe it is "van Essen", dear. Who can say how long they will stay? But they are welcome to be with us for as long as they need to. Wouldn't you want them to do the same for us if we had to flee?'

'Will we have to flee, mother?'

'I don't know, dear. I really don't know.'

2

Childhood

The van Hessels were not made to flee.

It was a few days after Germany had invaded Belgium when the van Essen family arrived, and they stayed with Arthur and his family until the war ended. For Wilhelmus and Mr van Essen, the war was an interminable political madness, but to the children, who remained relatively sheltered from the reality of war, the whole mess seemed like a surreal and distant adventure.

During this time Maria and Irma were too young to attend school. Anna and Alice went to the girls school in Vlijmen, while Arthur and his brothers went to the boys school. Initially, the van Hessel boys avoided the van Essen girls and the children all kept to themselves. But time tested them and, day by day, they found ways to play. They would hide and chase and tease and trick, and at times they would bicker and cry and threaten. Then they would forgive and forget, and fight, and repeat the cycle over and over.

Wilhelmus rarely spoke about the war. When he did, he told his sons that, being a rural town on the outskirts of the much larger 's-Hertogenbosch, they were lucky that it didn't affect the day-to-day life of people in Vlijmen very much. The townspeople were on rations, but his business, Hestana, was manageably unaffected. People still wanted coffee, tea and tobacco, and his shop provided those. The van Hessel and van Essen families were never short of food either, as Wilhelmus owned a lot of the land around the village, though he never worked it himself. On the whole, the war was a tragedy that unravelled itself around them and, eventually, resolved without them.

When the war ended, Arthur and his family attended a party. And at that party it rained – for that was the principal feature of Arthur's memory of that day. Or rather it half-rained, for it only fell across one side of the estate. Arthur and his brothers, as well as many of the other children, ran through the house, racing from end to end, through front and rear doors, with a kind of crazed excitement. The adults there were not at all interested in the whole thing for they had more pressing matters at hand, but the children were incredulous. They searched along the side of the house to find where the rain stopped and where it started. A rainbow had half its reach erased. The sky was in two parts – half blue, half grey; half clear, half cloud, like the shoreline where ocean meets sand. When they found the dividing line, they stood along it and laughed. One foot in and one foot out. Then they jumped back and forth, crossing and recrossing the border between drizzle and downpour. It makes sense that all things must start and stop somewhere, and for Arthur, on that day, it was just a matter of finding where that point was.

Sometime after that, when Arthur was almost twelve, a boy named Alfred and some of his friends were planning to skip school for the day to go on what they considered to be a grand adventure. The war was finally over and everyone, it seemed, felt that every hazard in the world had been dispelled with it – as if a new order of perpetual peace and security had established its reign. The friends invited Arthur along, their faces beaming with excitement. It seemed the war had made them grow up faster than nature intended and this behaviour was born of a suddenly acquired sense of safety. But at the same time, they were rebelling in silent protest – retaliating against the adult world of work and responsibility that awaited them. They wanted to cling a little longer to the remnants of their stolen childhood.

Instead of travelling east to 's-Hertogenbosch, the boys cycled west for what Arthur imagined to be almost three hours before they decided they had journeyed far enough. They had found a small river system, or rather, an offshoot, a backwater, only a short distance away from the road. The water was the creamy greenish-brown of a turtle's shell and pimpled by the insects that flittered about, their buzz and click swimming in the hiss of the reeds and the sigh of the sleepy stream. They let their bikes nap by the bank in the deep, frost-kissed shade of a weeping willow tree. One of the boys was named Ruud and he had brought two fishing poles. When they had arrived, he had withdrawn a soup spoon and with it busily dug around in the mud at the water's edge until he unearthed a clew of worms. He cradled a crumbling cluster of wriggling dirt in his upturned hand and smiled triumphantly before shaking them free on the greasy clay. Then he threaded several of them onto the hooks, one at a time, and cast the lines into the water. Still itching to explore, Alfred and Pieter went for a walk. Arthur remained with Ruud, a little unsure of what to do.

It didn't take too long for Alfred and Pieter to return, and when they did, they seemed disheartened and disappointed. They sat next to Arthur and Ruud for a minute or two, but watching lifeless poles suspend a slack line doubled their boredom. Their fantastic adventure seemed to be a lot less exciting than they had hoped. The wind was slow and damp in the shade. Even the river taunted them as it washed by nonchalantly, as if there was nowhere it needed to be other than where it was in that moment. The hustle and bustle of the town seemed distant. They briefly entertained the idea of stripping off their clothes and going for a swim, but their enthusiasm waned and, feeling defeated, they decided to head home. They woke their sleeping bikes and prepared for the return journey.

One thing Arthur hadn't considered was Andre and Bauke telling their father that they hadn't seen their little brother at school that day. The thought never crossed his mind until he had made it back home and started walking up the path. The realisation hit him at once, an unexpected punch to the stomach. His brothers would have heard about what he and his friends were up to – there was no way they couldn't have. Any and all news, big or small, spread through the school like wildfire.

As Arthur sneaked inside, he readied himself for what was to come – but it never did! His parents greeted him in their usual way, his father as stoic as stone, and his mother as welcoming and as pleasant as the familiar chime of a church bell. He waited for the inquisition. He waited for the scolding. He waited for some form of consequence. But there was nothing. There was only one plausible conclusion: for whatever reason, his brothers had fashioned an alibi on his behalf. Perhaps they had helped him so that he would owe them a favour in the future – a deposit made in good faith, he guessed. Whatever the reason, Arthur respected it.

When they crossed paths the next morning, at two separate junctures, one for each brother, they needed no words to communicate their understanding. Arthur looked at Andre and Andre looked back at Arthur. Arthur gave him a nod. Andre gave Arthur a nod. That was all. His interaction with Bauke was the same. It was the beginning, he thought – he hoped – of what would be an unspoken pact of brotherly honour.

3

Madeleine

Arthur's first kiss was with a girl named Madeleine. They were fourteen. She was from Lille, France. Her family had come to Vlijmen for business. Arthur and Madeleine's fleeting foray into love and lust was brief, to say the least. But there was a physical attraction – although Arthur was too young and naïve to make much sense of it. What the two had was a healthy and natural curiosity. At church, Arthur would notice her looking at him from across the nave. He thought she was pretty and liked looking at her. Her eyes were the colour of autumn and seemed to absorb everything around her – alive with energy, as though she were seeing everything for the first time. Her hair was thick, dark and wavy, and never fell in a way that didn't look perfect. When he watched her in church, Arthur often thought how nice it would be to bury his face in her hair, to kiss the smooth white neck beneath and feel her soft feminine figure press against him from under the thick padded fabric of her coat. Her lips were supple, and the way they moved when she breathed seemed to summon him to them. He could only imagine how tender they would have felt against his own. Arthur fancied himself speaking to her – saying her name. It was such a pretty name and he liked the way his mouth was made to move when he said it. It was like his fumbling boyish lips were pushed through the motions of kissing simply by saying 'Madeleine'.

One still, dry winter Wednesday, Arthur was set to visit Hestana As he arrived outside the shop, Madeleine stepped from within, carrying a brown paper bag. Having never considered that she could exist beyond the walls of the church, it took Arthur a moment to realise who she was. While he worked on solving the mystery, the smell of coffee floated in the air around them. He had, at least, worked out what was in the bag. As she stepped closer, he cast his eyes to the snow-speckled pavement. A pair of shiny shoes, black as buttons, stood before him. He was all nerves as he followed the line from feet to the face. The shape of her calves was scarcely disguised by thick black stockings. A black knitted dress came down to her knees. But what caught Arthur's eye was her red coat which, slightly open, revealed the top of the dress, which was almost like a long, fitted sweater. The outfit complemented her pale face, which was aglow with her usual radiant enthusiasm. Finally, a black felt beret nestled naturally atop her hair. His mouth moved through the shapes of a kiss as he remembered her name. He managed an awkward smile and Madeleine smiled back. It was all the incentive Arthur needed to finally break the silent nature of what he supposed to be their mutual interest in one another.

'Hallo.'

'Goedemorgen, Arthur.'

As they talked, they walked, and soon they unwittingly found themselves staring at a construction site for a new factory. It looked like nothing more than a large, empty shed, and with the war over, everyone was used to seeing new buildings sprout from the earth as if overnight, like massive man-made mushrooms. Stopped and silenced, they stared at it together, or rather, beyond it, because the sky that had maintained a steely shade through the morning was now consumed by a wave of ravenous clouds, rolling heavily and ready to rain. This time, it seemed, the dividing line had found Arthur and it would cross over him.

They watched a while longer, until the sky above them was dark and rumbling. They couldn't help but look at each other and laugh at their situation. They could have avoided the rain, but neither of them moved. Arthur didn't move because Madeleine didn't move. He couldn't understand why she didn't move, but as he watched her watching the clouds roll over them, he saw she was transfixed by them. They were at that age when boundaries are to be tested, and perhaps the situation they were in simply prompted her to conduct an impetuous adolescent experiment. It was no surprise to either of them when the rain started, thick and fast. It was cold and sharp and stung their hands and faces and soaked through their clothes in seconds. Yet they remained, planted to the spot, until Arthur felt a cold, slippery hand grip his. It pulled his arm without warning and he had to run to keep their hands from coming apart. Madeleine was making for the shelter of the construction site, taking him with her. A short verse of excited laughter escaped her and flowed through him. In that moment, she could have dragged him anywhere. Arthur had surrendered himself to the other side of the line – into whatever the next stage of his life would bring him – to find whatever new wonders awaited him there, where he must leave his childhood behind.

The roof was watertight and provided refuge from the battery of rain that had dowsed them thoroughly. Though it could no longer reach them from above, it persisted in its quest to find them. So, without walls to keep it out, the water slithered through countless shallow channels carved into the muddy earth. It snaked its way along until it arrived and pooled into pots of murky water. Arthur shed his jacket, for it had grown unbearably heavy, rain laden as it was. He peeled it from his undershirt and draped it over a section of scaffolding to dry – or to at least prevent it being ruined any further. If it had not been soaked through, he would have offered it to Madeleine, but instead he helped her out of her coat and placed it next to his.

Madeleine sneezed suddenly, though it hardly seemed a sneeze at all, more a quick hiss like a candle wick pinched out between moistened finger and thumb. She still held the Hestana bag, and from it she withdrew a small packet of cigarettes and a box of matches – both inexplicably dry. She slid one slim white stick out of the packet, placed it between her lips and, sniffling, struck a match. The warm orange light coloured her face momentarily, passed its glow to the cigarette, and was cast into a puddle where it fizzled out with a wisp of smoke. She drew in a lungful, and Arthur watched the tip of the cigarette burn to life. She exhaled and disappeared for a moment behind a plume of smoke. When her face returned, she offered him the packet. He didn't say no, but instead gave a friendly, dismissive wave to indicate his answer. She held the cigarette between her fingers. Arthur took a casual step towards her, reached for the cigarette and looked at it. He could feel her watching him as he studied it. He placed it to his lips the way he had seen others do. He imagined that in some way he was kissing her, and with that in mind, he inhaled. He envisioned his lungs filling with the spirit of her. He held it, then let it go. She smiled a bemused smile. Arthur returned the gesture in kind. He closed his eyes and almost immediately felt her hands brush against his cheeks as she slowly slid his rain-specked glasses from his face. He watched, his half-blind eyes pried wide, as she placed his glasses on an upturned bucket. Arthur passed the cigarette back to Madeleine offhandedly. She took it, flung it to the ground to die, pulled his face towards hers with both hands and pressed her lips to his.

Arthur didn't know how to respond. He was stunned for a few seconds: overwhelmed by the way it seemed to shut him off from the world around him. His mind had stopped working. He must have shut his eyes, because the world seemed to go black. Every fibre of his being seemed to exist at his mouth. He felt her lips press onto his, softer than soft. Smoother than smooth. Nicer than he thought nice could be. He felt her small cold nose glide along his. And then he slowly returned. Puff for puff. The clamour of slanting sleet thundering onto the roof above him resumed its applause. The cold air lashed his wet clothes. He was relieved to learn that his body was still holding him upright. When he opened his eyes, he was looking at the pretty girl he knew from church. She was smiling at him with a perfect row of teeth, with dimpled cheeks and with eyes that sparkled like stars. Her hair was wet, yet still it hung in flowing waves around her face.

'You have a nice smile, Arthur,' she told him. 'You should smile more often. You're always so serious. And you sure do stare a lot at people – at me . . .'

'Dank je,' was all the reply he could manage.

'Why *do* you stare at me so much, Arthur van Hessel? Do you think I'm pretty?'

'I . . . I don't know,' he fibbed. 'I guess so, yes.'

Madeleine smiled her approval. She seemed older than him somehow, more mature – as if she had travelled further, grown up around older people, or simply possessed some innate wisdom beyond her years. It may have even been her mother's influence – not that Arthur knew her mother, but Madeleine certainly resembled, in many ways, a woman more than she did a girl. She should have been too young to have mastered the art of seduction – if that's what it was. It may have been all she had known and what she knew to be. To her it may have been simply normal behaviour: a perfectly natural and ordinary thing. Or perhaps she had known other boys before him. Perhaps she had known men. But Arthur preferred to think she hadn't. Or at least, not many.

Several months later, Madeleine and her family returned to Lille. She was too exotic to survive such a humble habitat as Vlijmen for long. Arthur didn't hear from her. They hadn't really spoken much in the first place. But ever since then, whenever he happened to hear that name, Arthur would think of her. And when he did, what came to mind wasn't so much an emotional reaction, but rather a sensory experience. It was the blurry light and the total dark. It was the sweet, rich smell of coffee, girl and tobacco smoke. It was long, damp hair, tender lips and chilled skin. It was a half-built promise that provided shelter from the rain. It was unfinished floors and unexpected downpours. And it was the way his mouth moved when he said her name . . . Madeleine.

Part II

January 1988

Two gold rings gleamed and mirrored two golden faces. The quick click of a door jolted Arthur from his daze. This, and the sound of feet and chatter, told him the first of the workers had arrived.

'Goedemorgen, Meneer van Hessel!' called the men, but Arthur did not meet their reply. Instead, he sent them a cursory glance and casually turned away and inward. He was too far in – too lost in the past to relinquish his grip on it.

Arthur took one last look around. Everything seemed like nothing – the nothing was everything. All he knew was that he wanted what he couldn't have. He felt closer to finding the answer. He saw his name branded on the walls, the machines, his workers clothes . . . AR – *Arthur*, VA – *van*, H – *Hessel*. His once grand ambition. Was *that* it? Was *that* the answer?

The mystery continued to vex him. Whose was the name? Whose was the face? Were they one and the same? He knew the answer lay somewhere in the past, and he had to find it. Hack. Dredge. Sort. Seek. To let the past return, Arthur fixed his grip on the broom and put it to use. He found new sand to shift. He scratched and he scratched at it. To the scuff, scuff, scuff of the broom, a memory was slowly roused, set upon a new stage. And as the workers started the machines and got to work, once again, he let his mind wander into the past, lulled by the almighty pull of nostalgia and contentment.

4

ARVAH

In 1924, a coffee-singed wind welcomed seventeen-year-old Arthur into town as he dawdled down the slowly changing street of his childhood. Along the way, he took several long pauses to admire Vlijmen. Smoke streamed from the farmers' and labourers' homes, which were scattered in rows and plots, brown bricked, white framed, and with steep tiled roofs the colour of earth and moss. As he walked, the icy breath of a northerly breeze whispered, sentence upon sentence, through the canopy of the centuries-old oak trees that lined the path. With each stop Arthur noticed something new. He had started to see things differently. Had his town always been so quaint? Beneath him, the pattern in the pavement was scarcely visible, concealed by layer upon layer of rust-coloured leaves.

His final pause stopped his stroll in front of the big house at Grootestraat 37. He tried to imagine how the house might have looked to a stranger. Like its neighbours, it was a brick house, but it was certainly larger. There were two main levels, indicated by their rectangular windows, and an attic with a central oculus below the roof's ridge. The property was fenced by black steel bars poised to skewer the sky, like a line of antique lances propped point-up. From the perspective of a newcomer – one unfamiliar with the street and town – Arthur tried to imagine, to guess at the kind of people who might live in such a house. He acted the tourist even as he approached the property.

'Hoi! Could a kind family shelter a weary traveller?' he called. The steady drone of cicadas filled the short silence before his name was returned.

'Meneer! Saint Christopher has guided Arthur home,' said Wolf, his timbre low and coarse.

'Thank you, Marinus,' came Wilhelmus's firm voice, from closer than Arthur had anticipated. Rigidly formal, Wilhelmus refused to adopt the nickname by which Marinus was more commonly and affectionately known – earned, despite his nature, for his scowling, furry, ruggedness. In his gruff manner, Wolf opened one of the two gates to let Arthur in from the leaf-covered pavement.

'Dank je, my good man,' Arthur said, remaining in character as a polite and curious traveller. The hinge bolt whined in its socket until the latch was caught with a confident clunk. The pebbles crunched and shifted underfoot as he strayed from the square-bricked path. The sun had set the horizon ablaze and it glowed like heated glass, yellow-orange-red, as it fell behind the fence railing.

For Arthur, his father was both the greatest platform and the greatest obstacle to success. He wielded a well-polished intelligence that sliced through nonsense like a cleaver. Arthur knew that his father's cynical practicality could serve his purpose well. His father would be his first hard sell.

As if carefully mapping the best route through turbulent waters, Arthur tried to anticipate the course of conversation, for he knew he would be met with many challenges. In his mind, he could say what he needed to say, and could control his reply. He could edit his rebuttal until he had established an unassailable case. Any victory must first be achieved within the mind. And in his mind, he knew he could win.

Arthur approached the porch where his father sat puffing his cigar, with a glass of red wine. He caught a fleeting glimpse of Wolf heading off to tend to some project or to give his masters their privacy. As for the rich scent of coffee that still suffused the air – that was Wilhelmus. Arthur knew his father's rituals well, and he knew Wednesdays were for roasting coffee beans. Wilhelmus had been awaiting Arthur's return for an hour – contemplating his son's decisions. Wilhelmus's eyes, gazing from behind his gleaming glasses, had fixed on Arthur as he wandered through the yard – on and off his father's path. Arthur knew he was being watched, like a hunter silently studying his prey. He was a mouse caught by the inescapable eyes of the owl. Wilhelmus was reading his movements . . . gauging his resolve . . . anticipating his arguments . . . searching for a weakness. All the while, fine strands of smoke slowly swirled upwards from the smouldering stub of cigar that sat wedged between his fingers. His hair was as white as wool, as thick as a brush and neatly combed. His short, ashen beard was well groomed. He was the picture of success – and he knew it. He whirled the wine with the slow gyration of his wrist, letting the dark claret lap around the glass before lifting it to his narrowed lips. He dampened his mouth before he spoke in notes that were deep and full.

'How did you fare in Gompel, son?' he asked with a cadence that lacquered his words – rich and befitting a man of his stature and self-importance.

Knowing his father well, Arthur took a moment to measure his response. 'I fared well. Better than I would have had I stayed at school in Den Bosch.'

'What about the company?' Wilhelmus questioned quickly, clearly displeased with his son's decision to leave school.

Arthur took a moment to consider his first impressions of Gompel's glass manufacturer. 'It will be a useful business connection,' he answered, flattening his pitch while his father remained unmoved in his chair. Arthur rethought his approach. His lenses caught the flare of the setting sun and the glare broke his father's hold on him. Wilhelmus lifted a stern hand to his mouth and took a long draw from his cigar. His unsmiling face sank into shadows behind a veil of silky smoke. Arthur seized the opportunity and continued. 'It shows promise, I think. Though it has not yet been open a year, it has already secured several large contracts.' He knew he had to present his father with a case from a place of logic and practicality. Seconds passed. Wilhelmus exhaled and fixed his look upon his son. Arthur knew that at least he had not lost the argument. He was prepared, for the time being, to accept a draw.

'Did you get what you were after?' Wilhelmus asked, apparently more interested in the burning head of his cigar than in Arthur's ventures.

'I believe so,' he said, keeping his composure. 'I suppose we'll see.' His sight was fixed. His body, braced.

'Yes, I believe so,' Wilhelmus replied as he stood from the bench. His eyes focussed again on the slowly sinking sun. 'We'll see.'

The morning chill lifted early and the day was likely to remain dry, warm and pleasant. Arthur felt especially focussed and took the opportunity to hone his craft and to trial the advice he had received from the glazier in Gompel.

After making a breakfast of milk tea and the bread his mother had baked a day earlier, he whistled contentedly to himself as he walked several doors down from Grootestraat 37 to the galvanised tin shed that he had rented and established as his office and workshop. It was a lustreless, dot-dimpled, tin box that occupied a narrow space between two large sheds, each adorned with boldly coloured signs. Unlike them, Arthur's shed attracted no special attention. It dissolved beneath the boundless ceiling of a concrete sky and sank into the grey landscape of steel, brick and cobblestones. Even so, for Arthur, it was the beginning of bigger and better things, and he was profoundly proud of it.

He turned the key in the padlock, released the bolt and slid the door open to the grinding sigh of metal on metal. Everything was arranged the way he had left it the day before. He found the light, made his way to the crate in the corner and released the rope that had fixed the glass in place. He lifted and lay and aligned a sheet onto the drawing board and carefully unpacked and propped the others against the timber frame that was fixed to the wall. He withdrew the steel wheel cutter from his satchel and set the head of the T square against the edge of the glass. He held it tight and guided the wheel along the lip, scoring the sheet with a shallow streak to make a nice clean cut. The glass squeaked in resistance, like wet skin on a soapy china plate. With a straight and subtle scar scratched upon its surface, Arthur applied a firm, constant pressure until the sheet snapped along the line. The edge was a little rough, so he rubbed it with a whetstone in long, flat strokes until it was smooth and faultless.

In the back corner of the workshop, though he didn't use it often, was one of his father's retired desks that found a new place furnishing Arthur's office. After making a few more practice cuts, he traded one tool for another and spent the rest of the day sorting through paperwork while contemplating how and where to make business connections. Arthur knew it was important to rehearse his trade, but years of being his father's son also taught him that to succeed in business, one must be organised and willing to work when others won't.

Wilhelmus was never a man to do things simply for the sake of his own amusement. If he saw value in something – a benefit, practical application or lesson – he would share it without hesitation. If not, he would discard it without a second thought. For this reason, his advice had merit.

With thoughts of his father's doubts heckling Arthur, afternoon faded into evening to a different sort of tune – the flick of paper, the scratch of a pen and the tapping of feet. It was eventually a beckoning breeze that told Arthur the sun had started to set. He glanced outside. Twilight ripped the satin sky into a bleeding ribbon of fire that tinged the room red. The men of the town would be returning home from building, crafting, dealing, farming, fixing, trading, weaving and working. With that in mind, he stacked, straightened, sorted and packed his things, readied his bike, locked his shed, and set out to find work. To promote his services to the good people of Vlijmen, Arthur pedalled from door . . .

'Goedeavond, my name is Arthur van Hessel—'

'Not today, thank you,' said Mr Hauer.

To door . . .

'I am a glazier, ready to cut and install glass for any project, large or small—'

'My husband isn't home at the moment, sorry. Do you have a card?' said Mrs de Bruin.

To door . . .

'If you know of anyone who is in need of my service, please tell them to remember the name: ARVAH.'

'Yes,' said Mr van Veen. 'Well, maybe . . . but . . . well, no . . . not right now.'

The last of the boys who had spent their day chasing after one another through the streets and parks were making their way home for supper when Arthur happened by the church. The air was light and quick and crisp, as most of North Brabant lay above sea level, and the evening seemed to hint at the impending winter. He whirred along the cobblestone road, which made his bike lurch and jut and shake in unpredictable ways. On occasion, Arthur's wheels would get stuck tracing worn-in grooves, and with his future prospects relying on the delicate transportation of glass, he was thankful for the relatively flat topography of the town. All the while, above him, in the rusted dusk of autumn, the 73-metre spire of the church of Saint John the Baptist seemed ominous and surreal. Its thirteenth-century architecture still revelled in its past – concealing dark and timeless secrets.

Arthur noticed a spindly man striding towards him. His motion was graceful and poised, as though running were a form of dancing, and he floated towards Arthur as if flown upon a seraph's wings. Arthur stopped, kicked out the bike stand and dismounted, ready to enact every good measure of etiquette he could muster.

'Good evening, Arthur,' said the man, his hand outstretched. Arthur was surprised to find that the man didn't seem to be short of breath at all and spoke with a voice younger than his face, but he was undeniably well mannered and elegant. With him, it seemed, talking was merely a simpler form of singing, and the way he sculpted his fine features meant that his face was one not easily forgotten. In the dying rays of sunlight, a golden halo seemed to form around his head and, on the breeze, Arthur caught his scent – something akin to sawdust and the odour of sanctity.

'And it is indeed,' Arthur replied, reciprocating the gesture to shake hands, mutely hoping the man would give him the name he had forgotten or never knew.

'I hear you are making a name for yourself in your trade. You call your business ARVAH, right?' He paused long enough for Arthur to prepare his answer but not long enough for him to give it. 'And I understand that you will meet orders to cut and fit glass,' the man stated kindly, yet still with the inflection of a question.

Arthur nodded with a hopeful smile. 'You have heard correctly, meneer.'

'Excellent! I knew I had found the right man. And your workshop . . . it's only a short way from your father's house on Grootestraat, right? I do believe I will have need of your services, if you have the time? Not now, but soon, if you may?'

'Of course!'

'Hoera! That's wonderful! I'll meet you at your workshop tomorrow morning, then? I am certain I know the one.'

'Tomorrow morning suits me perfectly.'

'See you then, mijn snelle paard!'

'Vaarwel!'

The man left, his name still not known – or not remembered, whichever the case may have been – and, standing in the street alone, Arthur was left to ponder why he had been called a 'fast horse'. But he didn't think on it long, for he suddenly became aware of the cool dark night that had settled upon the town. The warm yellow glow of life flickered through the windows of homes and businesses yet to close, and he felt a similar warmth, peace, hope and contentment ignite in him. It compelled him, with gentle affection, to return home to his family.

Saturday found Arthur awake before the day had begun. Though he would often start work before first light, his enthusiasm that morning roused him particularly early. He was compelled by prospect, eager to meet his first real customer and start taking measurements. Arthur knew that to build a positive reputation, he had to satisfy his clientele, work hard and complete the job quickly.

Careful to not wake the house, he slowly descended the staircase that groaned in practised protest as the timber echoed his footfall. Cool moonlight filtered through the windows and fell softly upon the lifeless room. The dining table and its coterie of chairs seemed lonely and forgotten, as if patiently waiting for company to grace their station once again. Beneath a cloth on the tea trolley, Arthur spied the butter cake his mother had baked a day earlier.

He cut a slice of cake and selected an apple from the basket, and then took a moment to look at the boy whose portrait adorned the parlour wall. Wilhelmus had painted it. Arthur was not yet five years of age, and yet it was clear that Wilhelmus had, in a way, already started shaping his son into the image of his own ideals. His hair, like his father's, had been brushed across his head – the only difference was the colour. Wilhelmus's transitioned between white and grey, like the ash from his cigars. Arthur's, on the other hand, was like the youthful brown bark of an oak tree. He stared at his younger self, who stared back out. However, the younger Arthur did not meet his elder's gaze as he watched him – not looking at his father as he painted him but, rather, casually beyond him. Arthur believed he had been looking at his mother. He'd wanted to smile at her but his father wanted him to remain serious, and Arthur was too disciplined to defy his father. Serious though Wilhelmus was, it seemed he had granted Arthur the hint of a grin – perhaps as a lasting remnant of his childhood innocence and naivety. The thing about the portrait was that, like all paintings, as Arthur grew older it had always remained the same, a constant reminder of who he once was. He also knew that, when his father passed away, he would inherit this time-mocking memento crafted by the man who he knew, in some small way, he was likely to become.

Then, like a fire iron prodding lazy embers until they flared, an electric jolt of ambition shook him free from his reverie and he was spurred to action once more. Revitalised by purpose and motivated by promise, he left the house at Grootestraat 37 and pushed through the front gate into the dawning day and the wide world that awaited him.

Together, Arthur and daylight arrived at his workshop. The first light of dawn struck the glass fastened in the frame against the inner wall wherein it reflected the eastern horizon. The reflection was ghost-like, hollow and dilute – the colour thin, dull. And therein is the very nature of glass. In ornate fashion, it detaches one thing from another. It brings them closer, but keeps them apart. Even so, Arthur knew he would always see the world best, for all its vibrancy and clarity, through glass.

While he waited for the man to arrive, Arthur, never one to relax while there was work to be done, busied himself with sweeping out what little remained of yesterday's mess. As the brush head's bristles scratched at the crumbs of crystal and dust, he suddenly discerned the distinctive secondary sound of scraping steel. He looked to the floor and spied, among the debris, a nail that had been bent to form an L shape. He picked it up and turned it through his fingers. As he did so, he assessed that its injury was not fatal. A well struck mallet could straighten it out. Yes, it could be given a second chance. It could be made useful again. He tossed it into an empty paint tin that had once kept a solution of solvent, and resumed sweeping. And as he swept, Arthur amused himself with thoughts of his place in progress. Western industry, influence and innovation had begun to infect Vlijmen with change, hope, wealth and prosperity. Arthur pictured his father as the forerunner of this, and himself, in many ways, as the perpetuator.

Arthur was working the broom in a repetitive pattern, a little lost in time, when, like the dust from his workshop floor, his thoughts were suddenly swept from his mind as he became vaguely aware that he had been whistling, and that a slender shadow had started stretching its way through the door frame. His sense of sight and sound were soon attracted to the song-like tune of a man's voice.

'It's the snelle paard! Goedemorgen!' bellowed the man with a friendly wave and a generous smile.

'Good morning, meneer!' Arthur said cheerfully, propping his broom to rest against the wall. 'And how do you do?'

'Hail to you, my good fellow. I fare finely, but it appears I must first apologise to you. It was awfully remiss of me to not give you my name yesterday. You see, so many know it and I rarely need give it, and knowing your father, well – I knew yours . . . so please know I am truly sorry. I humbly implore your forgiveness. My name is Frans – Frans Engelbrecht. I'm a builder, of sorts . . . or rather, more of an all-round tinkerer,' he raced fluidly, his words forged with finesse: well-shaped, polished and intonated.

'No, not at all,' Arthur replied. 'Perhaps it is my fault for being so reclusive.'

'Agh! You're young! It's hardly an error on your part. Anyway, let us move on and discuss matters of business. I have several new builds and repair jobs that will need glass fitted over the next several weeks. What do you say?'

Arthur was excited by the assurance of a promising commission and a wave of relief and optimism washed over him. He stuck out a hand and Frans took it with a genial grin. Eyes wide, Arthur answered, 'I say, we'd best get started!'

Frans handed Arthur a detailed list of what he needed and it didn't take long for Arthur to cut the glass to size. As fate had it, there was exactly enough to complete the first of the repair jobs. Frans had decided to run a few errands around town while Arthur worked, and he returned with impeccable timing. Arthur was giving the final sheet a polish when he heard Frans' golden voice warble its way in light lilting loops towards him.

'You work well, Arthur – like you've been doing nought but this for a thousand years!'

'Dank je, but that's really too much,' Arthur deflected. 'All the same, I'm honoured to hear such a flattering appraisal. Do you have far to travel? Will you need help with the transport?' he added as a thought after the first. Delight stretched its way across Frans' face. He was clearly grateful for having a solution to the problem he had neglected to consider.

'That would be fantastic! But surely it's too much to ask of you.'

'It's really no problem at all,' Arthur assured him.

'Well, it's settled then. I'll help you as best I can. Besides, you might teach me something along the way. And I'll never pass up an opportunity to learn . . . especially if it will save me employing someone else to do it next time!'

Having anticipated this very situation, Arthur had purchased a disused trolley from a local carpenter and, for a small additional cost, had him fashion a frame upon it to support the carrying of glass.

'Perfect!' said Arthur. 'I've just got to load this last sheet onto the cart and we will be ready to go.' With the glass secured, the cart looked like an artist's easel on wheels, supporting back-to-back transparent canvases. Arthur carefully wheeled the cart out of the shed and followed Frans as he led the way through town.

His place wasn't far from Arthur's workshop, and when they arrived Frans insisted on helping him install the sheets. He had designed the property with a side path that led to the road and was wide enough to fit a carriage. Arthur made mention of it to him while they worked and Frans explained that he had designed it that way to accommodate a motor vehicle. This casual comment about his preparations for the future offered Arthur a valuable lesson in foresight. He reasoned that they couldn't always live the way they used to, and those who innovate will be those who succeed. It's important for life's apprentices to learn the basics first, but as entrepreneurs, man must find better, often different, ways to do things.

While they worked, Frans managed to evade any discussion on the topic of himself. Instead, he directed all dialogue back to the subject of Arthur.

'Please don't misunderstand me,' Frans said animatedly. 'But you could have pursued your studies – am I right? Become a scholar of sorts? From what I understand, you were rather passionate about a range of subjects: politics, language, but art and geography, too. Even I have seen the way you watch the sky. What an education! You can play too, I bet! Let me guess – piano? All that aside, you could have inherited a great deal of fortune from your father. You could have claimed his success. I mean, you had yourself made from the start.'

He didn't need to finish on a question for Arthur to understand what he wanted to know. Before he answered, Arthur looked at the man again and realised that there existed a quality in him that was in him too. Ambition, pride, adventure, independence . . . if it was one of those specifically, he couldn't say, and perhaps it was a combination of them all. In truth, it could have been something different entirely. Whatever the case may have been, Arthur knew he could have simply turned the same questions back on him. But he didn't. He simply smiled back, and said, 'You're right, I suppose I could have, but I didn't – and I won't. I'm sure you can understand that.'

Before driving a nail into the sill timber, Frans had to read his young friend's face to measure his expression against the tone and nature of his words. In that moment, he understood that the two of them were cut from the same cloth. He turned back to the task at hand, plucked a nail from between his teeth, and readied his hand to strike. 'I sure do,' he said bluntly, as the end of his sentence was punctuated by the successive *thid-thid-thud* of his hammer.

5

Maria

On Christmas Day of 1928, Arthur was overcome with the feeling certain times of the year always manage to bring about in people – the feeling that diverts one's attention, no matter how fixed, away from work and towards thoughts of romance and sentimentality. When the van Essen family came to dinner, as they had done for as long as Arthur could remember, he noticed something different about the youngest of the family, Maria. It could have been the season, but that night he was struck, unpreparedly, by her glow – a kind of womanly warmth that emanated from her. Since she had arrived, Arthur had felt her eyes flick on and off him. To and from, and away. Back, and gone. It was soft and subtle, like a fly that kept coming back to the same spot on bare skin. At one point he returned a furtive glance, partly wanting to avoid her eyes and partly hoping to meet them. The last time they had met, he had not seen her as he did now. The little Maria who, only one year earlier, had sat smiling on his knee as he told her stories – as he would to entertain a child – had changed in undeniable ways.

As they supped, Arthur felt the caress of a cat. It rubbed against the leg above his ankle, slowly, thoroughly, as cats are wont to do. Only, there was no *cat*. There was only Maria. Arthur could perceive by the feel of it that she was unshod. She had pushed heel to toe and slid stocking from shoe. She had levered her leg and her foot had found his. Yet her gaze was fixed elsewhere. He reasoned that it must have been an accident. She must have been stretching. Her foot must have felt too hot or cramped. He was sure she didn't mean to find his leg with hers. As for recognising her mistake, she gave nothing away. Indeed, even while she playfully pawed at him beneath the table, she gave no sign of it above. No one was wise to it. And Arthur felt he was probably the dumbest of all. Then the cat fled, startled and chased away by noise or shadow.

While he silently hoped for its return, Arthur listened indifferently to a conversation between Andre and Alice about fashion trends. Then a dainty arm stretched across him, reaching for the drink in front of him . . . his drink! Maria's petite fingers curled around the glass. With an invitation plainly gifted, Arthur let his eyes meet hers, and there he stared in blank assessment while she replied in kind. She lifted the ale to her mouth and, with eyes shut and with lips puckered, sipped. So, so slowly, slowly . . . sipped. She placed the glass back down and bit and licked her lips. Her mouth was moist and smiling. She did it so naturally that the company gave her no notice. Arthur couldn't think of how to react. He masked his shock as best he could and simply smiled back. Ordinarily, he would have disapproved of sharing a drink quite so literally, but something about her behaviour invited an intimacy he enjoyed. The glass sat slowly dripping onto the table, frosty in parts where her hand hadn't reached, clear in those parts she had. Arthur placed his hand around it to overlap her print. He sought the mark left by her lips, and when he took his drink he indulged in the idea of her mouth against his. His muse distracted him from the chatter that continued around him, that was until it was all at once interrupted by a question.

'So, Arthur, how is business?' inquired Mr van Essen, who had been speaking to Wilhelmus about the details of his youngest son's prospects. Mr van Essen was a round-faced, bearded man with beady eyes and stubby fingers. In many ways, his appearance was very much the opposite to Wilhelmus's. The pair were an unlikely match – at least on the surface.

'As well as can be expected,' said Arthur. 'As a matter of fact, I have some business in Mol next month.'

Mr van Essen's eyes were livened with a spark of paternal pride. 'Some business in Mol, you say? Well, you're welcome to stay with us for as little or as long as you like. After all, you're practically family to us.'

'Thank you, I might just take you up on that offer.'

A moment elapsed before Mr van Essen spoke again. 'I don't think I've mentioned it yet, and it's not too important, but you might like to know that Maria will be boarding at school as of next month.' He looked at his daughter, whose disposition changed at his words. A stern look overcame him as he fixed his eyes on her. His mouth was shut and straight.

Maria dispensed with her concern for public appearances, and met her father with a childlike defiance. 'But Papa, I don't want to go. I like living at home.'

'Maria, we've been through this,' Mrs van Essen said from across the table. 'Please don't make a scene.' She had been in quiet conversation with Hendrika until she had heard Mr van Essen raise the subject.

'Yes, we've been through this. You are going!' Mr van Essen stated, the volume of his voice rising in flustered aggression.

'No! I won't go! I'll run away! I'll hide! I'll stay here!' Maria yelled as she slammed her fists upon the table. Cups and plates and cutlery jumped and clattered and shivered still. For a moment, all were stunned into silence.

'Let's not have this conversation now. It will spoil our meal,' Mrs van Essen proposed. 'But we will be discussing the matter again later . . . in private.'

Mr van Essen was about to say something to Maria that would undoubtedly upset her further, but Mrs van Essen quickly shot him a look that stopped his tirade in its tracks. She sent Maria the same look, and Maria sank into her chair and apologised to the table. The drama dissipated, and everyone returned to making a meal of small talk, punctuated by pauses to eat and drink.

A short while later, as the room buzzed with conversation and laughter, the earlier drama forgotten, Maria's voice, like the chiming of a cat's collar bell, sought Arthur's attention.

'Hallo, Brother.'

'Good evening, Maria.'

'Could I talk with you later – just the two of us?'

'Of course,' Arthur assured her. 'Yes, of course you can.'

After dinner, Arthur and Maria slipped outside while their brothers and sisters stepped into the parlour and their fathers smoked cigars at the table. Their mothers busied themselves in their own way – discussing the lives of their children, plans for tomorrow, and days past. How Andre and Bauke entertained the van Essen girls, who can say? There was likely no natural attraction between them, so they would have simply practised a routine of social etiquette – despite Andre's crass gift for conversation. Alternatively, they may have separated, Arthur's brothers with their father and Maria's sisters with their mother. But none of that concerned Arthur. All that mattered was that he was let alone to be with Maria, if only for the briefest of moments.

The night was bright and cool. Arthur and Maria walked a little way down the path before they stopped at a tree, garbed in its shimmering moonlit shawl. The breeze washed by them as, after a moment of dawdling, Maria looked him in the eyes and went to speak. She held, in her modesty, his full attention. Then she stopped. Her eyes, suddenly lacquered grey like a pair of cat's eye marbles, shone with sadness.

'Maria? Whatever is the matter? You look like a lost little kitten.'

'Sorry, Arthur. I'm a little out of sorts this evening. And I'm quite embarrassed because it's for such a silly reason.'

'No, no, no! There's no need. Please don't feel bad about it, Maria. I'm sure it isn't silly at all. I'm sure if you tell me what's on your mind, it won't feel as bad as all that.'

She hesitated for a moment, but the delay helped her. 'Well, it's just that I am being sent to live at school next year and it's really not fair.' Arthur twisted away to escape the sudden seduction he felt in watching her pretty, pouting face, and by suddenly noticing the womanly scent of her perfume.

'You know, I think you'll be fine,' he replied, collecting himself.

'Do you?' Her words were quiet – almost a whisper.

Arthur turned back to face her. 'Certainly! You may even have fun! Just think of all the friends you could make!' But his contention was brushed aside with an air of juvenile disinterest.

'Will you visit me when you come to Mol?' she asked.

'Yes, by all means. I said to your father that I would.'

'No, not my family . . . just me. Would you see . . . only me?'

'I'm sure I could,' Arthur replied after a moment of indecision. Maria's countenance softened and seemed to assume that all powerful, all seductive, seasonal glow. She stared blankly at him, the hot emotion slowly cooling. Without planning it, he pulled her close. It was because it was her. It was her and who she was to him. Had it been anyone else, Arthur could have distanced his emotions. Maria was impulsive – perhaps too impulsive, chronically naïve – and he knew it. But it was that very quality that he found so endearing. He ran his hand through her thick brown hair and felt the warmth beneath it. The clouds were stretched thin, as if sketched by pencil, as they sailed like listless lanterns near the cool blue moon. A muffled murmuring came from within the house and floated on the night. All but Maria seemed cast into shadow. Arthur soon realised that he was holding her hands in his. Her porcelain skin reflected the silver-blue light. Her eyes shimmered like glass and caught the brightness of the night sky.

Suddenly, her voice assumed a tender tone. She had one more question to ask. 'Can I write to you?'

Her question undid him. He had to respond, this time, without a hint of hesitation and before her boundless innocence corrupted him.

'Maria . . . I would love for you to write to me.'

The two returned to company. Wilhelmus was stood talking to Mr van Essen who was, by now, well warmed by his wine. Though he masked it well enough, Wilhelmus twitched almost imperceptibly, like a rabbit's nose when it senses danger in the air. He stole a stealthy glance in Arthur's direction as if to ask him something, but decided against it. Arthur reckoned that his spending time with Maria may have been worrying his father.

Arthur moved to a window that, during the day, offered a generous view of the yard. At night, however, the view was veiled in darkness and so he simply stared, past his reflection in the glass, into the world hidden in front of him. Before long, Maria sidled over and stood beside him. He could still feel the ghost of her young hand in his. They wanted to look at each other, but instead they shackled their eyes to the darkness beyond. They idled with indecision. Arthur waited for her to look at him, yet he couldn't look at her. He wanted to, but instead he had to stand next to her, knowing that he could not openly console her. He could not hold her. He could not *have* her to himself. He could have spoken to her, he knew that much, but he couldn't bring himself to speak the words she needed to hear. His eyes found his reflection – faint and hollow and incomplete. He could tell that Maria had started doing the same, but, of course, he couldn't know how she saw herself. They stared, into the pane, and found each other's timid, reflected gaze. A fleeting smile flickered across their faces.

Arthur could sense their collective return from the surface of the night and suddenly felt the resolve to speak to her. He shifted slightly and prepared to whisper in her ear, but had little idea what to say. While he searched, she welcomed his cheek with cool, soft lips. She shied away and smiled nervously through the emotion welling up inside her. Her lips parted and two words floated towards Arthur like music.

'Goodnight, Brother.'

Maria had him abstracted. They had been corresponding with one another since a few days after Christmas and, in his most recent letter, Arthur let her know that he would be making a trip to Mol. He had an order of glass from Gompel's glass company and so he suggested they meet somewhere for food or coffee and conversation. Arthur told her that he wanted to hear about her transition to boarding school, and he figured visiting her might offer her some form of short respite from the dreary dormitory life she had complained about in her letters. But he didn't confess the whole truth. He didn't mention his other, more selfish, reason for wanting to see her.

Arthur had borrowed a friend's truck for the expedition. After what was a rather ordinary journey through several small towns and along roads that cut through fields and farms and forests, he had arrived in Mol by lunchtime and had checked into his reservation at a rather unremarkable hotel. He wasn't procuring his shipment until the following day, so he decided to spend his time walking about town, if for no other reason than to distract himself from his attentions to Maria. Before he left, he made arrangements with the honest-faced man at reception.

'If my friend is to arrive in my absence, you must let her know that I will be returning momentarily,' Arthur explained. 'Please, permit her to wait for me in my room.'

The man was an accommodating fellow and graciously accepted his mission without reservation.

Beneath a lavish blue sky, several people on bikes cycled by at a purposeless pace. A cluster of clouds collected in the east, but their cool, shifting shade was far away. Children romped and raced and rolled and rollicked on luscious lawns while their parents watched and smiled and chatted. Pedestrians strolled in all directions, though most followed the path around the lake and through the gardens. However, despite the dreamy scenery and favourable weather, Arthur only walked for half an hour. Concerned Maria might miss his message, he returned to his evening's lodgings, resolving to wait for Maria to arrive.

When he got back to the hotel, he scanned the lobby left and right but couldn't pick a familiar face – save for the man at reception.

'Hallo, meneer. Back so soon? I hope you enjoyed your stroll, brief though it was. Unfortunately, no one fitting your friend's description has been through that door since you left.' He motioned towards the entrance.

'That's a shame,' Arthur admitted. 'Well, thank you all the same. I will be staying in my room until morning, should anyone—'

'If anyone arrives asking for you, meneer, I will let them know that you have been expecting them. If it is quite alright, I will give them the number of your room.' His professional demeanour and alert countenance reassured Arthur, and he felt his trust in him was not misplaced.

Arthur spent that evening perusing the newspaper he had brought with him. From there, he sifted through the letters he carried among his effects and, later still, double-checked the dates in his diary. Regrettably, all matter of reading failed to occupy him and so, as the night nestled in, he quit waiting and put himself to bed, feeling more than a little pathetic and disappointed; unloved, misled and forgotten. His once glorious hope had deflated. His enthusiasm wavered. And Maria . . . never arrived.

It had been a week, at least, since his visit to Mol. After the usual business rigmarole, Arthur came home from work to find the gate had been left unlatched. After ensuring it was securely shut behind him, Arthur drifted in diagonals on and off the path until he arrived at the front door. As dusk fell and settled into the cradle of night, the sky retained a soft yellow hue, like that of sweat-stained cloth, which gave it the effect of a bruise healing upon its flesh. Clouds were merely wispy white threads streaked with grey like an old man's hair. Arthur imagined that the painter, frustrated by his decision to hide the sky, had smudged the paint and smeared it across the canvas in dismay.

Yes, it seemed the sky shared the very same feeling of dejection that afflicted Arthur.

Then a miraculous cure for his sickness was borne towards him on the breeze. The homely scent of Anneke's cooking made him realise his hunger and he snapped suddenly to attention, like a sail pulled taut under the strain of a sudden gust. The smell of roasted meat was proof Wilhelmus had been hunting, and with the taste of it all but on his tongue, Arthur left the sky to sulk on its own and went inside.

Anneke had been with the van Hessel family for as long as anyone could remember. She was, in many ways, like a second mother to Arthur and his brothers. Her meals were made of the flavours and fragrances of home, and she seemed to always smell of freshly baked bread. Even though she was under Wilhelmus's employment, the family always felt she was more than just a worker. And yet, while she cooked them meals, she rarely ate with them. And though she cleaned their clothes, hers were not the same. She was well looked after, but if something happened to her, she would have been missed for a moment or more, then replaced. Arthur used to think he loved her, but perhaps he – and his family – only loved the idea, the convenience, of her. He wasn't convinced that anyone truly knew who she was as a person, and this thought bothered him.

Arthur, his brothers and his parents, were sat around the dinner table. Andre, as always, salted his vegetables heavily before tasting them. Men are creatures of habit, and Andre's trait was quite trivial, but it bothered Arthur at every meal they sat together. Whether they were tired or hungry, Arthur didn't know, but that supper started off as a quiet and dull affair. At every turn, Andre stuffed too much food in his mouth, chewed briefly and swallowed loudly. No one raised a word against it. And as Arthur ate with a pitiable slowness, he fell softly into a shallow meditation on business and found it to be a pleasant digression from his incurable spate of discontentment. Without diligence or method, he mentally experimented with materials, money and measurements. As was his ritualistic overture, Wilhelmus had said grace, and everyone was well into their meal before a coherent conversation was established.

'We received letters from the van Essens today,' announced Hendrika, recalling Arthur from his thoughts. The name slung him back into the stupor he had temporarily remedied. 'They say they are doing well and everyone is in good health.'

'Yes, very well. All good news, I'm sure,' Wilhelmus declared with detachment.

'They say they are looking forward to Easter with us again,' Hendrika added. Arthur could feel his parents' eyes on him, but he wasn't sure why. What did they know? How could they have known anything?

Then, quite unexpectedly, Bauke saved him from their stares of assumption. 'Oh, brother! Arthur! You should have seen it! It was incredible!' he exclaimed, his face pulled tight – almost too tight in fact, for him to talk at all. 'Andre's shooting was so bad today, I don't think he could have even hit the bushes!' He laughed, but he was alone with the joke. 'His head will probably miss his pillow when he goes to bed tonight!' He convulsed with laughter. His hysteria melted away the gloom and the others at the table were soon infected with it, too. Even Andre laughed along at his own expense. But as the hilarity simmered down, Arthur knew he would have to say something to allay everyone's unspoken concerns.

'I'm letting you all know now that I will have to work on Sunday,' he said, wanting to change the subject.

Andre looked at him sharply for a moment. Over the years, he had developed a handsome face, an athletic build and a charming, dimple-cheeked smile that always won him the attention of women. But his looks served him a second function – for they also worked to make men feel inferior; competed against. 'That's hardly to do with hunting!' he countered with an arrogant smirk.

Arthur felt himself shrink under the weight of his older brother's disdain. Bauke slid a sly smile at him as though he suspected something, but unlike Andre's, Bauke's smile wasn't flashy and full of insincerity. He was a humble man, quiet and closed-off from people. Unlike the rest of the family, he wore a darker complexion – his hair and skin and his grave expression gave the impression of being thoroughly adrift in thought.

Thinking it best to put their suspicions to rest, Arthur shook free from their eyes and subdued the room by taking a deep drink from his cup before finishing the conversation. 'Well, I know it's not . . . but business is business, and . . .' He utilised the silence for dramatic effect. 'I'm sure we can all relate to that.' Arthur smiled in his triumph. And, surely enough, with his secret safe, a unifying sense of family enveloped the room.

The following day, Arthur came home from work to find that, among the mail of yesterday, he had also received a letter. His mother was always a kind and practical woman who stayed out of her sons' private affairs, so when she handed him the envelope, Arthur had some idea who it was from. Had it been business-related, there would have been no call for her discretion. He slid the envelope into his pocket, thanked her for passing it on, and continued to his room. He tried to act as though the paper was commonplace; no big deal, yet all the while he felt it throbbing in his pocket, like the heart of a kitten pulsing against his chest.

As Arthur had suspected, the letter was from Maria. He had been losing sleep thinking of her – sleep he couldn't afford to lose. His thoughts weren't elaborate or fantastical in anyway, just musings. Relentless, perpetual ponderings. But when, on occasion, she had made her way into his dreams, he focussed every effort on staying asleep; for that was where he could do what he could not do in reality. And that night, as Arthur readied himself for bed, he did so with a great anticipation.

He opened the letter. The lamplight spilled through the room. His mind swam in a sea of Maria and, there in his bed, he tried to be with her: to think that she lay beside him. He dispensed with reality to live the lie in his mind – at least for a moment – and imagined a scene where he held her so closely that every part of their bodies were touching. And in that letter, her vulnerability melted the remnants of his reason. Every time she said she was sad, her words furled his fists and unfixed his face. His eyes stung as he squeezed them shut. He reached for the lonely pillow next to him and pulled it to his chest. He clutched it tightly. He held her. He breathed her in to feel something real. But she wasn't really there, and he surprised himself to find in that moment that he revelled in her sadness – for he wanted to be the one who could hold her when she cried. So, to learn why she never met him in Mol, and with the tangled threads of thoughts knotting and intersecting and running through his mind, he read the letter he had held so close to his heart. He inhaled her fragrance from deep within the paper. It was a scent far sweeter than any plume of perfume or field of flowers, for it spored the beguiling blossoms of womanhood. He felt the soap of her saintly skin smudge against the page whereupon her hand rested as she wrote. And he let her words fill him like a fine, fine, wine . . .

Beloved Brother,

You will wonder why you get a letter from your Little Kitten and you will wonder even more for the reason why I write. I will tell you soon. Never had I thought the day I left would be like this, because you stayed at home and I had to leave.

In the train I could not read my book. I tried hard not to cry too much. Then when we arrived at Driest, Alice and Irma asked me if I was ill. Had I been on my own I would have seen you that night in Mol. I would have tried hard not to be in Thienen, but we ended up there anyway.

As long as I was with my girlfriends, I could stop myself crying. But in the evening in my bed, I sobbed and sobbed. The First Matron came to console me, but you can understand that she could not do it. I only wanted to be home in the family circle, especially because you were still there. I could not even bear her talking to me.

Nobody could console me other than Papa, Mama and you. It must have been midnight before I could sleep, then I woke every five minutes and started crying again.

And when I am here, I cannot eat anymore and cry all day long. Even in the evening when I am in bed, I feel like getting up and running away. Och, you cannot believe how I miss you and how unhappy your Little Kitten is in her prison. I feel my heart has broken from sadness. And I cannot bear the nuns anymore. They only believe half of what we say, and don't understand me at all.

They say that I do not have a heart – that I do not love anybody but myself. That for sure is not true, is it Thurke? Och, I am so unhappy. I don't want anybody and yearn to go home to stay. I am so hoping to see you again at Easter, for the dinner, for the Holy Communion of Irma.

It's good that I have two good friends to whom I can tell everything, and they understand and console me so well. One is a boarder, the other is a day student. I have asked them to write to you. I tell them everything, even my deepest secrets. All day long you are in my heart and I feel quite nauseous.

You will want to know why I write all this to you. I am hoping to get a long letter back from you which will cheer me up a little and console me, my dearly beloved brother. Then you will say 'Well, why not write when you are at home?' Yes, but you don't know the life of the 'boarders'. We cannot even write to our parents to tell them that we feel unhappy, because they simply tear the letter up and tell us to start again. And a secret letter to home is impossible, because then Mama and Papa will pick me up and the Mistress will know that I have written a secret letter home and they will kick me out (which would be better for me, but it would ruin our family's name).

And when I write to you, and receive a letter from you, I will feel a bit better and the nuns will never know. I hope it does not put you off to write to your Little Kitten, but of course not to the nuns' address, but to the address I will give you here. So don't forget what I have told you because it is very dangerous to seek consolation the way I am – by writing. But please write to me, my dear Arthur. I yearn for that. Your Little Kitten is so unhappy she is ready to run away. I cannot stand the nuns and no nun can stand me. None of them like me and I cannot live anywhere without love. Write to me as quickly as possible, dearest Arthur. I have to finish, although that is not my fault. Do not forget the two points.

Your Little Kitten, who would sooner die than live,
Maria

6

Windows

One night, in 1930, after a long week of work, Arthur had a dream. In that dream, he was with Maria. Her hair fell around her face. She wore her school uniform. But him having never seen it, she could only model what his mind fashioned for her: a white shirt and navy-blue blazer, dark stockings, and a pleated skirt, the same deep blue, that fringed her knees. She made him weak and pathetic, stealing into him with a look of infinite longing and she was smiling seductively. Teasing.

'Oh, Brother,' she moaned, 'let me sit on your lap like I used to. Read to me. Play with me.' She wriggled. She pressed her hand to his heart. Her eyes were wide and wet and wilful and wonderful. There was a pain for wanting in them that pleaded. 'Oh, Arthur . . . Oh, Thurke! Please make this happen. This moment. This, right now. You need to . . . you must make it *real* for us.' And then she was crying and sobbing, and crying and weeping, and crying and whimpering, and crying and crying and crying. And Arthur was holding her. He was holding her to his chest and breathing the natural scent of her hair. Despite the fact that the dream had not fooled him as well as he would have liked, he wanted to please her. And then, suddenly, they were on his bed. And they were undressed. But they just lay there. They lay there, and he held her, and she snuggled into him – bare body on bare body.

But, against his wishes, he awoke and she vanished, dissolving into the dismal darkness of his bedroom. Arthur lay there in that state for some time. His eyes were open and he stared blankly. His dream replayed and the mood of it echoed through him as he drifted, lost in unfettered thought. He thought of the real Maria. Then of the false one. He felt himself, still swollen with his longing to lie with her like lazy lovers, unhindered by the hassles of the adult world. His guilty longing made his thoughts licentious. He turned from the window and stared restlessly at a windowless wall. He imagined, in the privacy of his mind, one forbidden outcome – desire unshackled, lust run rampant. His hand was put to work and he found a hollow comfort that made him feel, somehow, both more and less alone.

The world beyond his room was sapped of life and colour – grey and still – and somehow the morning fog reminded him of his childhood. He suddenly remembered walking to school with his brothers one uneventful morning. To him, they seemed generations older and lifetimes wiser than he was. The world seemed larger back then too. And as they walked, Arthur watched their breath condense into mist as it collided with the air, curling and climbing like smoke, before quickly fading away. He remembered seeing adults standing around the fronts of shops, chatting, women pushing prams, men shovelling and sweeping the streets, loading and unloading carriages, and otherwise occupied with matters of severe importance. Then, as suddenly as the memory appeared, it was replaced by a more current and pressing issue. He was reluctant to leave the warmth of his bed, but persuaded by the call of nature, Arthur hobbled to his window, opaque with frost. Without wiping the frost from it entirely, he wrote a name on the sweating sheen of the glass. As if of its own volition, his finger cut through the dew like a skier through snow, and limned the shapes to form the name his mind spelled out . . . *M*. As he wrote, he thought about her, whimpering and shivering in her bed at night, lonely and starved of the love she needed. Then he imagined her confessing, in the noble confidentiality of a late-night conversation with the girls in her dormitory, the agonising attraction she had for him . . . *A*. They would ask, 'Who is this boy you are always thinking about, Maria?' And she would initially resist divulging the details. She would say, 'I have no interest in boys.' And in some capacity, she wouldn't be lying. But they would press her as girls do. They would beg her to tell them. And through their persistence, they would eventually earn the information . . . *R*. She would say, 'Yes, in truth there is someone.' And they would say they knew it. She would say, 'But he's not a boy – he's a man.' And they would tease her, but she wouldn't let it bother her too much because she would feel good about finally sharing her feelings aloud . . . *I*. She would say, 'I always used to think of him as an older brother. But my feelings have changed. When I think about him, I get a little flustered. I can't see him as my brother anymore – it's just too strange.' The girls would go on to tease her a little more, but Maria knew the information was safe with them, and she would smile at their jest . . . *A*. And from there, Arthur delighted in the idea of her shunning naïve boys who frivolously flirted with her in the schoolyard – though there wouldn't have been any male students at her school. But then his musings were interrupted for, through the clarity of the letters, he thought he saw movement in the garden. Compelled by a sudden sickness of guilt and embarrassment, he hastily cleaned the remaining frost from the glass and *MARIA* was gone. It was a strange thing to find himself doing. He was longing, languishing, as though *he* was the love-struck teenager. He had always been sure of himself, yet his feelings for her were shrouded in a vague and unfamiliar uncertainty.

Arthur questioned his convictions. His resolve was teetering, but he couldn't help that he was so suddenly and so overwhelmingly compelled to see her, speak to her, listen to her – to simply be in her company. He dispensed with reason, poised himself at his desk, plucked a pen from its pot, and upon a blank piece of paper, he wrote . . .

Dearest Maria,

I apologise for taking so long to reply and for not writing the long letter you asked for. Work has kept me busier than I wish to explain, and kept me at a distance to serving anything but its own selfish needs. In fact, I scarcely find the time in a day to eat or sleep. Before I know it, I realise that several weeks have passed by and I begin to regret letting work get ahead of friends and family.

It has been too long since I have seen a friendly face and I would very much like to get out of the workshop for a while. I am planning another business trip to Mol in the coming month, to collect a small shipment of supplies and to meet with some associates and other enterprising men to discuss business affairs. While I'm in town, I would very much like to hear about how everyone is doing. If you would like to, and can find the opportunity to meet and talk more about school and life, I will do everything in my power to set time aside to see you and your family.

I hope to hear back from you soon.

Your loving brother,
Arthur

When the time came, he rode the routine road to Mol. He was fortunate to have had pleasant weather for the journey because it seemed, at the instant of his arrival, that the sky had turned from grey to black, and it rained pipestems. It fell by the veritable bucket, thick and fast. Arthur and his motorcycle idled together in the flooding streets as he searched the signposts for his night's lodging. Distant thunder grumbled and growled while the all-consuming darkness cast the lustre of midnight upon the drowning town. Steam escaped from his mouth and smoke puffed steadily from his mount's exhaust as the road leapt with water dimples. Then he spied a sign for the inn and, pulling back on the throttle, accelerated towards it, the roar of his bike almost drowned out by the crashing of rain on roofs and windows and roads.

The inn was not a classy one and it had clearly fallen into disrepair sometime over the last several years, however, it still possessed a certain charm, a kind of admirable pride simply in standing despite its injuries – like a castle flying its banner after surviving siege after siege. The rain continued to fall hard and, with the weather the way it was, and the evening growing colder and darker, Arthur wasn't going to be too fussy over the condition of an inn for the sake of a night's stay.

He entered the building through the front bar. In his weather-beaten state, he was immediately directed by a young porter to a glass-windowed door with the word FOYER printed on it in gold lettering. Arthur gave a nod of gratitude and a casual salute and made his way further inside.

The next room was a practical one, furnished only with a lonely, flowerless vase on a square glass-topped table and a peculiar pastel painting of a sour-faced old man with a crooked mouth and small deep-set eyes that dared its visitors to be outstared. Arthur declined the challenge and made his way past the portrait to the booking desk. Caged within, like some long-forgotten fowl, was a thin-haired man with a blotched scalp who was busy scowling down his nose at a newspaper through thin, gold-rimmed glasses. Arthur had hoped to draw his attention without having to disrupt him, but he hoped more still that he could collect his room key without having to engage in the civil rigour of longwinded discourse on matters of no interest to him. Eventually the man discerned a presence and responded to it as though Arthur had arrived as the long-awaited audience to his pessimism.

'Bah! Fools and their followers! The world's a right mess, you know?' The man tapped the newspaper resentfully.

'Good evening, meneer. I have a reservation in the name of van Hessel.' Arthur was careful to not allow the interaction to be led astray by this caged man's desire for dialogue.

The man was silent for a while, as though he hadn't heard the request. Suddenly he lifted his face – wrought with a lifetime of disgust and cynicism. He squinted his beady eyes at Arthur and tilted his head slightly as though he were half-deaf and half-blind.

Arthur thought it prudent to repeat his earlier request. 'I have a reservation for van Hessel.'

'Who?'

'Van Hessel.'

The man nodded slowly. He moved the newspaper aside and stroked a slender finger down a lined page in an open ledger. 'Van Hessel . . . Yes, here it is.' He pressed his finger into Arthur's name where it was scribed upon the paper – as if to prove his point. 'Room Four,' he said as he stood, slowly straightening his spine. He made his way to a cabinet on the wall and withdrew the wooden tag affixed to the room key.

'Thank you, meneer. I hope you have a pleasant evening,' Arthur said hastily as he was handed the key. But his regards remained unreturned, for the man had already resigned himself to his perch, where he murmured wordless angst to the world as he recommenced reading the newspaper.

After securing his belongings in the room and running some cool water over his hands, face and neck, Arthur made his way down to the ground floor barroom to pass the time.

A man of about Arthur's age was there, sitting at the bar, dressed in a suit a size or two too small for him. Arthur gave him a friendly smile. There was also, stooping by the fireplace, an ancient man who appeared as rundown as the inn. It was clear his mind had been long lost to the past and he belonged nearer to the order of furniture than to that of man. And then there was the nonchalant barman. Arthur made his way to a stool to peruse the wine selection. He ordered the cabernet sauvignon, which seemed to cause the barman some bemusement. He made a short show of the uncorking, and invited Arthur to sample the fragrant notes as he did so. The other young man had kept his face fixed on him as they did this, and as Arthur lifted the glass to his mouth the man removed himself from his stool and exited the bar.

Before Arthur had finished half the drink, the public access door gasped open and the roar of rain spilled into the room with a violent flood of noise, drowning out the silence that had held reign. He soon discerned that the noise had brought with it a girl with drenched hair, a wet coat, searching eyes and an excited, almost absurd, smile. He was immediately drawn to her and he instantly understood why. Leaving his drink at the bar, Arthur rushed to her and dragged the door shut to keep the weather out. He helped her out of her coat, passed it to an attendant who had suddenly emerged from who knows where, and guided her to the fireplace.

'Maria!' he exclaimed. 'What are you doing here?' Her sudden and unexpected arrival banished the disappointment that had lingered in him since his previous visit. Arthur had all but come to accept that her affections for him were not as he had initially read them. He had endeavoured to not allow himself to build things up in his mind until undeniable proof presented itself. But now, here it was, standing in front of him, soaked and shivering and surreal. He had to collect himself from disbelief. 'You're soaked through,' he continued, yet she hardly seemed to notice. Her mind, as usual, was fixed on one track.

'I walked all the way here from school and this was only the second inn I tried! I hardly noticed the rain at all, I was so excited to know you were in town! Oh, Thurke! I just wanted to see you!' She smiled an intoxicating smile. It might have been Arthur's imagination, but it looked to him as though a yearning had broken her veneer of indifference and sat glimmering on the rain-glazed surface. And it made everything worthwhile.

'Won't you get in trouble?'

'Trouble? Well . . . maybe . . .' she replied with a sudden hint of nervousness.

'Have you brought a change of clothes? Where's your luggage?'

'Oh, I haven't brought anything!' she announced, seemingly surprised by her own forgetfulness.

'I suppose we can sort something out later,' Arthur said, conveying patience as best he could. 'But in the meantime, we should get you warm.' He took her cold hand in his as they stood and he guided her to his room, the opportunity to tend to her thrilled him to no end. The barman shot a curious frown in their direction as they passed. 'My little sister,' Arthur said as they glided by and made for the stairs. The barman simply shrugged and busied himself polishing the glassware.

Arthur sat on the bed and sifted through fanciful thoughts and memories of Maria – yet there she stood before him. He imagined holding her, even kissing her, but at the same time, a part of him felt uncomfortable with the stark reality of the situation. Thoughts were one thing, but acting on them was another thing all together. They were separated by nearly six years, but it was the fact that she was still in school that made him remember that she was, in many ways, still a child. To complicate matters further, his attraction was countered by feelings of family and friendship. But he knew their relationship was changing.

The room was cold and the rain fell steadily. They had removed their shoes as they entered and placed them side by side by the door. Arthur's seemed nearly twice the size – though the difference was not that great. They creaked barefoot over the floorboards and hovered awkwardly in the half-dark, for neither of them knew what to say or how to act. Eventually, clumsily, Arthur broke the silence.

'It sure is dark in here,' he said, stating the obvious. 'Perhaps I'll find the light . . .'

'No . . .' Maria's tiny voice stopped him. 'Could you light a candle instead, please?'

'Shall I light it for the warmth?' he joked. But Maria remained silent and he was suddenly afraid she might consider leaving.

'Yes, please,' she replied, her voice fading away and returning again. 'But also . . . because we're here together and I want to see all of you. I don't . . . I don't want to have to close my eyes and pretend anymore,' she finished, her concern contorting – corroding – chipping away at the corner of her words – changing their shape. Without delay, Arthur searched the room for the candle that had caught his attention earlier. He struck a match and navigated his way through the room with its sputtering yellow flame. He spied the candle and passed the glow from wood to wick.

'There we are. Now, would you like me to step out of the room so that you can get dry? You can borrow one of my shirts, or I could ask for help at the reception . . .'

'No. I mean . . . you don't have to leave,' Maria replied timidly. Arthur could feel the distance between them, the tension and the strangeness, lessening with every passing second.

'Actually, I have a robe you can borrow,' he suggested, moving to sit on the bed's edge.

Without a word, Maria sat next to him, turned, and wrapped her arms around him. He was taken aback, but embraced the opportunity to hold her in return. He could feel her tiny, frozen frame trembling, the icy dampness of her clothes. And he held her, and he held her, and he held her. He rocked gently to comfort her but she wriggled a little and swung her legs over his. Her white waxen feet were exposed, stripped from their wet stocking skin. Arthur cradled her in his arms and on his lap, and she looked as though she might slip suddenly to sleep. He watched her face as it relaxed. It was so pure and unburdened. Her eyelashes merged, meshing into one another, upper into lower. Her lips – lips that Arthur wished to feel against his, were slightly parted. To kiss . . . to kiss . . . oh, to kiss those lips! And all of him yearned for it. And for a moment, it seemed, he was enraptured.

They remained still until Maria slowly twisted her body to prop herself more upright. Her eyes were still shut softly and her lips, her mouth, her nose, were slowly steering towards his. Reaching. Arthur's lips wanted to move in reply, but he stopped them; he repurposed them to stop hers. He willed his voice to act but he struggled to say her name.

'Maria, wait . . .' It was his sense of duty to protect her – to love her in some other way. *Was it right to act like this?*

Maria's eyes opened and she shivered. She made to stand and Arthur let her move as she wished. She shied away from their embrace, carefully removed his glasses, placed them on the dresser, and slowly stepped her way across the room before turning her body back in his direction. She kept her eyes to the ground.

'Maria . . .' Arthur tried, but he could see that she wanted to speak. He stayed where he was. He watched her. The transparent barrier between them had been removed. He waited for her to move or talk. She shifted her hands to her blouse and unbuttoned from the top down. She curled her shoulders back and pulled slowly at the hem until it fell, spilling so softly away. Next, her fingers found the zip at the side of her skirt and, slowly, she drew it downward. She lifted her hands away and the skirt slipped down her legs, falling to the floorboards with a damp slap. Maria paused, took a step closer to him, and reached both hands around to the middle of her back. She unclipped her brassiere and, taking it in one hand, let it drop to the floor. She stepped out of the clothes gathering in wet clumps at her feet and stood, arms a little out from her side, palms forward. Arthur pored over her body as he would the archaic painting of a maiden. She bathed before him in the glow of the wintry-blue moon that filtered through the rain speckled glass – her figure polished by the golden flame that stretched and swayed in the corner. Her body was bare and natural and alive. Her hair fell in dark waves around her young, fresh face. Her frame was small and svelte and her budding breasts were like those of the bare-chested women of Renaissance art. But Arthur's study was stirred when Maria lifted her head and her eyes found his.

With discernible difficulty, she drew a shallow breath and started to speak.

'Arthur . . . I am a woman now . . . can't you see?' She begged him to see her the way he might see other women – the way she didn't know he already saw her.

'Maria . . .' he began, but again couldn't finish. His voice trailed off. Instead, Arthur sat on the bed and stared to where she stood before him, vulnerable and bare, in their makeshift chamber, alive with nerves and uncertainty, pale and pure. The candlelight shuddered and he found himself standing. She stepped shyly forward and he stepped carefully forward in reply. A step. Again a step. And another. When they were only centimetres apart, their breathing melded and he held her face with the tips of his fingers. He found the words and whispered.

'Maria . . . Maria, of course I can.'

A sudden recollection of his kiss with Madeleine flashed into his mind. He wondered, but only briefly, if it was going to feel any different. He also wondered whether his role had been reversed. Then all thoughts ceased and only Maria occupied his mind. His hands slid down her back and then up through her hair as she held him and their mouths met and their bodies merged. Her body was cold and yet had a soft humidity to it, and his touch had sent a shiver through her that made her skin rise into a thousand fine bumps. They moved instinctively, gravitating back towards the bed to steady their spinning, swirling world. Everything faded away . . .

Everything . . .

Except . . .

Maria . . .

He knew he loved her. He knew he wanted her. But, above all, he knew he had to wait. He had to do what was right. He had to stop.

'Maria . . . I'm sorry . . . I can't – no, I mustn't . . . not yet,' Arthur said.

'But . . .' was all Maria could manage. 'But . . .'

A wild, whistling wind whipped at the window and Arthur felt her silk-smooth skin turn to Braille again under his fingertips as he traced the length of her arm from shoulder to wrist. Maria curled in at his side, her head pillowed on his chest.

After several seconds passed, Maria started to speak. She spoke what must have been on her mind ever since she had arrived, and Arthur was glad she did.

'I'm so sorry about last time, Arthur,' she whispered, her words wrung with disappointment. He could see the regret written on her face, and she looked as though she might cry and the ink might run and ruin the page at any moment.

'I'm so, so sorry. I really tried to see you, but . . .'

He gently guided his hand to her cheek to hush her. 'I know,' he said tenderly. Arthur felt a repercussive resentment rise in him, and then, as quickly as it rose, it faded away, liberated. 'But you're here now and that's what matters.' A fleeting stillness fell around them. It was an intimacy they felt they could live a lifetime in. Their moods were subdued by the taste of the air they shared.

'Do you love me, Thurke?' Maria's eyes were alive with affection, and even though it was everything he had ever desired, it made him nervous.

'Of course I do.' Arthur knew his reply would lead to another question.

'But do you *really* love me, like . . . like you would love a woman? Will you love me again? Am I not too . . . young?' Maria's questions hung on the silence that settled upon them like drift upon drift of snow.

'Maria . . .' Arthur restarted. He wanted to say what she wanted to hear, but some deep sense of morality stopped him. Or perhaps it was something simpler – like guilt or cowardice.

'If you can't say it now, you don't have to,' she interrupted. Her words were slowed by the sleep that crept over her.

'Maria . . . I love you in the way I can, but your age . . . and our families, our history . . . this is more complicated than you might think . . .' He knew how flimsy and pathetic it must have sounded.

'No, I know . . .' she said softly, the final syllable sloping upward into a mellow yawn. 'Maybe, one day we can be together . . .' And as she faded into sleep, Arthur realised that this time it was her voice that trailed off.

Maria was still sleeping when he woke. She lay on her side facing him, half-covered by sheets and blankets, her knees lifted slightly towards her chest. The morning was grey and rain dappled the window of their room. Arthur could hear the nearby rumble of horses and their carts, as well as the humming murmur of motorcars and motorbikes. This was all accompanied by the near-muted mumbling of morning greetings. He propped himself up onto an elbow and lifted a hand to guide back the hair that had fallen across her face. At his touch, her body stretched out and her eyelids slowly fluttered open.

'You were purring,' he teased. 'You really are like a little kitten.'

'What time is it?' she asked mid-yawn.

'Does it matter?'

'A little . . .' she said sleepily. 'I'll need to get back to school soon.' She stood and was a little unbalanced from rising too quickly. Then she started to move about, growing gradually more and more frantic.

Her hair was tousled on one side into a static mess, like a kitten's fur after being licked by its mother. But despite, or perhaps due to, her dishevelled appearance, she looked more real and human than ever before, and she was temporarily reformed in Arthur's mind as the cute child he had once known her as. Then she stopped pacing, and he smiled when he saw her wince at the idea of climbing into the sodden clump of clothes that bulged from the floor like seaweed strewn upon the beach.

Maria reluctantly squirmed into her cold, soggy clothes, and assembled herself the best she could. Arthur paused to watch her for a while before dressing himself, and as they collected their scattered pieces from about the room, he felt his reason return.

'I'll give you a lift if you like . . . my bike's parked out the front.'

Maria was still a little flustered – probably overwhelmed by the night's events – and Arthur hoped to remedy her evident embarrassment and panic as best he could.

'Umm . . .' she murmured in delay, as she took a moment to consider the offer. 'Sure.'

Arthur smiled and rested a hand on her shoulder. He acted calmly, but inwardly he was far from composed. They were engaged in adult affairs and so they had to conduct themselves accordingly. Maria had ignited a desire in Arthur to be the man she imagined him to be. He felt an intoxicating resolve simmering deep within. But more importantly, he felt enlightened – as though from that moment on, he would see beauty in things, the way an artist does, and know how to appreciate it.

'Don't worry . . . it'll be fine,' Arthur said.

Maria smiled then, and her shoulders relaxed as she exhaled the pent-up tension. He could tell she was still a little concerned with whether or not things would be weird between them – whether they had somehow, irreparably, changed their relationship. He could understand her concern. But above all, he believed that it may well become the most satisfying pursuit of their lives.

'And we'll be fine, too,' he assured her. He gestured for a hug and Maria ceased fussing and, half-dressed and damp, pressed against him. Arthur folded his arms around her. 'We'll keep it quiet – for a while at least – and think more about it later. But let us, for now, focus on the present. I'll help you get your things together, take you back to school, and if I can, I'll see you again before I travel back to Vlijmen.'

He could feel her head nod against his chest, and they held each other.

They travelled through town as inconspicuously as possible and took the least populated roads. As they rode, Maria's arms were wrapped around his waist. Fortunately, the weather being wet and miserable, there weren't too many witnesses out and about.

On Maria's signal, Arthur pulled to a stop at a residential address across the way from where she boarded. She swung herself from his bike and fiddled with her hair and face and tugged at her clothes to fix her appearance as best she could. Her hair was still quite matted and her clothes were crinkled like paper that had been scrunched into a ball and unpacked again. Even still, something about her seemed to conceal these faults. She checked herself over one last time and shrugged. Then, before parting ways, she withdrew a length of white ribbon from her pocket. Arthur had thought she might fix it in her hair, but instead she took his wrist and tied a bow.

Then she found she had one last thing she wanted to say. 'Maybe you'll love me one day . . .' she started. She wore a wistful smile that seemed to contradict the mood of the moment. 'The way I want you to. The way that I love you.' And on that note Arthur thought she might stop, but her sad smile suddenly seemed to support her sentiment when she added one more hard-told truth. 'But for now, I guess . . . this . . . *this* is enough. Goodbye, dear brother. I look forward to seeing you again soon.'

And with that, Maria waved Arthur away. He realised something of her would still be with him for at least a while longer – a residual passion that would keep him company for the journey home. It was, in a way, like the warmth that still clung to the blankets where they had lain together. And just like the bedding's warmth, Arthur knew the feeling would eventually fade. For the time being, he smiled, nodded gratefully, and waved back.

Before he pulled back the throttle and merged back onto the road, he called out one last time, 'Farewell, Maria, my little kitten! Take care of yourself!'

After several weeks in the working world of men, Arthur was revisited by a familiar and salacious fantasy. He had been sleeping very little – trying to squeeze as much work into every day as he could, but eventually it all caught up to him, and he slept deeply and well. He was in a dreamlike daze one morning when, unexpectedly, he imagined Maria, under the fresh-pressed sheets and itchy blankets of her bed in a room she shared with two or three other girls at the boarding school. He imagined her, unable to sleep while the other girls dreamed of their families, boys they knew, teachers they hated and the futures that awaited them. Then he imagined her imagining him . . . imagining them together. He pictured her, enveloped in her linen shell . . . exploring – her fingertips slowly skating their way across her skin . . . sliding down . . . down the side of her stomach, down beneath the lace-lined waistband of her underwear. Her hand carefully traversing the soft bristles before nestling into position. She would melt into the fantasy. Arthur imagined her with her eyes closed, her face undone for the first time by a strange new ecstasy. Then like all things, it came to an end. He drifted into reality and his dream dissipated into the ether of daybreak. He thought he felt the grip of a silk band around his wrist, soft like her hand. But it was in his head and nowhere else. He was warm beneath his bedding, but he could feel that the morning was unseasonably cold. Rain had come and gone, and a misty film of condensation coated his window. At first he thought his eyes were deceived by a trick of the light, but suddenly he noticed that, stencilled on the frost-glazed glass, the shape of five discernible characters were daubed dull by the ink of a grease-tipped finger. Upon the glass, the letters he had once imprinted upon the world had come to life again, limned by lust, to display her name. Arthur could do little but stare transfixed. His heart pulsed with a painful pining as the emptiness, the loneliness, stole his breath. The isolation made him long for her again – to feel human intimacy. He felt she could fill the void he had never known existed.

And so little – oh, so little – did he expect to fall so suddenly, and so thoroughly and entirely, in love with someone he had not yet met.

7

Jo

In 1931, another weekend had fallen upon Arthur's anticipation like the return of a long-lost friend. He embraced the opportunity to let his mind wander from work and from Maria, and though it passed quickly, he caught frivolity before it fled.

Sunday was sunny, and after church an old school friend invited him to lunch. Alfred, being a gentleman of the town, was one whose good word was conducive to business. Struck as Arthur was by the weather as he exited church, he embraced the rare occasion for social discourse and accepted Alfred's invitation.

Merriment manifested in sunlit splendour. Roughly two dozen men and women dressed in their Sunday best chatted coquettishly in a thrum of summer fever. Arthur meandered among them until he spied his host across the lawn, speaking with an elaborate flailing of hands, one of which waved a slender glass. Strips of sunshine streamed, twinkling effervescently, through both champagne and crystal. Alfred was entertaining a throng of several guests and so, not knowing anyone else, Arthur thrust himself into his company.

'Alfred! How are you, old friend?' he announced, acting as cheerful as he could.

'Arthur! How frightfully fabulous!' exclaimed Alfred, flourishing his flute. 'I was just talking about our adventurous school days together! Everyone, this is Arthur van Hessel – the dashing young entrepreneur.'

'I'm surely not all that,' Arthur demurred in temperate embarrassment, 'but he had my name right. And though I may not remember each of yours, it's nice to meet you all the same.'

Alfred gave him a sudden look, as though he had been instantly struck by inspiration. It was the same look he used to make in school when he had invented some new game or fantastic scheme for his friends to have a bit of fun.

'Arthur! My, my! I've just had a stupidly splendid idea! You must get to know Johanna here.' Alfred gestured towards one of the ladies, a guiding hand placed at his friend's back. She turned towards him, still smiling from her previous conversation. Her hair was centre-parted and bounced in soft blonde curls. Her floral-patterned frock fell just above the knee and her shoulders were bare. She sported a glass of sparkling white wine, but Arthur guessed it was more for accessory than for function. Her posture suggested she was probably wishing, like Arthur, that she had already had a drink or five to numb the nerves.

'Conversation can be used for more than filling the silence, you know,' said Alfred, winking knowingly. 'How about I leave you two to get acquainted,' he added, before turning back to his livelier company.

'Johanna, was it? How do you do?' Arthur greeted, offering a smile and a hand.

'It's nice to meet you . . . Arthur, right? Please, call me Jo,' she corrected. 'Also, I feel a little uncertain of Alfred's introduction.' Her eyes were gentle and content, and they smiled when she spoke, and something about her expression conveyed a certain passivity, a desire to be pursued, a willingness to be taken away.

'Well, I will admit that his suggestion for conversation has merit,' replied Arthur. 'Would you like, perhaps, to go somewhere, quieter than here, to talk?'

Jo looked to where Arthur's hand remained on offer, and smiling, she took it. 'Why not? I think that sounds rather nice.'

They found a spot upon a bench beneath a cider-scented sycamore, and Arthur listened as Jo regaled him with an account of the man she had once loved and who had died last year at only thirty — a concert pianist by the name of Lars Hermans. She told him how deeply it had upset her and that the thought of another man had not crossed her mind since. By her account, Lars was well mannered and his family was well-to-do. She described him as tall and handsome — but stressed moreover that he was honest and gentle, and that she was convinced that no better man had ever existed. And yet, though she spoke so openly of this other man, and though he should have found this to be in poor taste — as she may well have intended it to be — her ardour was alluring, her elegance irrefutable, and her affections admirable.

Hours passed while they spoke, heedless of time and place. The glass of wine that Jo had earlier sipped at had long since lost its fizz. Had the truth been told, she would have confessed she had no intention of finishing it in the first place. Alfred and his energetic assemblage had, on the contrary, grown thoroughly red-faced, dishevelled and incoherent. Their glasses had been loved and abandoned, one after another, smudged with the prints of lips and fingertips. They were a rowdy crowd. But Arthur's interests had shifted to loftier heights; Alfred and his party were elsewhere and far beyond and, with genuine intrigue, he attended to Jo. At seventeen, she had moved in with her older sister, Grada, and her husband, Jan, to help them look after their six children. Jo was the third youngest of eleven children. She had five older brothers – Romos, Jan, Hans, Claes and Stephen – and three older sisters – Grada, Maria and Cato. The two younger siblings were her brother, Tom, and sister, Tien. Her father, Albertus de Haas, had died in May 1918 and had made his living as a builder. Her mother, Janneke, died four years later, in February 1922. Arthur learned that Jo was a sensible woman, well-practised in all matter of household duties, yet he found that these chores had not robbed her of womanly charm, but rather added to it, layered it with maternal empathy and maturity.

The pair went on talking in this friendly fashion until their conversation was cut short by a slurred interruption from Alfred. 'Arthur . . . Arthur – my fabulous, fabulous friend . . . be good . . . be good to this one.'

'Dank je, Alfred, naturally.'

'Right, right . . . Jo! Oh, Jo . . . you be good, too!'

Alfred saluted, came close to losing his balance, and then slapped his feet against the grass as he toddled away, wide-stepped and listing to the left. Arthur and Jo smiled together at his expense and were abandoned in a sudden and surreal silence.

Arthur knew that it would be getting dark before long, so he ran to catch Alfred before he was out of earshot. 'Vaarwel, Alfred! I must go. Miss de Haas and I . . .'

But Alfred simply waved him on and he had no need to say anymore. Arthur and Jo shared yet another smile and they knew it was time to say their farewells.

'Thanks for a lovely afternoon,' Arthur began.

'Yes – yes, it was,' she said politely. 'Sorry for prattling, but thank you ever so much for listening all the same. Dank je, Arthur, I had a lovely time.'

'Well, how about I write to you?' Arthur offered, suddenly inspired and hoping her response would indicate whether he had truly made a positive impression.

'That would be nice,' she smiled.

And with that, they parted, yet her distance from his heart was not depleted in the least. In their time apart, his thoughts drifted into the week of work ahead of him, the weather, and an array of other subjects, but each time, all things circled back to Jo. His ruminations were meshed with fragments of their conversation, recollections of her face, her subtle beauty, the scent of a sycamore – and from dream to dream, a new optimism grew.

Letters still came from Maria in Mol – letters penning promises, letters of longing and loneliness and love. And Arthur would reply to them in time, but the tenderness, care and passion no longer lived between the lines. Arthur's affections were drawn elsewhere. And as they grew, he was made to wait, delayed in part by work's constant demand. But eventually – within the week – he wrote:

Dear Jo,

Here you hold the letter as proof of the promise I made to write to you. I most earnestly hope it finds you well. Ever since we met, the weather has seemed unusually favourable. But perhaps I am mistaken. Perhaps it isn't the weather at all that has suddenly made things so blissful. I think it is, rather, my state of mind. Ever since Alfred's party, I have thought about our conversation many times over and I would very much like to have another one. Your company that day saved me from what could have been a rather ordinary outing. I hope you don't find it too presumptuous of me, but do you think we could meet again?

Yours sincerely,
Arthur van Hessel

In turn, and without undue delay, Arthur received her reply.

Dear Arthur,

Thank you for the kind words in your letter. I agree that the weather has been unusually pleasant. I was certainly relieved to hear you appreciated my company as much as I found comfort in yours. I think arranging a time see each other again is a truly lovely idea.

Faithfully yours,
Jo de Haas

From there, everything happened quite quickly. Within the following two weeks, Arthur went to visit Jo at her sister Grada's place in 's-Hertogenbosch. They had tea and cake as several small children played and slept and rolled about on a flatweave rug. The older ones tested him with a field of difficult questions of the type only children can devise – each one followed up with a 'Why?' – and Arthur tried to answer them as best he could, until he was finally rescued by his hostess. Grada was in many ways an older and more sleep-deprived version of Jo. She maintained a resolute posture, but the signs of stress were pressed in fine folds on her face.

'So, Arthur . . .' Grada queried. 'Jo tells me you met at one of Alfred's . . . *social events*.' She placed a certain sarcastic emphasis on the last two words and mimicked a reverent twist of her wrist to flout sophistication. 'You probably know this, but I've heard that even though he might seem erratic, he has a highly developed business acumen. And yet, you don't seem to belong to his usual crowd. In fact, you present as a gentleman of a different sort. And you act it too – from what I understand.'

Arthur understood the compliment, but took a while to decide how to reply.

Before he could find the words, she continued. 'So I suggest you take my sister for a walk. Get her out of this dreadful domesticity lest either, or both, of you are put off by it.'

'Dank je, Grada, but your home is lovely. I am quite at ease here,' he smiled, humbled by her suggestion at their relationship developing into something serious and long-term. Then, reflecting on her tone, he continued. 'But why not? The weather is lovely for the minute and it might change the next, so let us enjoy what we have while we have it.' He smiled again, motioning to stand.

Jo lifted her eyes from where she watched the children on the floor, then to her sister, then to Arthur. 'Yes, why not?' she agreed. 'Let's make the most of it.'

Arthur and Jo strolled along the street, stroked on occasion by a sweeping gust that picked up and softly spiralled the white, pink and purple petals that dotted the pavement like confetti. Arthur felt an urge to whistle but restrained himself. Instead, he imagined the two of them as the very picture of blossoming romance. He felt proud to walk with her in public. Outwardly, he acted suitably indifferent, simply content, but inwardly he was immersed in the illusion of them as a married couple. They had not known each other for long, but Arthur felt favoured by fortune, filled with a love for life, and he decided that he would let Jo know it.

'What a beautiful day! In fact, I don't think I can recall a nicer one,' he began. Gauging her polite, reciprocal smile, he continued. 'But I feel the company might be more pleasant still.' Jo shied away at his advance, and he could tell she was hesitant to be courted too directly. It was likely that she was thinking of Lars and was, at least momentarily, in two minds.

Arthur reflected on his flattery and attempted to make amends. 'I'm sorry . . .'

But Jo was quick to allay any need for an apology. 'Oh, please, no. There's no need – no need at all. It's quite alright, really!' She smiled reassuringly and Arthur smiled in reply before they continued along the path.

A sudden curling gust tumbled by like a whispering wave, stirring the petals once again, and Arthur felt Jo's hand in his – but whose had reached for whose, neither knew. They stopped and stared ahead.

Then Jo faced him, he faced her, and she spoke. 'Actually, I think I should be the one to apologise. You were being so nice, and I didn't know how to respond.'

Arthur was impressed by her humility. 'I suppose it is nothing for us to fuss about, then. Let's move on. I was a little too forward and it caught you off guard – and if you'll forgive it, it needn't be a big deal.'

'Very well,' Jo agreed.

They strolled for a while in shared tranquillity until Jo suddenly breached the sealed surface of her feelings.

'To be honest,' she said, 'and I hope this isn't too forthright of me . . . but I felt perfectly confused – not by you, I assure you, or at least not directly. But you see, I hadn't expected to feel . . .' she paused a while to choose her words, to muster her courage. '. . . to feel this comfortable with a man, so soon. You know, after Lars . . .' She waited, uneasily, watching closely for Arthur's response.

'Well,' he began, 'I'm glad you feel comfortable with me.' He was unable to stop the smile that had fashioned itself so fixedly on his face. 'Would you like me to take you home now?'

Jo slowly shook her head and looked down at the petal-peppered pavement. 'Not yet. That is, if you are happy to stay with me a while longer.'

'I will stay with you for as long as you like.'

And together, hand in hand, they walked on to find where the path might take them.

Several glorious weeks passed and, one fine summer morning, Arthur and Jo decided to picnic on Wilhelmus's land. They had arrived at the point in their relationship when Arthur felt it was necessary to show that his interest in her was more than a social one. He wanted to prove his affections were romantic, too. And so, the stage was set. They rode bikes that wobbled as they fought the handlebars and pedalled over the unsealed country road in pursuit of the perfect place to set up.

They left the bikes propped up by the wayside and trudged on foot through wild, knee-high, needle-like grass that caught on their clothes and scratched at their skin. Eventually, after some time skipping and scrabbling and stumbling through the copses, they found a shady spot beneath a sycamore and laid out the blanket. They stretched out the stubborn fold lines and smoothed the lumps that the uneven ground and weeds and stones beneath it produced. With their square of coloured cloth placed on nature's skin like a mismatched patch, they proceeded to unpack the basket. Jo had packed bread, cheese, fresh fruit and sweets. Arthur had raided Hestana the night before and brought a bottle of wine from his father's stock. Beneath the sycamore, their feet soaking in the sun, their heads in the shade, they made idle conversation about the weather and the view. They weren't quite hungry enough to have lunch. As they spoke, Arthur watched her face and casually edged closer to her. Birds and butterflies flitted about. She let him approach her and smiled approvingly. The shade shifted. Her fingertips caressed the blanket, tracing the tessellating patterns. Sunlight showered them. Arthur watched Jo's hand for a while, then stilled it and stole her attention by placing his hand on hers. He had made the first move. It was her turn. A gust rustled the leaves above them. Their eyes met. Her chest rose as she inhaled deeply. On cue, their heads tilted slightly. Their faces moved closer together. Their eyes closed and their mouths melded. Lips locked and they held it. They responded to each other's subtle cues. They harmonised. There was a certain pulsing rhythm to it and it worked. It felt right to them, as if it was how romance ought to be. Then they stopped. They looked into each other's faces. And, half-squinting into the sun, she said the best thing he had ever heard. 'I have never been so happy.'

They continued to meet each other as often as they could – mostly on weekends. More often than not, Arthur would travel to see her in s-Hertogenbosch, but she visited him in Vlijmen on two or three occasions. But each time, he was a little embarrassed to still be living with his parents – it certainly marred the image of masculine maturity he had rather hoped to convey to her. But at that point in his life it was convenient and made the most sense financially. As time passed, their visits became routine, and it was clear to their friends and family that they had fallen in love. So it came as no surprise to anyone, except maybe to Jo, when Arthur sought her answer to an important question.

It was on yet another sunny Sunday morning, two-month since the day they first met. They had decided, ahead of time, to skip church and find one another at a particular bench beneath a certain cider-scented sycamore. The fresh smell of lawn lingered in the air as Arthur waited, slowly pacing and contemplating every conceivable scenario, over and over, again and again. He knew what he wanted to do but, as it turned out, had put little thought into how.

He spied Jo approaching. He tried to act calm and composed, yet scraps of scripts unravelled in his mind. Sentences disintegrated and reformed – mutated. Poetry eluded him. And soon – too soon – she was before him. He feigned composure as best he could.

'Begroeting!' he announced with a needless salute.

Fortunately, his awkwardness made Jo laugh. 'Begroeting!' she replied, a charming chortle slipping between the syllables. Arthur caught hold of Jo's friendly face and found himself starting to relax. This was the feature, he realised, that distinguished her from Maria. It was in her response, and it was written well upon her face for him to read. Where Maria's features and its separate elements, her eyes in particular, were bright and hopeful, Jo's were calm, wise and content, and seemed to reassure him that she understood everything he could ever think or feel. Arthur knew her tender affection and refined intelligence was what he was drawn to and found most endearing. He also knew that their conversation would have to be natural, that he had to read the mood, to let the right time present itself, and trust himself to find the right words.

'A lovely day,' he announced, gesturing to the world around them.

Jo smiled kindly, but her eyes suggested she was a little suspicious of his behaviour, though she humoured him all the same. 'Yes, truly, it is a lovely day.'

'Do you remember Alfred's party, when was it? Two months ago now?'

'I remember.' Jo smiled in reverie.

Arthur took her by the hand and continued steering the conversation, wholeheartedly, to where he needed it to be led. 'And do you remember when I said I would stay with you for as long as you like?'

He lowered himself to one knee.

Jo's hands leapt to her face and pushed in at her cheeks. She was piecing the puzzle together. 'Yes?' She squeaked.

Arthur's nerves made it difficult for him to think. He felt outside himself. He continued before he lost all ability to speak. 'Well, will you stay with me forever?' He opened the velvet-covered box he had taken from his trouser pocket. A diamond-crowned ring sparkled in the sunlight. 'Johanna de Haas . . .' His voice sounded like a stranger's in his ears. 'Will you marry me?'

Almost immediately, and with tears welling in her eyes, Jo squeaked again. One. Short. Perfect. Word. 'Yes!'

The moon burned like a sombre fire sinking low on the horizon as Arthur made his way up his father's path. The sky was a mess of colour as clusters of charcoal clouds drifted nonchalantly by in contrast, like heavy misshapen balloons. The atmosphere was cushioned in perfect stillness. Everything was peaceful. As he walked, he habitually thought to veer off the path, and he anticipated feeling the loose gravel sink and shift underfoot, but he refrained. Perhaps it was a lapse in stubbornness, or maybe he no longer felt so compelled to make things more difficult than they ought to be. Either way, it didn't bother him. He was visiting for another reason.

In the shed, Wolf was whistling as he tinkered with his tools, the tender chinking of steel tapping steel punctuating the melody. A light shone from Wilhelmus's office window and Arthur knew his father and brother would be working late into the night.

The warm waft of freshly baked bread welcomed him inside. The sound of pots and plates splashing softly into the kitchen sink accompanied the gentle notes of Anneke singing to herself. Arthur passed the portrait that perpetually shared its opinion of the past, and trekked towards his father's office. The door was ajar, and as he neared it he could hear fragments of conversation between the two men within. He stood for a while and tried to plot what he had to say and how he had to say it. He knew his father well enough to know that to keep him onside, he simply needed to avoid saying anything foolish.

After letting his grip rest on the handle for several moments, Arthur opened the door. He saw Andre first, his face in the partial shadow cast by the desk lamp, as he worked at his father's desk – a seat he would likely occupy when his father was no longer at the helm. Wilhelmus stood next to him and over him, reading figures from a thick wad of thin papers. They each gave a casual glance in Arthur's direction, as if to acknowledge his presence and to let him know that they would only be a few sums longer. Wilhelmus continued reading numbers in baritone monotony while Andre kept his pen busily scratching and stabbing at the ledger in front of him. Arthur left the door slightly open behind him and skimmed the shelves of leather-bound accountancy and reference books. Only a half-minute passed before his father's voice shifted from numbers to words.

'Arthur, to what do we owe this visit?' Wilhelmus was granting Arthur a limited window of opportunity to give what he expected to be a business update. Andre kept his head down, adding and subtracting figures, marking memoranda, writing, correcting, and rewriting.

Arthur answered his father's question without further digression. 'Goedenavond, Father. I have come to tell you that I am to marry Johanna de Haas.'

Wilhelmus looked up and his eyes were temporarily lost behind the reflection of the lamplight on his glasses. He reached into his suit pocket, withdrew his cigar case and clicked it open, found a cigar and snapped the case shut. Arthur had seen him do this before. He was recalibrating himself, preparing his mind to deal with matters of family instead of those of business.

'Well, congratulations,' he started, then paused to light his cigar. The scented smoke puffed into the air. It grew and thickened, stretching its shadow over Andre.

'Yes, congratulations,' Andre added uniformly.

'When do you plan to have the wedding?' Wilhelmus asked.

'It will be at least a year away,' said Arthur, vouching for sensibility.

'If I recall correctly . . . Johanna's brother-in-law, Grada's husband Jan – he's an architect of sorts, is that right?' Wilhelmus asked in a tone of assessment.

'Yes, from what I understand he specialises in homes and small buildings.'

Wilhelmus gave a slight nod, more to himself than to Arthur or Andre. And that was the end of the conversation. The window was closed. As Arthur left, the methodical murmur of numbers resumed.

Several days passed. Arthur was in his workshop until noon, cutting glass for several jobs around town, and spent the rest of the day travelling from place to place fitting the sheets into their frames. It was late in the evening when he finally locked up the shed and made his way home.

His brothers caught him by the hall, both arrayed in new suits. They had their hair neatly combed and their faces were cleanly shaved. He could smell their cologne and knew that it meant they would be going out for drinks. They were in a loud and cheerful mood, and genuinely excited to see him.

'Hè! Welcome home, little brother!' Andre announced. Bauke smiled, sauntered towards Arthur and casually extended a tumbler of mahogany coloured spirit. Arthur accepted it and the three clinked their glasses in cheers.

'Proost!' Andre grew more excited – more energised – more ecstatic, by the second. 'Get dressed in your best, little brother. Tonight, you are coming out with us!'

The establishment – dimly lit by half a dozen sizzling yellow bulbs – echoed the raucous chatter of its patrons, each of whom was well dressed and well respected in town. Around Andre, giddy girls and gaudy young men gathered to listen and laugh, while Bauke caroused inwardly in his introversion and watched Andre's antics from a safe distance. Arthur was in a third state – drawn inward, a little like Bauke, drunk on fantastic romances, on an indulgent muse of his wife-to-be. And as the evening settled in and excitement tapered, there was a discernible lull in the conversation, and Arthur found himself approached by a half-remembered face.

'Arthur! We don't see you here often at the kroeg! What's the occasion?' asked the man, sweating beer. Arthur smiled through him in false sincerity, annoyed to some extent at having his thoughts disturbed.

'A celebration. I'm getting married.'

'Well, well, well! That's fantastic!' the man replied in inebriate excitement. Fortunately for Arthur, the man was suddenly summoned by a friend. He tipped his head, flashed a grin and turned quickly away. His place was taken by his brothers.

'Are you having a good time, little brother?' asked Andre, grinning.

'I suppose so. It's nice to be spending time with you two.'

Andre winked in reply and Arthur could see that he was refining yet another impulsive idea. 'I'll be right back,' he said before disappearing through the crowd.

Bauke moved in closer and spoke with his usual tone of reservation. 'You know, Arthur,' he started, 'it's incredible. Andre and I might be your older brothers, but you give us a lot to look up to. It has always been what makes you different from us.' He paused for a moment and Arthur waited in patient anticipation. Though the detour wouldn't last long, he appreciated the serious direction in which his brother had taken the evening. 'Andre will inherit Father's land and business, and I will benefit from the work he has done too. But you have made something of yourself, more or less, on your own.' He paused again. Arthur was humbled and taken aback by his praise. 'Love is a splendid thing, brother. And now you are engaged to be married. It's wonderful, and I know you and Jo will make each other happy.' Bauke had said what he wanted to say and he didn't say any more. He didn't need to. He simply held out his drink, raised it in a silent toast, turned his face to the ceiling and resolutely poured the contents of his glass into his mouth.

A moment later, Andre returned with three more drinks. He handed one to Arthur, one to Bauke, and kept the last one for himself. He held out his hand, gestured that they do the same and, to the chime of their clinking glasses, made a short dedication.

'To the van Hessel brothers!' And the three of them, in strident unison, saluted the sentiment.

'Proost!'

To inform the van Essens of Arthur's engagement to Jo, Wilhelmus wrote to Mr van Essen and extended an invitation for a celebratory dinner. Jo, as well as Grada and Jan, were also invited.

Anneke, with some help from Hendrika, had prepared quite the feast. The banquet was spread before them on their best dinnerware. Steam rose from pots of potatoes, gravies, roasted meats and assorted vegetable dishes. White wine glistened gold in shimmering glassware, and the room buzzed with festive merriment. Unfortunately, Andre and Bauke had other engagements, as did Alice and Irma. So the table consisted of Wilhelmus, Hendrika, Mr and Mrs van Essen, Maria, Grada and Jan, and Jo and Arthur. Prior to the evening's formalities, Arthur had made a point of introducing Jo to the van Essens. As the host, Arthur knew his father would preface the occasion with a customary detailing of who was who, but he figured his father's introduction could act as a reiteration and elaboration upon his own. Of course, the person Arthur most wanted Jo to meet was Maria. A strange sense of pride rose in him, a pride he attached to his connection with each of them: Jo for her sophistication, maturity and kindness, and Maria for her youthfulness, enthusiasm and playfulness. Arthur had hoped their meeting would allay any awkward tension. As he spoke each name to the other, he seemed to lose all sense of time and place. It felt to him like watching night meet day, winter meet summer, the past meet the present.

After his father's predictably efficient and cursory introductions, all were seated for their meal. A collective conversation quickly commenced above the unobtrusive clamour of crockery, cutlery, and glassware.

'It's a shame that we couldn't all be here,' Mr van Essen asserted. 'But it can't be helped. Still, a shame all the same. I know Alice and Irma always enjoy it when everyone is together like this.'

'It is nothing less than a shame,' Wilhelmus echoed. 'The same can be said for Andre and Bauke. But they are busy men, always involved in matters of importance.' Then he smiled at the table and spoke once more. 'Now, please join me in prayer so that we might eat while the food is still hot! Bless us, O Lord, and these, Thy gifts, which we are about to receive from Thy bounty. Through Christ, our Lord. Amen.'

'Amen!'

With that, they ate. And while they ate, quiet, confluent conversations broke out intermittently between neighbours.

'So have you decided on a date for the wedding?' asked Mrs van Essen.

'We aren't looking to hurry things,' Arthur declared. 'I imagine we'll find a time late next year, probably sometime in November.' But she had heard enough of the answer and Jo saved him by sharing the particulars.

Then Arthur caught Maria watching him from across the table, but only briefly. When he looked her way, she withdrew into herself and sent her eyes to the entrée – untouched in front of her. Her chin was cupped in the palm of her hand, while the other casually chased a grape across her plate. Before long, she earned her mother's frown by unintentionally flicking the fruit to the floor. As Arthur watched her, he realised it was something other than her disposition that had altered her appearance. It was her hair – it was near half the length it had been when he last saw her. Arthur's study was suddenly interrupted by a conversation that, for one reason or another, caught his interest.

'So, Jan, I understand you are something of a draftsman?' Wilhelmus asked in the officious voice he adopted when he spoke about business undertakings and other matters of financial consequence.

'Well, I have some experience in the field,' returned Jan. 'Actually, I have designed several homes and buildings around Den Bosch.'

'How about I commission you to do some work for me?' Wilhelmus smiled and schemed through his wine.

'Certainly, I would be happy to help if I can.'

'Excellent, how about we discuss it further, in my study after supper?'

And with that, Arthur's musings were suspended and he was caught in conversations of enterprise.

Wine glasses were steadily emptied and refilled, emptied and refilled again. Dinner plates were cleared and conversations were steered in all directions. Maria still sat, painted with a polite veneer of quiet contentedness, evidently preoccupied with her thoughts. She was occasionally forced into short interviews, mostly regarding her progress in school, but her half-hearted smile would linger no longer than it had to, and after the questions were answered and the interrogator turned away, she would slip back into misery, eyes to the table. Wilhelmus suddenly stood and gestured Jan towards his study. They left, with Mr van Essen in accompaniment. Jo and Grada were speaking to Hendrika and Mrs van Essen about babies and children, then about cake recipes and other topics Arthur held limited scope for contribution towards. Instead, he started planning a conversation with Maria in his head. He wanted to talk things through with her. Seeing her so depressed afflicted him with guilt, and in some way he felt like a failure for not being able to console her. As he tracked and rerouted several directions for discussion, he became suddenly aware of a hand resting on top of his own. It was soft, warm and kind, and managed to calm his concern. He traced the arm to Jo, and her smiling eyes met his.

Jo must have recognised Maria's temperament and read Arthur's thoughts for, with a sympathetic smile and almost in a whisper, she said,

'You should go and talk to her.' And in that voice there was no malice, no judgement, no hint of any untoward feeling, only compassion and understanding.

'Yes, I will if I may?'

Jo's unspoken reply revealed there'd been no need to ask. He stood to the groan of his chair grinding rearward against the timber floor. A lively discussion on draperies continued unabated and Jo gave Arthur a reaffirming smile before returning to a tutorial on interior decorating.

As Arthur walked behind Maria, he placed a hand on her shoulder. She slowly woke from her daze and looked up. Her eyes were wide and pained by melancholy confusion.

'Would you like to talk?' he asked, without expecting an answer. She nodded in polite, yet uncertain, agreeance. Arthur carefully lifted his hand again and made his way out of the house.

Recalling the night two years previous to this one, Arthur stood by that same tree and waited. A full moon, heavy and whitish-blue, cut through the black sky like a hole in black fabric exposing the pale flesh beneath. As he waited, he stared at the stars, searching his feelings for guidance. He suddenly heard hesitant, irregular footfall on the pavement and listened as she carefully crunched her way across the gravel. Then the sound stopped. Arthur tried to guess where it ended – to determine where Maria might be standing. He imagined her, halted by shyness and uncertainty, standing on the other side of the tree. They waited in silence for several seconds. Arthur knew he would have to be the first to speak.

'Maria . . .' He did not expect a reply – and he considered that perhaps it might be easier for him if there wasn't one. Yet he had very little idea as to what to say next. As he searched for words, a crooning voice caressed the silence.

'Well, this feels familiar.' Arthur could feel the smile in Maria's words. It gave him the reassurance he needed to face her. He moved around the tree and found her standing there. Before he could say anything, she took two small steps towards him and threw her arms around his waist. She pressed her head to his chest and her body trembled as she began to sob. Arthur let his arms fall around her, and held her.

'Maria,' he started. But his speech was fragmented. 'You know I still love you, right? I always will . . . but . . . I love Jo, too . . . it's different, I'm sure you can appreciate that . . . and no matter what, I will always be here for you . . . so, please . . . don't hate me . . .'

And at that, he waited. He had spat his heart out and whittled it into words, clumsily and without warning. He could feel Maria's body relax. She had stopped crying. She stirred ever so slightly and the two of them loosened their arms. Maria stepped back and looked up at him, tear-glazed eyes shimmering like the moon's reflection on a quivering lake. Her face softened a little and she lowered her eyes to focus on Arthur's collar. She patted a soft fist to his chest like a hammer hitting fruit without the means to bruise it – blunt, and heavy with helplessness. Maria was hurting, and in some way she wanted to ensure he hurt too. Her fist pounded tenderly at his heart and he could feel the emotion in it, the frustration. And it hurt him.

After the third half-hearted hit, she stopped and clenched a fistful of fabric from his coat. 'It hurts though,' she trembled quietly through her tears. 'It just . . . hurts.'

Her words rattled him. He melted inside, but his resolve kept him from showing her how much her pain wounded him. Arthur was on the brink of speaking when he felt his clothes pull tight across his shoulders and back as she doubled her grip. Her small voice spoke again. 'I don't hate you,' she resumed quietly. 'And . . . and I like Jo too.

She's really nice.' She managed to smile, and Arthur knew they had said almost everything they had needed to say.

'I'm glad you think so,' he replied. And they moved towards one another for another hug – a different hug – not one of tears and consoling, but one of love and understanding. Then, after enough time had passed, they separated again, looked at each other and laughed. It was only short and quiet, but it brought a great comfort to them both. 'Would you like to go back inside?'

'Yes, please,' Maria smiled, patting her eyes with the sleeve of her coat.

And, taking each other by the hand, they walked back to the welcoming glow of the house that babbled with the laughter and jovial voices of friends and family.

Part III

January 1988

Two gold rings gleamed under the white light of a dozen electric suns. The backs of his hands and fingers were thin, wrinkled and blotched with age spots, but each ring was as clean as the first day he wore it.

Hunched over the handle of the broom, Arthur continued to push and pile the sediment – the tiny scraps of paper and granules of glass that littered the factory floor. He turned the head on its heel and buried the bristles into the lines in the concrete and carefully scraped out a steady week's silt.

He realised the incessant chit-chit-chatter of people and machines had stopped. He was alone, and yet it affected him very little. He propped the broom against the wall and made for the lunchroom.

As he left the factory floor, Arthur passed by the main entrance and, instead of looking beyond it, he temporarily caught the faint, fleeting world it reflected. And he lived in there, in that moment, as if he was outside looking in. However, his reflection remained difficult to discern – made transparent in the bright midday sun that shone through the glass, and he was temporarily denied access to the view of the outside world.

Arthur didn't feel much like talking at lunch, so he sat by himself. To add to his sense of isolation, Bert had a team of young workers on staff, and when they talked to one another about their interests outside of work, the words they used and the subjects they referenced were completely foreign to him.

Careful not to attract too much attention, Arthur fished his food from the fridge and found a spot in a quiet corner. He just wanted to be left alone – to eat in peace, while he lost himself in the past. He opened his lunchbox to find several sandwiches, half of them sweet, the others savoury, each neatly cut. As he carefully slid a wedge away from its neighbours, like one would a card from a deck, he felt contentment. Arthur smiled to think of Jo preparing them . . . but jolted himself into correction as he recognised his error.

Had he missed something? A hint? Some important clue? What was the question? Did it matter? Arthur wasn't sure. But he knew he needed an answer and he wouldn't rest until he found it. He knew this much: it was a feeling – a person – and it gave his life meaning. He had to try the past again. Plough. Comb. Track. Find.

The scent, taste and texture of the bread, cheese, salad and meat sent him to a time long passed. As he ate, he retreated into reverie and he let his mind wander into the past, lulled by the mighty pull of nostalgia and contentment.

8

Married

Arthur sat at his parents' piano – a dusty relic from his past. After a few clumsy chords and a stray note or two, he managed to recall the patterns to several simple songs. Wilhelmus must have heard him for, in his own time, he entered the room and casually sauntered into Arthur's proximity with a glass of red wine cupped in his supinated hand.

'Well now, my son, this takes me back,' he announced in the silence between songs. Arthur knew his father was leading to a grander point. He pretended to search the old song book for something to play, but he didn't really need to – he wanted to improvise as he searched the scales further for forgotten chords. He also knew that his father would much rather be an audience to his struggle through an attempt to play something he knew – something classical and Dutch, like Sweelinck or van Wassanaer. But Arthur had no intention of pleasing his father.

'I must admit, none of you boys ever had much of an ear for music.' Wilhelmus was right. Each of his sons, in their own way, could play the songs they had been made to memorise through repetition, but they were never good enough to play for an audience. But Wilhelmus had not simply interrupted his son's playing in order to criticise it, and so Arthur waited a while longer before lifting his hands back into their position above the keys. 'Anyway, Arthur, I won't bother you for long. I understand you have set this time aside from work for reasons of your own. I have come to let you know that I have organised a wedding gift for you. You will find it on Julianastraat. Your mother and I expect you and Johanna will find it a modest but suitable first home.'

It took Arthur a moment to comprehend what his father had said. He had articulated it clearly enough, and he wasn't the kind of man to joke around, but the scale of the gift surprised him. Lost for words, Arthur sat silently, and a little rudely, too. He was dumbfounded. He gave up the idea of fumbling through the fragments of forgotten songs, and carefully dropped the cover back over the keys for what could well have been the last time. As he did so, Wilhelmus spoke again. 'You will need a home, of course, and I knew you would decline my offer had I asked you prior to having it built. I understand you have a penchant for doing things yourself, but we wanted to give you both something practical. So, there you have it . . .' he finished somewhat awkwardly.

It took Arthur half a minute, but eventually he stood and approached the man who was attempting to quell his tension by drowning it in wine. Arthur waited for his father to meet his eyes. His stiffness and straightness seemed forced – as if it was more an act than a fixed aspect of his character. Arthur offered a hand but as his father moved to grip it, Arthur surprised even himself by wrapping his arms around his father and embracing him in the briefest of hugs. He couldn't remember the last time either of them had shown any affection towards one another, but it didn't feel as strange now. Wilhelmus didn't move his arms in return, but nor did he express any objection. In some way, he wanted to hug his son, but he denied himself and resisted the natural human response to reciprocate.

Arthur released his father with a pat on the back, and as they straightened their shirts and jackets, he found the appropriate reply not only to the wedding present, but for everything his father had ever done for him. A lifetime of thanks that Wilhelmus had never asked for, nor needed to hear, was spoken in two words: 'Thanks, Dad.'

The wedding was set for the fourth Tuesday of November 1932. Arthur and Jo's wedding ceremony was a swift affair attended by a hundred or so of their closest friends and family. At Arthur's request, it was held in Vlijmen, at the church of Saint John the Baptist. The day was cold and windy, and yet the slicing sound of the icy wind was washed out by the ceaseless murmuring of excited guests.

As he waited at the altar, the priest busying himself to one side, Arthur stared into the chatting sea of faces that filled the church. The van Essens sat several rows from the front, and at the very centre of that pew he spotted Maria. Finding her face was like plucking a pretty shell from a wave-beaten beach. Only, he didn't scoop it from the sand, he didn't hold it, didn't think on it, for long. He didn't let himself. He simply admired it, appreciated its natural beauty, like any other thing pleasing to the eye. Unlike the other guests, Maria stared impassively to where Arthur was stood. He tried to imagine what she was thinking, and whether she was happy or sad or neither, but he promptly reminded himself that his feelings for her existed in a different place at a different time, in a different way. He had made a commitment to Jo. Arthur had once entertained the idea of marrying Maria, and if things had been different he might have done. But now he reminded himself that how she felt, or what she thought, must not matter to him.

Arthur's contemplations were interrupted by the sonorous ceremonial notes of the organ, signifying Jo's arrival. The figurative shell was dropped and dragged away by the roaring tide – strained back into the hushed sea of friendly faces. The sacramental sound solidified his resolve and straightened his posture.

When Jo appeared and commenced her walk alone to the altar, Arthur saw the approval and adoration on the faces of the people in attendance, and it filled him with affirmation, a measure of confidence that told him he was doing the right thing. Any doubt that may still have haunted the neglected crevices of his conscience dissipated like sea foam.

Arthur wanted to paint the image of her in that instant so vividly upon the canvas of his mind that whenever he wished to recall it, he could see it as clearly as he could in that moment. Her ivory gown flowed down the length of her body with a lace as thin as the finest film of mist ever caught in the morning light. She moved and hovered and halted and moved again, with every effort applied to not stepping too quickly. Arthur could not and would not unfix the trance that she had him in.

When she reached him and the music stopped and they stared into each other's eyes, they smiled. Arthur was simultaneously excited and nervous, but he found conviction in the woman before him, and a sense of comfort too, a comfort that he had grown to rely upon.

The priest brought their hands together, and as they each gazed into the other's eyes, the rest of the world seemed to melt away. His words merged into an incoherent mumbling that was muffled – muted to Arthur's ears by the stifling hands of Time that were firmly pressed to the mouth of the moment. Arthur and Jo exchanged smiles that spoke volumes. They were brimming with joy because they knew that the lifetime ahead of them was more important, in many ways, than a few uncomfortable minutes of attention.

On cue, Arthur slid the ring onto Jo's finger, and she did the same for him. The ring glistened gold against his skin.

When the ceremony ended, Arthur and Jo's first kiss as a married couple was welcomed with applause. They were congratulated in a tumultuous torrent of good wishes. Before they finally left the church for their new home, they met with their most immediate friends and family. Arthur's mother hugged him. He received handshakes from his father and from Andre and Bauke. A kiss on the cheek from Grada, and a handshake from Jan. A handshake from Mr van Essen, and a hug from Mrs van Essen, Alice, Irma and Maria. Jo received much the same – although people approached her with less rigidity, less formality. The interaction Arthur found most difficult to read was between Maria and Jo. He knew there would be no notion of malice on Jo's part, but he couldn't help but think of the misery Maria must have been masking. The two embraced and shared celebratory smiles. Arthur even saw Maria whisper sisterly secrets into Jo's ear like an old friend, and he was glad. He had been worried that Maria, in her youth, might get lost trying to navigate her way through the maze of thoughts and feelings that would swirl in a storm of emotion and etiquette.

After the two women parted and Jo had moved on to talk to the next guest, Arthur tried to catch Maria's eye and to communicate his thanks to her just through the expression on his face. When she eventually felt his eyes on her, and made herself look his way, she stared awhile as she read what he wished to convey. Then her face changed and Arthur knew his message was received, for she finally sent back a look that seemed to say *You're welcome*. After that final acknowledgement, she turned to her parents and disappeared into the crowd. Feeling a sense of accomplishment, Arthur duly returned to helping his wife with the task of acknowledging the well-meaning guests who sought to make their attendance known to them.

With their families satisfied, Arthur and Jo were deep in a state of romantic love. After the final few guests had departed, the newlyweds made their retreat into married life, and the future that awaited them.

Night had claimed its ephemeral reign over day. In the back seat of the car, seated beside Jo, Arthur gazed out of the window. Corrugated clouds creased the sky overhead, combed like ripples on a lake, and they were below the water's surface. A large cloud coasted by overhead, and it looked to Arthur like the pale underbelly of a giant turtle floating in a black sea. He was awestruck by an infinity of stars that perforated the canopy like pinholes pressed into the cloak of night. He stared up while they stared back down, blinking, squinting, twinkling. Then, as their chauffeur turned onto Julianastraat and Arthur snapped out of his trance, Jo grew visibly more excited. She had known about the house, but she had not yet seen it. In fact, even Arthur had only seen it briefly from the outside, so the layout and the furnishings would be as much of a surprise to him as to Jo. They stopped before a house that seemed to shine in the moonlight. The glossy fresh paint and unweathered windows were signs of the building's newness. Arthur tried to look at it through Jo's eyes, with all the comprehension that this address would be the start of new adventures and the laying down of memories.

As he was looking at it from her perspective, she spoke. 'Is this really our home now, Arthur? Isn't it too much? It's so new and exquisite. Don't you think it seems to sparkle in the dark? How do you suppose it does that?' Her questions sought no answers, they simply expressed her elation.

'Yes lieverd, this is our new home.'

It was all the confirmation she needed, and with that they exchanged yet another expression of anticipatory excitement. After signalling for the driver to leave, they went to the front door. The wintery wind that had lashed at the church walls during the wedding had abated, but the night was brisk. Arthur found the key his father had given him before they left, and slid it into the lock. With a clever click, the house was open. Guided by the light of the moon, Arthur lifted Jo into his arms and carried her through the doorway, down the passage and into the heart of their new home.

They were eager to explore every nook and cranny, but they both agreed that it could wait until morning. Jo removed her coat, and her scarf, gloves, hat and shoes too, and let them all fall to the floor. Then she sent Arthur a kind of wild smile and skipped and danced her way through the house in nought but her wedding gown, which she had hitched up somehow so that it hung to halfway between her knees and ankles.

When they found what they knew to be the master suite, Arthur looked to Jo, who seemed ready and waiting. He placed his arms into position and she leapt into them as he lifted her from the floor once more. She slung an arm around his neck, and playfully stepped her fingers down his cheek. A lamp at each bedside spread a dim light about the room, and he used this to his advantage as he carried Jo across the threshold and towards their bed.

He lowered her as close to the centre of the bed as he could manage, but with gravity's assistance, a little more quickly than he intended. She made a soft impression upon the quilt and pulled it into wrinkles that streaked from her in all directions. To Arthur, she seemed to blossom on the bed like a magnificent rose. She stretched her arms above her, slowly twisted her hips from side to side, and let the smooth skin of her legs glide over one another. She wriggled and writhed in a state of sensual rapture. Her hair fell across the fabric to frame a face that would have inspired any artist. Her look was soft, yet she had adopted an expression that beckoned him. Then, as swiftly as drawing a curtain or removing a silk glove, she slipped out of her gown and, after slowly sliding it across her body, let it drop to the floor. Her body – pale and pure, was laid bare before her husband. She spoke slowly and in an almost dreamlike fashion. Her arms reached for him. 'Well, what are you waiting for? Come to me, Arthur . . .'

And go to her he did. He propped himself over her. She held a hand to his ear and busied the other at his shirt, pushing button after button from their holes until his chest was bare. His feet pushed at his shoes and socks, and he used a hand to remove his pants, until, like her, he was bare. Then he lowered himself over her and pressed skin to skin, hip to hip and lip to lip. And then she reached down. She took him. Guided him. And with her warmth welcoming his heat, they were one.

When Arthur awoke the next morning, he felt perfectly at home, and he thought that for the first time in a long, long time, he had been cured of Maria. Since he had been with Jo, he had felt differently about Maria – his musings were not of a romantic or amorous nature, but he still thought about her as much as his love for Jo would allow. He thought of her as a close friend, a confidante akin to family, and then, when she sent him that last look before departing the wedding, it was as if he had been released from a spell.

However, while Arthur and Jo were touring their new home, just as they had arrived at the bottom of the stairs, Jo spoke in an uncertain tone.

'Arthur, you know after our wedding, when we were thanking our guests . . .' She left the question unfinished, and so Arthur knew she needed some encouragement to continue.

'Yes?' It was all he could think to contribute, but it was enough.

'Well, I don't think it's anything, and I had thought to keep it to myself, but that's hardly proper given the openness of communication

– the frankness, so to speak – that a healthy marriage demands . . .' She wavered again, so Arthur redoubled his investment in listening to what seemed so hard for her to say.

'What's on your mind, my dear wife? Did someone say something that upset you?'

'Well, yes, but I'm not so sure exactly. See, Maria – you know – van Essen, she hugged me, to give me her good wishes, or so I thought, but – and I'm sure I don't know what she meant by it – she said to me, so quietly that I hardly heard it – in fact, I almost thought I had imagined it – but I couldn't think what would make my mind hear such a thing if it *hadn't* been said, which made me think I *had* heard it, and instead I shifted the blame back upon young Maria, and wondered whether she even meant to say it aloud at all . . .' Jo was fumbling, trying to find a way to articulate what had been silently vexing her. Arthur recalled the interchange; he had watched them with such a careful eye that he could play it again in his mind like a film.

Jo finally arrived at the point she had wished to make. She was much more composed now and found the words without difficulty: 'Maria said, "*If you don't love him, I will*".'

Arthur was stunned. To what effect Maria had spoken those words, he did not know. He could have speculated, in fact reasoned, that her brazen words were a warning to Jo, laced with a polite hostility, but to allay Jo's anxieties, and to preserve Maria's position as a sisterly figure, he needed to find a logical explanation.

'I'm sure I don't know why she would say something like that. It just seems so out of character,' he began, hoping to ignite doubt in Jo's memory of the event.

'I'm sure I didn't mishear it. If I had thought I'd imagined it, I wouldn't have been able to find the resolve to tell it to you.' Jo spoke in a more patient tone now, calmed by finally having the thoughts that had festered through the night out in the open.

Arthur tried another tack. 'No, I believe you heard her right. But do you think perhaps she didn't mean it in the way you think? What I mean is, do you think she might have said it to you to give you peace of mind in knowing she can offer me the kind of family love and support I might need if something were to get in the way of your ability to afford me your affections?' He waited on the point, not completely convinced by his own arguments. He hoped it would be enough to dull at least some of the effect of Maria's oddly pointed words.

Jo thought on it for several seconds, before slowly constructing her rebuttal. 'I think . . . that if that were her meaning . . . she should have spoken it to you, not to me.'

Arthur wasn't surprised that Jo didn't buy into his flimsily constructed conjecture. His final solution was not a helpful one, and it ran some risks, but it was all he had left. 'I guess we may never know why she said what she said, and what she meant by it,' he reasoned. 'But I suppose one of us could ask her the next time we see her.'

At that, Jo, as Arthur had hoped, started to slowly shake her head. He could tell she had regained her usual humour, and would be able to forget the matter – at least for the time being. 'I don't think that will be necessary.' A smirk extended into a smile. 'But thanks for the offer.' Jo planted a soft kiss upon Arthur's head. 'I know I don't have anything to worry about. Today's our first full of day of being a married couple, so let's enjoy it together. Besides, I want to explore the rest of our beautiful new home!'

'Yes, I agree!' Arthur said, relieved by Jo's mature and rational response. 'Where shall we start?'

9

Birth

As new routines were established, Time made short work of burying the memories of the independent lives Arthur and Jo had led before marriage. They were living a redefined normality. Jo spent a good deal of her time at home, tending to household duties. Each week she would also spend a day or two a week visiting friends and family – both Arthur's and hers – and volunteering to help them however she could. She spent a good deal of her time at leisure, and for good reason.

It was mid-afternoon, a week from Christmas in 1933. Arthur and Jo strolled hand in hand along Grootestraat towards Visser's café-restaurant, beside the Vlijmen town hall. A pearly sun blurred into the foamy sky and everything was glazed by a dewy dampness, but some quality in the sleepy breeze declared that it would not rain again this day. As they neared the café, a flavoursome aroma teased their hungry stomachs.

They sat at a table beside the purring fire. For the time being, their coffee was too hot to drink, and so they sipped on conversation.

'If we have a boy, I would like to name him Bert,' Arthur said to Jo. 'But if we have girl, I think I would like to call her Maria.'

Jo reclined slightly and rubbed her lower belly for a few moments. 'I quite like Bert,' she said, 'it reminds me of my father, but I might have to give more thought to Maria.' She reached for her coffee, but when she kissed the cup it was still too hot and she burned her lips.

'Let it cool a little longer,' Arthur suggested after seeing her wince.

Jo made an effort to straighten her aching back. The chair was hard and poorly angled. 'Could you help me with my coat, Arthur? The heat is rather stifling.' Arthur helped Jo from her coat and then removed his own and took them both and hung them by the door.

'You know, Jo, my mother is sick with excitement,' Arthur said on his return to the table. 'She's always wanted to be an oma. She has said she'll help us in any way she can. But I don't think I'll call on her too often – her health worries me.'

'Grada was so happy too!' Jo said, finding her humour. 'But she was convinced that she'd known long before I told her. She said it was "something about the way I glowed" when I'd stopped by one day.'

'Andre and my father are happy, too, I'm sure, but it's not in their nature to admit it. Of course, they congratulated me when I told them, but their replies were recitals. Bauke, on the other hand – he seemed sincere when he expressed his delight. But all that really matters is that you and our baby are healthy.' Arthur thought back to when Jo's pregnancy was confirmed. The waiting since then had felt like an eternity. As a first-time expectant father, it was difficult for Arthur to comprehend that he would be responsible for a new life, and it was not something he felt fully prepared for. It was surreal and foreign, like a distant future, a separate life to the one he was living. He was excited to be a father, but at the same time he found himself stressed, restless.

The idea that Jo was bearing his child had doubled his need to care for her, provide for her and make sure that she always felt loved.

A waiter approached and placed two plates of cake on the table.

When the waiter was out of earshot, Jo said to Arthur, 'I hope the cake is better than the coffee.'

Arthur grinned and used his spoon to slice a piece. 'I don't see why we couldn't name our daughter Maria,' he said, resuming their earlier discussion. Jo was about to dig into her slice of cake, but paused. Then she carried on scooping a spoon to her mouth. In the time it took Jo to chew and swallow her cake, Arthur pried into her thoughts. He imagined her recalling Maria's words to her on the day of the wedding. He imagined how the idea of naming their child after Maria might bring on the same sense of nausea Jo had experienced early in her pregnancy. He realised how unfair his suggestion was, and how uncomfortable it made Jo feel, but how much she hated a part of herself for feeling that way and how she couldn't shake the queasy, uneasy feeling it gave her. Then Jo took a sip of coffee to swallow her cake and Arthur imagined how she wasn't fine with the proposal he had made, and how deeply she didn't like it, but how dutiful she thought she had to be.

Jo said simply, 'You're right, dear. I think, if we have a girl, we should call her Maria.'

Arthur half-smiled, half-scowled, as he tried to interpret her tone. 'How was the cake?' he asked, though he had tried it for himself.

'I believe you already know the answer to that,' she said, grinning. 'I think I'll have a cup of tea when we get home.' Suddenly the thrum of rain climbed over the murmur of people and the world beyond the window was one wet mess. A moment later, someone prodded the fire until it purred and purred.

Time crawled forward on its hands and knees until, finally, in March 1934, Jo's labour started. Arthur's sense of calm surprised him. It was a quiet Saturday and the two of them had been dawdling about the place in an uncharacteristically slow fashion. They knew they had nowhere to be and nothing they needed to do. Their only plan was to wait, and so they waited.

The sun shone at the start of the morning and Arthur tried to make the most of it. He was in the yard, but remained within earshot of the house. He swept. He pruned. He split some logs and loaded the barrow. He searched for weeds in the pavement. He traced a trail to a snail that moved with unbearable slowness. He found a stray nail, crooked and brown. He bent down and picked it up. He put it in his pocket. Then he just stood and enjoyed the greyness and coolness and peacefulness of the day. A fleet of soggy-looking clouds was sailing in. Arthur packed all the things away and was safe and dry inside the house before the first drops dampened the ground. He busied himself with preparing food and drinks and by returning things to their proper place. Then a sudden breeze bullied the grey clouds away and rays of sunlight refracted through rain drops, making the garden glitter. Arthur found himself searching the sky for the dividing line – to once again find that inevitable border between light and shade, though it impressed him only a little. He sensed he might soon be leaving his old life behind. And all in a day, the seasons came and went and came and went again, each cycle shorter than the last.

In anticipation of the due date, they had long since put their affairs in order. Jo had written the doctor's number on a card by the telephone. She frequently made a point of confirming Arthur's knowledge of this, but she did so in a way that didn't frustrate him. Instead, he felt all the more motivated to get things right and prove to her that he understood what he needed to do when the time came.

And so, while they were enjoying a leisurely late morning of casual conversation, sporadic snacking, menial chores and inconsequential reading, it happened. Arthur was disinterestedly perusing the day's paper when he sensed that something in Jo's manner – her posture perhaps – had changed. Although she held her book open on her lap, she had stopped reading. She was concentrating on the clock and applying a great deal of effort to quietly counting and making mental notes of the figures in her head. He suspected, without letting his mind jump to conclusions, that her labour was about to begin. Jo's eyes met his and she managed to force her face into a faint and fleeting smile, fraught with courage, nervousness and uncertainty.

She gave several short nods of her head and spoke. 'Arthur, the doctor's phone number is on a card by the phone. Could you call and let him know to make his way here now, please?'

Time looped in a peculiar fashion as they waited for the doctor to arrive. For some reason, Arthur found himself cleaning. Though the house was still in near-perfect order, he busied himself washing and drying dishes. The waiting was intolerable, and he was trying to distract himself with chores, accompanied by excessive checking of his watch and the clock. Time passed, as it inevitably does, and Arthur's activities were finally ceased by three sharp knocks at the door.

Despite knowing many people in town, Arthur wasn't familiar with the doctor Jo had chosen. He had only recently arrived from Poland and, being of a different faith, didn't attend the same church. Nevertheless, he was a well-respected physician, known for his expertise with modern medicine. Jo had met him on several occasions during her pregnancy for assessments of her progress, and to have him answer a number of questions that she felt silly – but all the better – for asking. Jo was well equipped for many aspects of parenting in the later stages of a child's life, having helped Grada regularly with her children, but she found she had an array of questions along the way that still needed clarifying. This doctor had come highly recommended by many of the women she spoke to, and so she had sought him out.

When Arthur met him at the door, they shook hands. He carried a large brown-leather bag that opened across the length of its centre like an oversized purse.

'Good day, Mr van Hessel. My name is Doctor Kugel,' he said with clinical precision. Doctor Kugel was a man of moderate proportions, perhaps a little thinner and shorter than Arthur – who was of an average height. On his head he wore a black homburg hat that crammed beneath it a frizzy nest of hair which, with hat removed, appeared to be thinning, receding and transitioning from brown to grey. To complete his ensemble, he held at first – in way of resting a hand upon it like a cane – a recently retracted umbrella that was black and bejewelled with droplets of water that clung to it like glass beetles. He had, before extending his hand to meet Arthur's, relocated the umbrella to a horizontal position upon his bag in order to produce a free hand.

It being mid-March, erratic changes in weather were to be expected, so while the morning was clear, cloudy, wet and windy, another sudden shower had been and gone and this doctor had clearly been wise to it. He must have travelled through winter and arrived in spring, for a wet wind whisked by as they stood in the open doorway. Standing a little behind Doctor Kugel was a rather nondescript nurse who, in a manner akin to the way Jo glowed with understanding, projected a tender, maternal quality. Doctor Kugel introduced her as his nurse staff, one Mrs de Jong.

The two needed no second bidding to enter. Arthur guided them towards the bedroom, where he had, only an hour or so earlier, helped Jo onto their bed. When she saw them, a clear wave of relief washed over her – but only for a moment, for it seemed that her concentration ebbed with an inner tide that demanded her unwavering attention. Taking his cue to leave, Arthur kissed Jo on the forehead, wished her luck and assured her that he would be seeing her soon, and that he would be eagerly awaiting news of the safe arrival of their child.

Arthur went out to the garden and paced for a while. Then he decided his bike needed polishing, and buffed it until it gleamed like new. He next went inside and tried to resume the newspaper he had started. He picked it up. He put it down. He picked it up again. Then he put it down again. He sought other ways to occupy his mind, yet all the while Arthur maintained a quiet prayer – or inner dialogue, as it were – that both his wife and child would be healthy when he next saw them. Eventually, after dark, he returned to the outdoors, and it was there that the noble nurse found him.

'Mr van Hessel, would you like to meet your daughter?'

In a trance-like state, Arthur went to the bedside. It was Jo's face that first broke the blur. She was propped up on a pile of pillows, and in her arms, with its face against her half-exposed breast, was a head so small that he, having not seen a newborn baby before, found it difficult to fathom that it could be human, and that it was his daughter. Jo's hair stuck to her face in places, and he could tell that she was beyond exhaustion. Even so, she gave her husband a look of complete contentment, and it calmed him instantly. She mouthed 'hallo' and he returned it in kind. He moved to her side and held her hand. He kissed her on the forehead, then quickly on the lips, and then knelt by the bedside, both to be close to his wife and daughter, but also to relieve his legs, which had suddenly weakened under him. When she released her latch upon the breast and, after Mrs de Jong swooped in and wrapped her in a blanket, Arthur was given his daughter to hold and he knew, with more conviction than ever before, that he loved her in a way that he had never loved anyone before.

It was his first time seeing his daughter's face, and besides feeling a complete sense of relief and affection, he surprised himself by unexpectedly finding traces of his parents – Wilhelmus's jaw, Hendrika's nose. After a moment of standing, his legs revitalised by the opportunity to hold his daughter, Arthur took up a position beside his wife on the bed. And, in that fashion, they rested. In his arms, his daughter slept, while Jo rested her head on his shoulder, his cheek upon her crown, and they were weary, and they were happy, and they were a family.

Early the next morning, Doctor Kugel visited. As he spoke to the new parents, he did so with a preciseness of tone that chiselled his words in bold print; each letter stamped with a clarity that ensured no room was left for error.

'At all times, a baby must be kept warmer than ourselves,' he started. 'Indeed, the cold will do no good for your baby – being premature, she is certainly smaller than she ought to be and I have several concerns about her survival.' Arthur was jotting the instructions down in his memory with a quiet desperation that placed every ounce of hope he had upon making an accurate record of the doctor's advice. 'I suggest you place her in a small box – closed in on all sides for the warmth it can provide, but also to keep her from falling out. Of course, you'll leave the lid off. The box could then be positioned by a fireplace, at a distance where you could sit comfortably. It will be a little like incubating a chick.'

So it was that they would often place their daughter in a shoebox above the mantelpiece to keep her warm while she slept. Yet still, they were told she should not have survived. Though Arthur presented a brave front to Jo and others, his thoughts were in constant contest against the concerns he had for his daughter's survival.

By the third day, Arthur and Jo had finally agreed. They named her Maria. Maria Josephine Theresa Martina van Hessel, and yet she was so small they hardly knew how she could ever bear so many names.

The first year of her life brought Arthur a great deal of joy, but it was not without daily doses of panic and regular calls and excursions to the doctor's office. Doctor Kugel attended as many of their appointments as he could. He seemed more pleased with every milestone Maria reached – to witness firsthand that her health had not deteriorated.

And so, Maria survived her infancy. Every day, Arthur and Jo celebrated her convalescence as she continued, slowly, to grow bigger and stronger. And when Arthur fell asleep early or slept through the night – deaf to the midnight cries that broke Jo's already broken sleep – Jo rarely asked for help beyond what he could give her. And though he searched, he found no note of complaint hidden in her words, nor was there any sign of it written upon her face.

Occasionally, when he felt he had enough energy to stay awake late into the evening, Arthur would let Maria fall asleep on his chest while he reclined on an armchair or lay propped up in bed. Oftentimes, when he did so, he would look down on her sleeping face, which was finally relaxed and calm and peaceful, not a single muscle tensed, and he would realise how unguarded – indeed vulnerable and dependent – she was. And when standing and holding her was all that would cool her temper, and Arthur's back ached and his arms were ablaze, he would feel her soft cheek press against his shoulder, and her impossibly fair hair tickle his ear, and he would find it in himself to hold her for a little longer.

10

Couples

Early in April 1935, after visiting at the weekend, Grada proposed that Arthur and Jo entrust their daughter's care to her for a night so that they could get away, rest, reconnect with old acquaintances, or simply enjoy some much-needed time together. After a short deliberation, they accepted her offer and so, the following Saturday, Arthur escaped work and drove Jo to Mol so that they might visit Maria and a man she had met named Henk Peeters. It had been a while since Arthur and Jo had been able to get out of town and they agreed that it would be nice to spend time in the company of adults.

Shortly after getting married, Arthur had purchased his first car – a black, two-door sedan. He knew he would need a means of transport that could accommodate the large family he planned to have. He still rode his motorbike and pushbike from time to time, for work and personal errands, but to take people with him, he needed something bigger. The car was the very embodiment of modernisation: the driving force behind the changing dynamic of a world in which everyone was becoming, gradually, more self-sufficient, and everything was in some way becoming closer.

Before they left Vlijmen, Arthur stopped at Garage Pulles to fill the tank. The garage was near the train line and was a popular stop for motorists arriving in or leaving town. The building had a predominantly stone façade, with two bowsers and a large sign at head height advertising motor oil. It didn't take a discerning eye long to realise that the building had once been home to another retail enterprise – but guessing at what specific business would be a far more challenging feat. While the stone front gave the place a solid, established look, a side view revealed that the back three-quarters, like the roof, were galvanised tin. Arthur took a moment to appreciate that the building, probably like others of its kin, had meshed old and new to form a hybrid habitat for human and mechanical activity.

As Kees Pulles checked the oil and pumped the fuel and so on, Arthur and Jo sat in the small dining area annexed to the store front. Kees' wife, Doortje, brought them each a tall glass of lemon cordial. As she approached and made small talk, she held a smile like the woman on the advertisement for detergent Arthur had suddenly spied in the shop window.

'That's a lovely motorcar you have there, meneer,' she said – yet her eyes never strayed from the vacant gaze she held in their general direction.

'Dank je,' Arthur beamed proudly. 'This will be our first trip out of town with it.'

'How lovely,' she recited dreamily. 'I hope you enjoy your lemonades.'

'Yes, dank je,' Arthur replied again, suddenly realising he had never heard anyone call a drink by that name before. He lifted the glass from the red and white checked tablecloth and savoured the tang of the cool, refreshing drink. He looked across at Jo, though his view of her had been, the whole time, partly and rudely obstructed by a vase of unusual flowers – unusual because they were too vibrant and too exotic and too perfectly shaped and unblemished to have been grown locally at that time of the year. He shifted the vase momentarily aside and Jo smiled. He could tell she was enjoying the drink, and Arthur gave her a nod of approval, as if to say that he too found it pleasant. Doortje hovered nearby, twirling a ringlet of her hair around a finger while she flicked half-heartedly through a catalogue of women clad in foreign fashions. Soon Arthur and Jo had reached the bottoms of their glasses and, as if scripted, Kees poked his head in the rear door and jingled a set of keys.

'She's all ready to go,' he announced. After a moment's confusion, Arthur realised Kees meant that he was finished tending to the car. Arthur passed Doortje a thin slip of paper and she took it between the scissored grip of her index and middle fingers. Having paid the bill, Arthur and Jo thanked the Pulles with the sentiment of satisfied customers. Then, with their destination awaiting them, they left town to the clean smell of gasoline, and the bitter-sweet taste of lemon and sugar on their lips.

As Arthur drove, thoughts drifted through him and he reflected on why he was never much inclined to take the train. He arrived at the fact that it was because a train is committed to its track and can never stray from it. A train is limited by a predetermined path, and as its passenger, he must surrender his autonomy. The freedom of a car or motorbike allows a man to navigate the roads as he wishes. Other thoughts came and went as well – thoughts of the past and the future, of work and home, of family and friends. All the untouchable and irreplaceable aspects comprising the human experience were awake and aching inside him.

He looked across to Jo. She seemed to be enjoying the serenity of the countryside and the reprieve from motherhood. She wore a short-sleeved cotton dress with a fine blue and white check. Careful to keep his eyes on the road, but drawn to her irresistible beauty, he briefly looked across at Jo. She had had her hair cut a few days earlier and Arthur admired how the light refracted through the soft blonde waves that washed, parted slightly off-centre. She casually tucked a loose lock behind her ear. Arthur felt her beauty was a picture to behold – like the hillside meadow that extended to the horizon, freckled with the sporadic scattering of daisies and daffodils that danced and curtsied and bowed in the breeze. A sweeping wind made the landscape shimmer like velvet in the sunlight. Her face was fixed with an immoveable smile as they drove, and she was as pure and as calm as the countryside. And cutting through it all, the motor droned like constant thunder before them, while the tyres whirred beneath and the spotless glass gave a view to think through. Instead of talking, husband and wife sat in a mutual and intimate fancy of observation, communicating through the exchange of glances and grins. At one point they lost the landscape when both sides of the road were lined with thick-trunked trees. Arthur felt as though they were being funnelled towards their destination and so, in defiance, he flung himself to distant memories of the past. He thought of Madeleine and of the young Maria he remembered from his dreams, and each and every time, he circled back to Jo – smiling beneath a cider-scented sycamore, sitting upon a checked cloth, stretched out upon her wedding bed, clutching a baby to her breast . . .

Then a soft hand upon his knee brought him back to the countryside cruise. Jo looked at him and smiled as if to welcome him back from the past. She could probably tell by watching his face, Arthur reasoned, that he had travelled somewhere deep into thought. Seeing her face, and with memories of her streaming through his thoughts, he couldn't help but feel an irresistible desire to kiss her. But he knew he would have to wait and so, gradually, each slipped silently back into their shared solitude.

The drive took a little over an hour and when they arrived in Mol, the city seemed to fish them from the deep fog of thoughts they had been wading through and left the couple cast mercilessly upon the roaring shore of civilisation. The streets were a hive of human habit and ambition as people hummed from place to place with pace, purpose and a palpable practicality. Arthur caught the contagion and drove fixedly until he had arrived, as if by instinct, at the address Maria had given in her previous correspondence. He cut the engine and was freed from the trance of single-minded navigation he had fallen into. Quickly checking his reflection in the mirror, he looked to Jo and was filled once again by a profound adoration for her. With his fingertips, he softly steered her face towards his and let nature pull them closer together until he could deliver the kiss that had been waiting so patiently upon his lips. They were joined at the mouth for several seconds, and would have been for several more if not for etiquette. They unfixed themselves to let the fever fade. Arthur looked and smiled and nodded. Jo looked and smiled back. He offered her a final look before opening the door and throwing himself from the car. He straightened his suit as he made his way around to Jo's door to help her out. Taking her hand, Arthur led her along the path.

Maria welcomed them at the door. 'Arthur, Jo! How nice it is to see you both looking so well! I hope the journey was pleasant.' She leaned forward to embrace each of them. 'Henk has been called away but he should be home for dinner. Please come in and make yourselves at home. I'll fix you each a drink.'

'Hallo, Maria,' said Arthur. 'Our drive was lovely, thank you. You appear to be doing well for yourself! Jo and I have been looking forward to meeting Henk. It's a shame he's been delayed, but we'll meet him in due course. A drink would be delightful, thanks.'

'Thank you for having us to visit, Maria,' said Jo. 'Yes, the weather has favoured us today. Lovely sunshine. Oh, and I can't wait to meet Henk!'

And the three of them disappeared into the house as the door slowly swung closed behind them.

As Arthur washed his face, polished his lenses, combed his hair and otherwise preened himself for dinner, he knew he did so with a less-than-honourable purpose at the forefront of his mind. He wanted, quite simply, to impress Maria. He wanted her to maintain an image of him as a handsome, desirable fellow. He also wanted to avoid having that image diminished in contrast with the intimidating idea he had constructed of the man in whose guest bathroom's mirror he now appraised himself.

After they were all seated to dine, Henk, who had arrived home just ten minutes earlier, poured the wine from a bronze-tinted bottle into a corpulent conical decanter. Then he poured it into the glistening glasses, the black-red, oak-scented fluid swirling. Arthur lifted his glass to his mouth. Stopped. Sampled the bouquet. Gave a smile to the table and pressed the thin rim to his lip. His tongue bathed in a warm, acidic puddle. And as the juice jolted his palate, he withdrew the glass, mouth closed, swallowed and started to speak.

'A fine wine, Doctor,' he decreed. 'Made the more pleasant by the company.'

Henk was a remarkable man by every measure. In his profession, he was the very embodiment, the epitome, of perfect practice – as though he was constantly, effortlessly and without fault, offering

117

everyone a tutorial in life. Arthur didn't know the particulars about what kind of doctor he was – in what areas, if any, he specialised – but he could tell he was a good one. He seemed a king among men. Indeed, a crown would not have looked odd on his head. Furthermore, he was built like an athlete, toned and tanned. Everything about him was defined and refined: his voice, his face, his ambitions. In addition to a lean physique, he was clearly well read, for he spoke like a poet. Arthur guessed his age was between Maria's and his own, and in every way, Arthur had to admit he was a man worthy of her. He smiled his approval at Maria and, turning to Jo, offered a matrimonial smile. For Arthur, considering Henk a rival would have been an easy, yet foolish, trap to fall into. But the manner in which Henk flaunted his fortune and qualities was subtle and not annoyingly pretentious. He was proud of his accomplishments, that much was clear, but he was more than happy to have other people hold the attention of the room. As a result, no rivalry grew and Arthur accepted Henk into an amiable coexistence.

As the evening wore on, Arthur felt the wine's effects doubled by his fatigue, and doubled again by a recent stint of sobriety that had reduced his tolerance for the drink. He was made to reacquaint himself with alcohol. But aside from a slightly increased fogginess of thought – or rather a decreased clarity of mind, a general light-headedness – he found his symptoms quite pleasant. Arthur felt a kind of peace and contentment take hold, and he revelled in it.

Time ticked by to the tune of talking and laughing and drinking, and the room fell into a collective sentimentality.

'We are fortunate people, aren't we?' said Arthur.

'To think we have all come together like this,' said Maria.

'Yes, we have each found someone so special to us,' said Jo.

'Proost!'

'Proost!'

'On the topic, our wedding will be early September, next year. You're both invited, of course. You should expect to find a formal invitation in the post soon,' said Henk.

'We wouldn't miss it for the world,' said Jo.

'We only hope it could be half as lovely as your wedding,' said Maria.

'Yes. How is married life treating you? I hear it came with a new house.' said Henk.

'Who knows something outside of ourselves, something different . . . something recent?' said Maria.

'I hear the new Vlijmen-Drunen water tower has been opened in Nieuwkuijk,' said Jo.

'Yes, I saw Burgemeester van der Ven's photograph in the newspaper just the other day,' said Arthur.

'Do you know him, or . . .?' said Maria.

'Not at all, I've merely heard the name.'

'And here we all are standing at the forefront of industry,' said Henk.

'It's all so practical – all these magnificent things made by man,' said Arthur.

'Yes, aren't cars simply wonderful?' said Maria.

'Wonderful indeed, but they could spell the end for trains,' said Henk.

'Do you really think so?'

'What would ever happen to all the railways?' said Jo.

'I suppose trains did the same for horse and cart,' said Arthur

'The next new thing always comes along and the old ways are forgotten,' agreed Henk.

'It would be such a shame,' said Maria.

'Trains have such a certainty about them. Such an efficiency,' said Henk.

'They're dependable – yes. There's no nonsense about them. From point to point. That's what they do. From place to place fixed to their track,' said Arthur.

'Must we talk of trains all evening? What else is there?' pleaded Maria.

'Did you hear about Truus van Vliet?' asked Jo.

'Oh yes! How horrible! It's all far too sad,' said Maria.

'Who is she? I know the name but I'm afraid I can't quite place the face . . .' said Henk.

'Can we please talk about something else?' said Maria.

'Yes, let's not succumb to gossip,' said Arthur.

'Well, now I'm curious, so I'd like to know at least a little more,' teased Henk.

'Her husband had an accident at work,' said Jo.

'An accident?'

'Oh, really?'

'Unfortunately, he didn't survive it.'

'It's so sad!' said Maria.

'What was his name?' said Henk.

'I think it was Pieter.'

'Yes, that's right!'

'And now she has some other man?' said Arthur.

'You think she just replaced him?' said Maria.

'Well, she's still quite young and really rather fetching,' said Jo.

'But do you think her beauty makes her behaviour permissible?' challenged Arthur.

'What do you suppose makes a flower a flower? And what, for that matter, makes a weed a weed and not a flower?' said Henk.

'It's hardly proper, is it? I mean, so soon and all?' said Arthur.

'Who can say? We're hardly in a position to judge. I mean, what would any of us do?' said Jo.

Then, in the midst of conversation, a *cat*! For, perhaps, a second or two, a . . . *cat*? Arthur wasn't sure. Had he imagined it? Had he wished it and dreamed it? He couldn't tell. Had he really felt it there, stroking itself against his leg as he had once, so many years ago? Would it return to him again? And from that point on, Arthur lost track of who had said what.

'That's right, we're only human after all.'

'I really don't think famous people are any more interesting than the rest of us.'

'No, no, most decidedly not, but they think they are – that's the thing!'

'I can hardly blame her. I'd hate to grow old alone – and to be raising children!'

'Well, I hardly think that is something any of *us* needs to be too concerned about.'

'Well, it might be now that Arthur and Jo have a daughter.'

'Of course! Yes!'

'You must both take extra care now!'

'And you named her Maria!'

'What an honour!'

'How is she? Is she quite healthy now?'

'A lovely name – I'm sure we would all agree.'

'That reminds me, Henk . . .'

'You might not know him, but the doctor who delivered our Maria was a man named Kugel.'

'We have sought for him since but can find no trace of him.'

'I think I have heard of him, yes. Jewish, right? Doctor Jakub Kugel?'

'He never gave me his first name.'

'Nor me.'

'I believe he still practises. He's quite widely known. If I hear anything, I'll let you know.'

'I hope you do.'

And from one topic to another, if conversation could be so easily mapped, theirs would have moved to each cardinal point – and to those in-between. From work to leisure, religion to the weather, politics to people. In that way, the four of them talked and laughed and enjoyed each other's company well into the night. The cat did not return to Arthur that night.

The next morning Arthur's head was heavy, and throbbed and spun with the effects of too much wine. In his stupor, he thought about the ephemerality of life for as long as his tired mind could bear it. He was in a friend's guest bed under blankets that didn't smell like his, looking out at a view that wasn't his, next to a woman who was his wife and the mother of his daughter, and she made it feel like home . . . and Arthur knew that he loved her. But mortality is a frail, fickle and flimsy thing, and one never knows when one's time on earth might end. His thoughts were drearily dark, but he was comforted by a strange sense of contentment. As he searched for shapes in the timber grain of the bedhead, soft morning sunlight filtered through the window and he suddenly found solace in knowing that he was alive, and that he knew love and that love lived in him. It might have been the exposure to Maria, or the distant effect of the half-forgotten story shared at supper of the wife-made-widow, or the mystery of the phantom cat's return beneath the table, or the warm and nostalgic scent that had recently begun seeping into the room, but Arthur had suddenly found himself thinking aloud.

'Jo, you know Maria has always been a close and special friend to me, don't you?' She shifted a little in the bed and he knew she must have heard him. He had started speaking, half thinking she was still sleeping. 'Well, I think that if she and I were, by some bizarre coincidence, the last of us remaining, I would in likeliness look to marry her.' Jo slowly turned and looked at him, but she didn't show any sign of shock or resentment. It wasn't a wise confession for Arthur to make, and he wasn't sure what had made him say it, but nevertheless he felt, for some reason, that he had to.

After several silent seconds she said, 'Yes . . . I know,' smiling that kind, understanding smile. 'I've known that since I first saw the two of you together. What she said to me at our wedding merely confirmed it.' She sat up, her back against the headboard. Arthur was still quite tired and so, feeling a deep compulsion to be close to Jo, he rested his weary head on the quilt that covered her outstretched thighs. She welcomed him and softly stroked her fingers through his hair as she continued. 'You love me, I know that. But I know that you love her too. And I know that you will do anything you can to support her. You're a good man, Arthur. You have your heart in the right place. I guess, the thing is that . . . I love you. That's why I trust you. That's why I married you. That's why I agreed to our daughter's name.'

Arthur kept quiet, enjoying his wife's comforting, calming voice. Her unquestionable faith in him was remarkable. There appeared to be no capacity in her for hostility, jealousy or mistrust. But after lying there for a few minutes, Arthur felt his lethargy lapse and took it as the opportunity to get out of bed. He lifted himself from Jo's lap and kissed her upon the brow, and they readied themselves for the journey home.

As they stepped onto the landing and into the parlour, they were met by Henk, who was busily preparing breakfast in a haze of coffee-infused air. Unlike Arthur, Henk was the kind of man, it seemed, to never suffer the after-effects of too much alcohol. His morning temperament was energetic and cheerful as he hummed about the house, as if he had been up for several hours already. He was brewing a large pot of coffee, knowing it would promote conversation that might aid everyone's convalescence, and he had clearly had a few cups.

'We'd best start your course of treatment straight away,' he joked. 'Please, stay for a cup, won't you?' He proffered a mug of steaming coffee. It was deep and rich and black and Arthur could tell it was a quality blend. In addition to not wanting to offend his host, he knew the coffee could provide some much-needed clarity of mind.

He turned to Jo and was met by her smile and a gentle nod that communicated her usual patient contentedness. Arthur eagerly accepted the cup. 'I think a little cup of solace is just what we need! Dank je!'

'I acquired the blend from a reputable, but rather bohemian merchant who assured me of its exquisite taste. He trades exclusively to high-end clients. Admittedly, I'm drawn mostly to this blend's aroma. I think a good cup of coffee can do wonders, don't you?' He handed a cup to Jo, and they took up seats at the same table as the night before, though the scene was painted in vastly different colours. Only minutes passed before the soft percussive pat of foot on timber echoed in the stairwell.

'Begroeting, mijn schatje! Arthur, Jo, have you ever seen such a picture?' chimed Henk, with his usual air of assuredness on all things.

'Good morning, everyone,' Maria said courteously, though with less vigour than usual, and clearly through the same dull ache that afflicted all but Henk. 'How is everybody feeling? I trust Henk has fixed you all with a hot drink?'

'Of course, of course,' Henk sang, moving to greet her with a cheek for her to kiss. 'Now come and join us. Take a seat and let us enjoy the pleasure of your company.'

They sat for a while and remarked on the qualities of coffee. Maria, however, couldn't stomach it. She said she loved the smell but couldn't acquire the taste, and Arthur was flung into quietly cogitating whether or not this was a fact he had already known. They also delved briefly into wedding plans, and commented in agreed protest against the unfortunate distance that kept the four of them apart. Eventually their cups were empty and the conversation simmered to an appropriate end. Arthur packed the car before he and Jo thanked their hosts and were ready to return home.

A few weeks after his trip to Mol, on a Saturday morning, Arthur was surprised to be roused by the sound of Jo whistling in the kitchen. He realised, as he lay and listened, that unlike his own, Jo's whistle was slow and flat, with very few abrupt or high notes. Even still, the sound wasn't melancholic, but rather effortless and peaceful, as though it strolled and rolled upon a soft breeze. When Arthur whistled, he favoured upbeat tunes with high rises, often in short succession – as if every second or third note gambolled on a gale. His whistle could have been likened to a pianist perpetually approaching crescendo without ever quite reaching it. Then Arthur thought of other people he knew and the way they whistled. He realised that there were many friends and family members whose songs he had never heard. He had heard both Andre and Bauke whistle while they strutted about town and through the house on a weekend morning, but their tunes were as different as Arthur's and Jo's. Andre's was quite unlike the violin he had played when he was in school. He was always quite the contemporary, influenced by British and American trends, often whistling whatever new tune he may have heard on the radio or at a concert. In contrast, Bauke whistled in long, sustained notes, and favoured slow tunes that felt profound and forlorn. Hendrika's whistle was much like a blend of everyone's – an eclectic symphony of genres. Interestingly, the two people he had never heard whistle were his father and Maria van Essen. It made him wonder if he ever would, or if he had but simply forgotten. Perhaps, he considered, they only whistled in solitude – or was it possible, he wondered, that they had never learned how? And to the tune of Jo's mellifluous morning melody Arthur fell, slowly and deeply, back to sleep.

11

War

Days bled into days. Nights never lasted long. Arthur was only sleeping for a few hours most nights. During the years of the war, he struggled to get much business in Vlijmen, which somehow meant that he rarely had time to rest. Wilhelmus had a similar issue. Partway through 1941, he had to announce Hestana's indefinite closure. But the business he loved and that had been his passion since 1889 was a supplementary one – a profitable pastime. The land titles Wilhelmus held meant that he had more than enough income to comfortably live out the rest of his days. But nothing, not even war, could subdue Arthur's romantic passion. His family was young and growing and he needed to provide for them. First, on Valentine's Day 1936, his second daughter, Grietje, was born. Then, in September 1938, his son was born and they named him Bert. In April 1943, they welcomed their third daughter, Maartje, and in August 1944, their fourth, Ingrid.

The German army had seized a large deal of his business. It frustrated him to no end, but Arthur had to comply or he would have been taken to a camp and put to work or killed.

One night of the war-ravaged many, Jo roused Arthur from his sleep. Despite the dark, he could see the panic in her eyes and it shook him to his core. He had never seen her face twisted with fear like that. His heart raced. A thousand thoughts flooded his mind, yet nothing coherent formed. He opened his mouth to speak but Jo pressed her fingers to his lips and shook her head.

'You need to hide,' she whispered. As a wealthy and influential businessman, Arthur was of interest to the enemy so he and Jo had discussed the possibility of his abduction. He had, early in the war, loosened several floorboards so that he could quickly hide below them. With Jo's help, Arthur managed to conceal himself before the German soldiers trod their dirt through his house – his family's home – stomping over their floors and carpets in hideous boots that stamped zigzag prints across Arthur's pride. Their raucous intrusion roused the sleeping children and the house became the theatre for a choir of wailing and shrieking.

As he waited for them to leave, Arthur reflected on the situation he found himself in. There he was, bound by war, to hide beneath the floorboards of his own home. Fear steers the mind in strange and scary directions, and he couldn't help but worry about his family. Arthur also found himself trying to imagine what his father would have been thinking if he was forced into hiding. But whenever he thought of him, he couldn't fold his father's posture into the positions that concealment demanded. Every image of Wilhelmus was unyielding, as though he were permanently fixed like the marble statue of a Roman god – only Wilhelmus wore a suit and glasses, and eternally held a glass of wine in one hand and a cigar clipped between his fingers on the other. Thoughts of his father aside, Arthur also found himself wondering what may have happened to Doctor Kugel. It was depressing to consider that a man like him – a man who had dedicated his life to learning everything he could to help others, might have had to suffer through unimaginable pain. Arthur hoped he had somehow managed to survive, even if it was only in a capacity to help others. But he knew it was wishful thinking. A man like Kugel – a man who gave so much back to the world, but a victim of time and place – would have been, one way or another, eradicated. Eventually, the fever of panic that had infected the house died down. The children were quiet. The footfall of soldiers had faded away. Arthur could bear waiting no longer and so he emerged, back into his home – though he had never truly left.

The war was tough on everyone. Had Arthur not been a father, he may not have realised it, but children suffer to no end when the world turns violent. There was one day in particular – a day in the summer of 1941 – when he had to admit that no more work could be accomplished – that he came home earlier than usual to find his eldest daughter, Maria, asleep on his bed. Jo hadn't told him where she was, but would have known he would find her there. Maria was asleep but it was clear that she had been crying. She was belly down, soft blonde tresses curled in sticky streaks against her puffy, tear-stained face.

Arthur gently sat on the bed's edge but his weight displaced the angle of the mattress and Maria sank into the depression he created, rolling on to her back. Arthur's leg prevented her from rolling any further. Half her face was reddened and wore the faint print of the bedding's creases. As he rearranged the hair from about her face and carefully cleaned away the crusted tears with his handkerchief, she awoke.

'Oh, hallo, Daddy,' she yawned. Her voice was hoarse and broken. She took a second moment to determine where she was and why. 'I fell asleep on your bed?' It sounded like an apology and a question rolled into one.

'That's fine, meisje. Did you have a nice sleep?' Arthur was carefully building to his real question. It was a strategy that he had learned from his own father.

She started her response with a purring hum as she stretched out her fleshy white limbs. 'Yep, I did.' She smiled with her eyes squeezed shut.

'So why did you want to sleep here?'

'I was sad,' she stated matter-of-factly. Her eyes opened and her smile quickly disappeared.

'What about?' Arthur asked, imitating his daughter's direct approach.

'I hate this stupid war,' she pouted. 'It's not nice.' It was a fair reason for her to be upset and there was little that Arthur could do to help. Once, when Maria had been angry about something that had happened at school, he had dug a hole in the garden and held out his hands. 'Give me everything that's bothering you,' he had said. She had looked at him oddly, but he kept holding his hands out until she played along. Then, with his hands full of her concerns, he dropped them into the hole, buried them and trampled the dirt flat. 'Now your troubles are buried. They won't be back to bother you,' he had told her.

But no one can bury a war. Arthur knew he couldn't protect his children from everything the world would throw their way. In that moment, all he could do was hold her. He held her close and consoled her the best he could. 'No, the war isn't nice is it? But one day it will be over, and everyone will live happily together.'

He could feel that she was at least a little satisfied by his answer, but for some reason, he wasn't. He thought more talking could help. 'I promise I won't let anyone hurt you or your sisters, your brother or your mother.' Arthur thought articulating his resolve would ensure he could keep his promise – that surely, in some way, if he willed it

130

enough and remained optimistic, then things would naturally work out. He believed that if he prayed for their protection, no harm would come to them. But he was wrong.

Their marauding knew no limit. They revelled in it. For several months, the German soldiers had been making a concerted effort to ensure their presence was known, enacting their authority in a cruel, abrupt fashion. They took what they fancied, and had no hesitation in using violence to settle even the smallest of disputes. The local businesses were ransacked and many collapsed under the burden of debt shortly after. ARVAH was under serious threat of being exploited beyond redemption. Many of Arthur's tools and resources were stolen by soldiers, and his workshop was raided sporadically for supplies. Despite this, he knew he had to keep himself busy. He had to salvage some semblance of life beyond the walls of his home, even if just to occupy his mind. Arthur understood the risks of getting caught, but being inactive had its own consequences. He was fortunate to retain his delivery truck and driver to help him transport shipments from the station. Although their operations were impeded significantly, this meant there was still hope. He had also managed to save a small kit of hand tools. Most of the work was out of town, but he still received a few small local jobs.

To avoid drastic losses, Arthur avoided unnecessary stockpiling. He bought stock on a needs basis. His strategy was inspired by something he had once overheard Jo tell little Maria. One lunchtime, to educate her on matters of food preparation, Jo tutored Maria in the art of sandwich making. After Arthur had eaten their masterpiece, he watched the two of them wash up. The soapy water had made the dishes slippery. Before long, the crashing sound of a dropped plate reverberated through the house like a shotgun blast. Maria's face distended with sadness, and she looked up at Jo expecting to be scolded.

But Jo, being Jo, and knowing that Maria had not come to harm, simply smiled. 'Don't worry about it, schatje.'

Maria's face was a puffy mess of unspoken apology. She looked at her father, then back at her mother. Not wanting to interfere with Jo's lesson, Arthur maintained an expression of indifference. He turned away – feigning a greater interest in matters of his own.

'As long as you're not hurt, that's all that matters,' Jo assured her. 'It just means we'll have one less plate to wash next time.'

And while, from a business point of view, Jo's argument had its flaws, the logic pacified their distraught daughter. Arthur appreciated the sentiment and simultaneously found in his daughter's lesson a lesson for himself. The loss of an asset is negligible when weighed against a person's wellbeing. In essence, people take precedence over profit. So, throughout the war, and while Arthur filled his tin with bent and jobless nails, he reminded himself of the broken plate and accepted that losing tools and resources was relatively inconsequential. But, as Arthur soon discovered, stealing stock is one thing, robbing a child of her innocence is another matter entirely.

It had been four years since the war started. Despite the dangers, Arthur was working in his shed. He was being as quiet as possible, yet the thin tin walls seemed to echo the bustling tension from the town outside. He operated by salvaging the scraps of light that stole entry through the gaps between the places Time exposed. Since he had left home that morning, he couldn't shake the feeling that something bad was going to happen. He knew each trip had its risks, but greater than the danger was the need. Arthur didn't tell his family where he was going. He reasoned the less they knew the better – but, naturally, they could figure it out.

Since he had arrived, Arthur had been arranging an area in which to work. He did so without making too much noise and painstakingly cleared a space and planned a system of operation. After measuring a sheet to the job specifications, he was ready to start cutting – but the moment he pressed steel to glass, he heard a gentle tap ring through the tin. In that moment, dread pummelled his nerves into doughy helplessness. That curt and singular knock sounded like the knell of death. Visions of soldiers in grey suits flashed into thought. He could have held his breath, stood silent, and willed his unexpected visitors to leave without inspection, but instead he mustered his courage and prayed he was wrong.

His grip was limp with fear as he opened the door. If his visitors were German soldiers, he could have been in a great deal of trouble. He tried to think of a story that might appease them and their insatiable appetite for violence, but Arthur found that the figure that filled the void was only half the size of a soldier, and he recognised the outline immediately. It was Maria, all of nine years old.

There was clearly something wrong. The pale hands she held to her mouth were streaked wet with blood. All she said – all she could manage – were four short words, but when she moved her hands to talk and Arthur could see for himself, his stomach churned and his heart sank like lead. Her gums bled from the holes where her teeth had been ripped. Every single tooth had been stolen.

'Day hur my moub.'

Fear and panic accosted him in the blankness. Arthur pulled Maria inside by the waist and slung the door closed again. He turned the lock. His hands shook. He fumbled for a clean handkerchief from his pocket and rolled and folded it into a wad for her to bite down on. Blood soaked it red in seconds. Arthur's legs collapsed beneath him but he managed to land himself into a kneeling position. Then, jolting, he pulled his daughter close. He wrapped an arm around her tiny, shaking body while he used his other one to steady her head against his chest. In that moment he felt he had failed her. He could not keep the promise he had made to her – to himself. It was his duty to protect his children, yet here was his eldest daughter, pointlessly maimed by man's senseless violence.

As he calmed her, the fact that she was still alive, standing and breathing, consoled him. Her sobbing gradually grew louder. He hushed her and guided a steady hand across her back and around her head in a gentle wading motion. Arthur's eyes stung with the tears he had hoped to hold back. He thought of the baby – the toddler – the little girl. She had grown so much, but she was still only a child – and she was *his* child, *his* daughter, *his* precious baby girl.

'I'm . . .' he faltered. 'I'm here . . . I'm here. You're safe now.' But he knew he couldn't promise it.

They held each other until their emotions cooled, and when Maria's body stopped shaking, Arthur brought himself to examine her face more closely. Her wide eyes searched his and her face, still wet with blood and tears, and heavy with swelling, seemed to relax a little. The thick-aired tension of the world outside seemed to creep in, seeping through the tin to shake the darkness around them.

'Do you want to tell me what happened?' he asked in a hushed voice, hoping for Maria's sake more than his own that putting the experience into words might offer a less painful perspective.

Maria dropped his gaze and pressed her face back into its previous position on his chest. Because this so clearly relaxed her, he let her snuggle in. He found some solace in it too. It made him feel a fraction less pathetic.

He waited a while and then, as gently as he could, Arthur repeated the question in the same words as before.

Her face eventually returned to his and she spoke, her small words muffled by fat lips. 'I jub wanded do h– h– helb dem.'

And then her voice was gone again and silence sat between them. He could see she was about to cry aloud once more but instead she burrowed back into coping with the pain, confusion and trauma, as best as a nine-year-old child can.

When Arthur withdrew the handkerchief from her mouth, the bleeding had slowed. They had been together for a while and though she was in pain, he knew Maria would be hungry. They agreed to try some of the bread he had brought for lunch. She had to break the bread into small pieces before swallowing it whole with water. After eating, she slept. While she slept, Arthur watched her beaten face rest. He listened to her breathing through swollen lips – too fat to close. Her eyes were puffy slits that twitched beneath their darkened drapes. And Arthur swore to himself that he would never let another man lay a violent hand upon her.

When the light that had previously skewered the dark around them had retreated, and the noise of the town outside dissipated, Arthur knew it would be safe to head home. His legs and neck and back were bent and weak and stiff and sore from sitting on the rock-hard floor. But all the same, he stood and carefully cradled his child in his arms and, in that way, carried her all the way home.

When she saw him step into the kitchen carrying Maria, and when he turned to reveal her sleeping, swollen face, Jo's legs all but collapsed beneath her. She was overcome with agony and despair and staggered towards them, arms outstretched.

'Oh, my baby . . .' she spoke in broken sounds. 'No, no, no . . . my baby girl . . . my darling little girl . . . who? Who has done this? Why? Why?' Jo wrapped her arms around them.

The weight of it all became too much for Arthur and, back to the wall, he slid to the floor. He had made it so far, he had held it together as best he could, but all he could do in that moment, was cry. 'I– I– I'm sorry . . . I'm sorry . . . I– I didn't . . . I wasn't . . . I couldn't stop them . . . I couldn't . . . protect her . . .'

A week later, a woman in town who had watched everything from a shop window, told him what she had seen. Her name was Edda Bakker. She was clearly distressed, riddled with guilt, but with fear as well.

'Oh, your poor child! Bless her! I'm so, so sorry. But I couldn't . . . I couldn't help – not with my own little ones to worry about,' she confessed. 'There were three wee ones – the baker's children: two boys and a girl. They were trying to steal back some of what was stolen from their pa. It was risky because those nasty Nazis had been inside the watchmaker's workshop for a while and I knew they would be out before long. They may have even been watching through the window. That was when your Maria happened along. And she was all by herself. Being a head taller, she just reached up and passed down a loaf or two, then those little ones scampered out of sight. Well, that was when those men – there were two of them – one just grabbed her by the hair and she . . . she was so scared. Those soldiers didn't care that they had stolen that bread in the first place, or that she was just a young girl. I'm . . . I'm just so sorry. They did it right there in the street. One grabbed a pair of pliers from the truck while the other just held her jaw open, as if she wasn't even human. And . . . when she screamed . . .' Edda was a mess. She wiped her nose on a handkerchief.

136

But she was determined to finish her story, and Arthur wanted her to. Indeed, he needed to hear the whole truth of it. 'That scream . . . that sound . . . there was so much pain in it. I had my hands at my ears but I couldn't block it out. She just screamed and screamed, and there was so much blood. I was so scared for her. I think I screamed too. Then they just dropped her there. She climbed to her feet, and she ran, nearly falling all the way. And they just started their truck and drove away, as if it never even happened.'

Though he hated every second, Arthur was glad he had heard it through. He tried to assure the woman that it wasn't her fault. She had no control over the events she had been made to witness. 'You did what any parent would have done. I would have done the same.' But he couldn't help but feel he was lying. Those soldiers had assaulted everything that had not yet been corrupted by a toxic world. Maria was a child. Her face, irrevocably and senselessly dismantled, mirrored the dreadful state of things – of civilisation, of humanity. She was the living embodiment of defiled innocence, a desecration of the world's once peaceful and optimistic future. They had no right. No reason. No remorse. No regard for the damage they did. And yet they did these things all the same. Only a child! Her jaw was swollen and there was blood and bruising around her face – mostly her mouth and cheeks. Her eyes were puffy from crying. When she said they hurt her – and he knew without having to ask who "they" were – it made him hate them even more. His helplessness fed a rage that had long been simmering in him. An accumulation of everything – all the evil they had done, every injustice – tumbled into a maelstrom of hatred and anger and frustration, but of fear too, for he knew they could have done much, much worse.

12

Family

After the war, Arthur was not short of work. It was 1948 and the world was rebuilding. Civilisation was scraping itself from the pavement. It was picking up its pieces, recollecting what it knew, and preparing itself to be recast into something better than it ever was before in the blazing kiln of industry and ambition.

Arthur understood that a region's glass was a sign of prosperity. In every disaster, whether it be the product of nature or man, it was the fragile shield from the world that shattered first. Likewise, when peace returned, so too does the glass. And that is where Arthur came in. During the war, he was, on the whole, hopeless – he wholeheartedly, yet regrettably, had to admit that to himself. His skills were largely and irredeemably redundant, but in the aftermath, he was at the forefront of recovery. He was, in his mind, tasked with restoring the dignity of Vlijmen and every nearby town that had been ravaged by war. At the time, and like many of his countrymen, Arthur was compelled by an altruistic force that inspired him to help any way he could. With his relatively undamaged facilities, he knew he could, with a small team, repair every nearby town and at least prevent the remnants of the war's chilling, ashen wind from blowing through the homes of innocent people. Arthur considered that, like a doctor or nurse, he could do next to nothing to prevent a man being shot; he could not stand in the way of destruction, but he could dress the wound and prepare it so that it could heal on its own.

Arthur had not only aided in the restoration and rejuvenation of Vlijmen, but many of the neighbouring towns as well. There was an abundance of work and Arthur had to employ more staff to keep up with the demand. Time to rest and spend with family seemed impossible to balance with the demands of work.

And one night, in the early hours, Jo, who had always taken everything in her stride, had reached her limit. The thought of facing another day kept her awake. Her list of duties seemed only to grow. And her need for sleep kept her from it. She felt tired. She felt pathetic. And so she cried. And slowly, her husband woke.

'I know I shouldn't be so . . . I should be grateful that we have what we have . . . and to have Nelleke – who does so much, but I can't have her do it all – there are certain things she can't – no, that I want to do . . . and there's always so much – so much to do . . . but I just can't anymore, Arthur! I just can't! I need sleep! I need to get out of this house, I think, just for a few hours, without having to take a child with me. Without having to try to think of what I'm forgetting – to think of what I haven't done. And I want to . . .'

Arthur took a moment to wake up and to sit up in bed. He lit his lamp and turned towards his wife. 'I know, dear. It isn't easy. But what else can we do? In a few hours you will have to do it all again. Then, the day after that, you'll do it again. And the day after that, and the day after that. And it won't get easier, but all the same you will do it, over and over again. And do you know why?' Arthur paused, but not because he expected her to answer. 'Because you're a mother. You are strong and you will survive. I don't know how . . . but I know you will. The war did not defeat us. The lack of sleep . . . the endless work . . . the time apart . . . these things will not defeat us.'

'That's easy to say for you though, isn't it?' Jo said, her sadness turning bitter in the ruddy hues of the light. 'It's just easy to say. But what I need is for you to help me, somehow. Not with words. Not with money. But somehow . . . I need you to do what needs to be done.'

Arthur gave her a long look of consideration. After several seconds, all he could do was repeat what he had said before. 'I don't know how, but I know we will survive this. One day at a time. We will do the best job we can and we will get through this together.'

In business, as in parenthood, no growth occurs without setbacks. In any line of work, in all aspects of life, there are times when things don't seem to go right. There had been a number of times when Arthur couldn't make the glass cut the way he needed it to. Whether it had something to do with the weather – the heat, the cold, the moisture in the air – or a fault with the material, the tools or the craftsman, it just would not work the way it should have done. And, when things didn't work, Arthur could get quickly and thoroughly frustrated. He was usually a patient man, but when he repeated a rudimentary task in the same way he had always done it, only to be met with successive failure, he would eventually lose composure.

Arthur knew that menial tasks weren't worth the pain and hassle they caused, but in the heat of the moment he could forget these things. It was easy to abandon sense when he focussed so single-mindedly on overcoming a seemingly insurmountable challenge. Each setback was like the tension served upon a string already pulled too tight to strum. Every turn of the tuning peg took its toll until . . . snap! The line recoiled and thrashed like a worm skewered upon a hook.

It was near noon and he had worked through the morning. An important client was demanding an expensive project and much of Arthur's profit had already been sacrificed to secure the contract. He also had a backlog of orders, but for whatever reason, on that day, the glass would not work for him. It would not cut clean. The glass was heavy and awkward. It was thick and fickle. And of course, the problem was not the glass at all. He was sweating, getting agitated and had lost the finesse required to grip his tools. He dropped things repeatedly, which only led to further irritation. He was tired, careless and clumsy. He could have stopped and delegated the task to someone else but the best of his workers were out of the factory making deliveries, picking up orders and running various other errands. All excuses aside, Arthur was stubborn beyond reason. He knew he had to succeed or he would never be satisfied.

It wasn't sudden by any means – in fact, it took several minutes – but eventually, while he was ablaze in a haze of anger, he was drawn a measure of patience. In all its sweet bitterness, perspective was pulled from within his well of weariness when a familiar hand rested on his shoulder and a soft whisper respired a name upon his neck.

'Arthur . . .'

Jo had appeared and yet Arthur's initial response left him quite uncensored and unrefined. He spoke out against himself. 'This is so infuriating!' he grunted.

Jo just kept her hand on his shoulder and placed her other at his back. She had been watching for a while, keeping her distance.

Then she spoke again, a little louder and more clearly. Her voice was imbued with patience and understanding, and it placated her husband with just three syllables. 'I know, dear . . .'

Her tenderness soaked his rage to a stack of softly hissing cinders. The coolness of her hands cooled his skin and fought the fever through it. She could have been easily annoyed by Arthur's juvenile agitation, but she returned his impatience with a tempered tone.

Jo didn't often visit Arthur at work, but he was glad she had done on that day. Once rationality returned to him, he learned that Jo had brought a box of sandwiches to share for lunch. Perhaps she knew, ahead of time, that her husband was going to have a bad day and would need something to go right. He had, indeed, been out of sorts – discernibly afflicted by a shortness of temper – well before he left the house that morning. When he got that way, it was usually a sign that he was about to fall ill. Arthur had been working long hours, so it made sense for him to be feeling run down.

The sandwiches were so neatly packed that he felt bad for eating them. They were cut into triangles. There were sweeter ones with fruit jams and chutneys, and then there were the savoury, meat and salad ones. And as Arthur ate them, he felt himself grow stronger with every bite.

After he had finished the final crust, Arthur gave Jo a smile, yet she had been smiling all along. He knew it didn't need to be spoken, but he wanted to voice his appreciation – not just for the food, but for everything. The sandwiches were delicious, but even if they weren't, he would have appreciated the love that went into making them.

'Thanks, Jo . . .' Arthur started, but she was quick to dismiss his gratitude.

'Anytime, dear. You're always working more than you ought to – and it's for us that you push yourself so hard. It's the least I can do, really. I . . .'

But this time Arthur was the one to interrupt. 'My thanks are not just for the sandwiches – which were wonderful by the way – but for . . .' He wasn't sure how to phrase it. He wanted to express himself as elegantly as possible, but he suddenly decided that he didn't need to decorate his words. He didn't need embellishments. He simply needed to say exactly how he felt, and so he did. 'For everything. Thank you for everything. I really don't know how I would manage without you.'

When he finished, it almost seemed, for the first time, like Jo was truly and deeply flattered. Her face swelled, but she managed to hold back the tears. She was silent for several seconds, then she looked at him, and in a clumsy yet irrationally elegant, lilting, stumbling voice, she cried, 'I love you, Arthur!' She fell into his arms. Her convulsive cry rippled through him and shook the silent air.

He held her and returned the sentiment without hesitation. 'I love you, too, Johanna.' And he knew that they each meant it more than they had in a very long time.

It was late September, and Maria and Grietje, all of fourteen and twelve, requested that they spend a weekend away with Maria van Essen-Peeters. Jo, who was pregnant again, and quite close to the due date, was about ready to burst. Arthur reasoned that the excursion could be a timely one – having fewer children in the house would be best for everyone. Besides, his children, especially his eldest two, were very fond of her. They treated her much like a second oma and they had come to affectionately call her 'Bonma'. So, after calling and confirming the stay with their host, they commenced packing – their past experiences guiding their future plans. And as they made no scruples over selecting a wide and mismatched collection of their belongings, they couldn't help but express their excitement.

'I really like spending time at Bonma's house,' declared the eldest through her gap-toothed lisp. As she spoke, Arthur had to shake away the guilt or shame or whatever the feeling was that hurt him every time he heard it. By now, all of her adult teeth had come through – but she didn't have *all* of them. She never would. Not really. The dentist said she would have to wait until she had stopped growing before she could have a special denture made and, hoping it would mend him as well, Arthur longed for that day to come.

'So do I! She's nice and gives us sweets to eat,' added Grietje. 'But only sometimes, of course,' she corrected.

But their father had full confidence that his old friend would look after his children as well as if they were her own, just as she had always done.

Deciding she should avoid too much travelling and that her attention could be better spent on caring for their younger children, Jo entrusted the transport of her two eldest daughters to Arthur. With their luggage packed – a few changes of clothes and other personal effects securely stowed in the trunk of the car – the three of them were bound for Mol.

Arthur found the drive quite pleasant. With the girls chatting excitedly to one another in the back seat, Arthur was left relatively free to sift through the various topics of contemplation his lack of free time had seen him neglect. He had banked a number of schemes and fancies and he was finally afforded the opportunity to form lists and formulate plans in order of priority, factoring in the cost of each in terms of time and effort. It seemed that no sooner had they left Vlijmen than they were parked outside Maria's house. He was quite unprepared to be rattled from his run of open cognition, so he sat a little stunned and disappointed at the sudden end to it. Several seconds passed before he sent his eyes into the mirror and saw the silent, smiling faces of his daughters. He knew that they were at the brim of their capacity for waiting, but being eager to stay in his good favour, they obediently awaited the cue to leave the car.

He gave it to them. 'Here we are girls,' he announced. 'Let's say hallo to Bonma and then we'll come back to gather your things.' The pair cheered in excitement, swung open their doors and dashed across the pavement, through the gate, along the path and up the steps to the front door. But as they readied themselves to knock, the door opened and their host stepped from within. Arthur watched as the girls flung their arms around her and Maria secured a hand to each of their backs. She caught him watching her and gave him a welcoming smile. Arthur smiled back and made his way from the vehicle, his thoughts placed on hold until he could attend to them on the journey home.

The girls had disappeared into the house after Maria invited them in to find their rooms. While Arthur waited for them to re-emerge, he met Maria on her landing.

'Hallo, Thurke,' Maria said, drawing him in to exchange kisses on the cheek.

'Hallo, Maria.'

'How was the journey? Not too noisy, I hope?'

'On the contrary,' said Arthur, 'it was a lovely drive. Perfect day for it too.'

'I'm happy to hear it. And don't worry, I know what you're thinking . . .' Arthur grew curious – even he didn't know what he was thinking. 'I'll make sure that the girls eat all their meat and vegetables . . . *before* they're given anything sweet!' There was a self-mocking twinkle in her eye.

'Thank you,' he said, smiling at her joke. 'That's very reassuring.' Then, as the joke's effect abated, their conversation seemed to vanish with it. Arthur was reluctant to impose upon her for a tea or coffee, or whatever it may have taken to extend their time together, and knew he ought not to stay any longer than was needed.

'I wonder—' he had all but uttered when his daughters suddenly burst between him and Maria.

'Father, can you open the trunk please? We want to get our things out now,' the eldest declared.

Arthur prepared to scold them for interrupting adults while they were talking, but lacking the energy required, and being in a rather pleasant mood, he forewent the discipline. 'Very well. Wait patiently please. I'll be there soon.'

But the girls weren't made to wait long, for he had lost whatever it was that he had thought to say only a moment ago. It made him wonder if he had had anything to say at all.

When he returned to Maria, who was still stood by the door, and as the girls heaved their luggage up to their rooms, Arthur attempted to resume their dialogue, but he was interrupted again – only this time it was not by his daughters.

'Would you care to come inside for coffee and cake?' Maria asked. 'I baked it this morning – as a special treat for the girls, I must admit. But there's more than enough to spare.' Arthur had no intention of foisting himself upon her, yet he knew instantly that her offer only had one outcome, one reply. It was clear to both of them that there was no way he could turn her down.

They spoke for a while about the weather and about work and about their families. But Arthur soon realised that he had seized a large share of the talking and so he gradually began to wonder if he was boring her, if she had become silent merely because she was politely feigning interest – entertaining him out of etiquette – or if she was enjoying his company and the conversation.

'I'm sorry if I've talked too much. I—' But he didn't get to offer a justification.

'No, Arthur,' she stopped him. 'I really ought to have spoken a little more. And I should have been more open with you. But let's keep our meeting jovial. How was the cake? I tried a new recipe.'

'It was lovely, of course,' he admitted with a smile.

'I'm glad,' she said.

And knowing it best to leave when things were as good as they could get, Arthur finally prepared himself for departure. With several crumbs of cake left on the plate, and a teaspoon's worth of coffee stretched into a waning crescent at the bottom of the cup, he stood.

'Thanks again for agreeing to have the girls for a few nights. If all goes well with Jo, I'll be back on Sunday afternoon to pick them up. If they give you any trouble, be sure to let me know.'

'Thanks, Thurke, but I'm sure they'll be fine,' she assured him. 'I'll see you again in a few days. I'll be praying to Saint Christopher for your safe journey home. Give Jo my love.'

They had extended their farewells long enough. Arthur spoke a few final fatherly reminders to his daughters and then, uncertain of feeling – unsure of thought – he returned to Vlijmen.

With several hours of daylight remaining, Arthur decided he would get some work done at ARVAH, but also, for whatever reason, negotiated with himself to do so after stopping in to see Jo. When he arrived home, everything seemed quieter. And it seemed it wasn't only his house that was inexplicably affected by the girls' absence. The town seemed quieter too – slower and sleepier.

He parked the car, unlocked the front door and walked around for a while, searching each room. Many were checked twice over before Arthur could confirm that Jo wasn't home. In fact, no one else was home. And even though he had spent the journey in a similar fashion, this wider space made the emptiness far more apparent. It had been many years since he had been at home alone, and he felt oddly lost for thought – as if he was stalking aimlessly through a strange dream. Then a sound like a hundred hands scrunching a hundred sheets of paper came from overhead, reverberating through the silence like the pitter-patter of a million mice stampeding in the ceiling, and then the whole house was overwhelmed by a deep, dark, dullness as rain pelted down.

Arthur caught his shadowy form reflected in the china cabinet's glass and considered his appearance. He searched long and hard for the ways he had changed and wondered whether he had started to look at all like a father and husband. Was there some characteristic that would mark him to others as a man who held these titles? And while he pursued this course, he felt another set of eyes upon him. These eyes were both his and yet, at the same time, not his own. He rested his quest for a minute and turned his attention to the portrait that hung like a faulty mirror upon the wall. The lack of light made him strain, though he had seen the painting so many times that he could picture it distinctly whether his eyes were open or closed. He knew that beyond the subject was nothing but a mossy curtain; a felt-like green veil – all but black now in the crumbs of light afforded him by the room and the painting's position in it. And deeper still, beyond and beneath the world of paint, was the brown hessian weave of a makeshift canvas. The foreground was a section of crude fencing: three horizontal rails and two uprights of raw tree limbs the colour of coffee. Indeed, the subject could be seen as caught in the painter's trap. Upon that matter, the subject was a young boy. He had a close-lipped smile, and one arm lay over the other, the fingers of his hand wrapped around the uppermost beam – or branch, as it might be considered. And though the boy was Arthur, it wasn't. It was the painting his father had made of him when he was a child, but the subject was a different character altogether. Art and photography . . . what peculiar means they are to forever capture a single and fleeting moment in time, Arthur pondered, eternally unchanged by the subject's age and experiences. Arthur once looked upon himself – the boy in this painting – with a good degree of contempt, for it was who Wilhelmus wanted him to be. Or at least that is what Arthur thought. But he couldn't be so sure. He could see the optimism – the joy and peace in that young boy's face – and finally, despite it all, he realised that he liked it. After being alone with himself in the silent darkness, Arthur realised how much he wanted his family to be home again. Then he thought about meeting his new son or daughter . . . and he smiled.

For the first part of the car trip home from Mol that Sunday afternoon, Maria and Grietje frantically tried to tell their father every detail about their stay with Bonma. All he could do was listen as best he could. He smiled and nodded and chuckled and agreed. Then their fever cooled and they spoke at a more casual rate about other things.

'Did you miss us, Dad?' Maria asked.

'Miss you? Of course I did! We all did.'

'Did anything exciting happen?' Grietje asked next.

'Nothing out of the ordinary,' Arthur replied, thinking hard on what had happened over the course of the days they had been away. 'Actually . . . Bert lost a tooth eating a carrot. He's quite frightened of eating them now.'

The three of them laughed a little at his expense. The consideration came too late and all at once Arthur realised the joke could have upset Maria. But she saw the humour in it – perhaps more so than anyone else. 'Oh, and there was one other thing . . .' Arthur teased. 'When you get home, you'll have to meet Alida . . . your new baby sister.'

'Dad!' Grietje laughed.

'You should have told us that first!' Maria said. 'That's much more important than silly little Bert!'

'Is it?' Arthur joked. The three of them were so excited that they laughed and talked the whole way home, and unlike their outbound journey, Arthur was out of his own thoughts, and right there, with his daughters.

13

Death

One mournful Monday morning in July 1951, death arrived.
Arthur had been with a client for most of the morning and by
the time he had returned to ARVAH, he was eager for lunch. He was
partway through his sandwich when he was requested on the phone.

'I beg your pardon, Meneer van Hessel,' called his assistant, Helma,
'but your father is on the phone and he has been desperate to reach
you.'

Arthur rested his lunch and puzzled over why his father might be
calling. He took the call in his office.

'Arthur, it's your mother . . .' came his ever-stern father's voice,
sounding greyer than silver. 'She isn't well.'

Arthur didn't need to hear any more than that to know what was
coming next. He acknowledged his father's news and ended the call.
He walked outside and stared at the sprawling town in the distance.
The ignorant sun was shining. The naïve flowers were in bloom. If it
were truly bad news, Arthur thought to himself, the sky would darken,
a wetted wind would howl over the weeping rain, and everything

would wear shades of black and grey. But the world was full of energy and colour and indifference.

The hospital room was lit both by the white bulbs overhead and by the beige sunlight pressed against the papery drapes. In the centre was a bed, the head-half angled slightly upward. Upon the bed was Hendrika. The lines in her face seemed deeper than Arthur remembered, but perhaps he had just never taken notice of how she had aged. A thin blue sheet was pulled taut over her chest by the weight of her resting arms. These, too, had changed in ways that Arthur had never realised – thinner, and like a dampened cloth, revealing the network of veins below. A machine blipped beside her bed. Arthur had not been the first to arrive, but nor was he the last. Wilhelmus and Bauke were there before him, standing side by side in a place neither the light of man nor that of nature seemed able to fully reach. Nothing was said until Andre arrived.

'How is she?' he asked. A slightly silly thing to ask, but no one was in the mood to mock him, and he hadn't said it hoping for an answer. The machine blipped again.

Hendrika's doctor, who had seen the room quite full as he was passing by, was the next to speak. 'If everyone's here, I think I should let you know . . . Mrs van Hessel probably won't wake again. I will check on her again in an hour or so, but I think now would be the most opportune time for you to say your goodbyes. Mr van Hessel . . . you'll let your sons know, I'm sure, but only a few hours ago she awoke and said that she knew you would all be here. She smiled, didn't she? And she wanted to let you all know that she had lived a full and blessed life.' The doctor accepted the silence for what it was worth, and departed.

Another blip. Wilhelmus remained stuck to the spot, stood awkwardly at his wife's side as a bright light beamed down upon her face while his was soaked in shadow. He could not confess his heartache. He would not reveal his despair. He was simply unwilling and unable to move. He was held up merely by a habit of years, but inside he was hollowed out, like a tree taken by termites. Then silence. More silence. And nothing. Not another blip.

As far as death goes, hers was simple. She had approached the end of her journey slowly, as if reluctantly returning home after a full day's festivities. Then she was there, but not. She was with Wilhelmus, Bauke, Andre and Arthur, but far away and not returning.

His mother's death challenged Arthur in many ways. He found some consolation in knowing that she died without too much pain. Arthur knew her passing was particularly hard on his father, but Wilhelmus was such a proud, stubborn man that he refused to express any sign of mourning, save for the sombre tone that unambiguously afflicted his every utterance. Arthur never thought he would witness his father weakened, but he was soon bowed by loss. He slowed. He slouched. He slurred. Day by day, he withered. In weird and worrisome ways . . . oh, how he withered.

At the funeral, Wilhelmus was stone – a bleak, grey, pale stone. Andre remained by his side, and his appearance was much the same. Bauke was with his family and Arthur with his. Every daughter sobbed, and Bert cried, too – as much as he tried to resist it. The church of Saint John the Baptist mourned with them, her windows dimmed by the murky sky beyond her ceiling and the candles' flames hugging tight to stunted wicks. The priest played his part and people were soon gathered around a grave. Hendrika was lowered while Wilhelmus stood, was offered a chair, sat for a second, then stood again. And after everyone had left, Wilhelmus stayed – still standing . . .

Then, in October 1955, Wilhelmus died. Arthur was made to learn that growing old meant losing those you needed. There had been two people with whom he had shared his growth – two people who had always encouraged and overseen his pursuits and who were always his greatest supporters. And in the space of a few years, he had lost them both. Arthur was truly saddened to have lost a man who meant so much to him, but at the same time, he found that he was a little relieved that the war his father had fought for so long had finally ended. Wilhelmus no longer had to compete against how he had to appear and how he felt inside. He could rest and could lie alongside his wife forever.

Unfortunately, death did not stop there for the van Hessel family. A year after Wilhelmus died, Andre passed away at the age of fifty-three. Even though he and Arthur had drifted apart over the years, from each other, and from Bauke too, Arthur still felt as if he had lost yet another huge influence in his life. It was only a week earlier that Andre had, for no immediately apparent reason, decided to visit Arthur at his factory. He had never shown too much interest in his brother's work, or in his life in general, so Andre's arrival surprised Arthur. As he walked in, he was clearly impressed by the extent of his brother's success and the sheer scale of his operation. And when Andre saw Arthur approach, he clapped an almighty clap as his approval stretched itself into an open, flashy-toothed smile while he announced his awe aloud.

'Well, how about that! I'd ask how business is going, Arthur, but I think I can see well enough for myself!'

Arthur simply grinned and held out a hand as he met his brother's praise. 'It's so nice to see you, brother. I don't think I've seen you since father's . . . well, never mind . . . yes, business is steady. You look well yourself! Tell me, what has made you want to see your little brother at work in his atelier on today of all days?'

The two shook hands and Arthur knew instantly that his brother wanted nothing from it but to see him. He was all smiles.

'Thanks, Arthur. Yes, my loving and worrisome wife has had me on something of a diet lately,' he gloated, making a show of patting his midsection, though he was in rather good shape for his age. 'She's had me cut back on taste, especially. Tells me I don't need to put salt on everything, but what's life without a little flavour? It all goes into one stomach, right? But never you mind about me . . . would you look at all of this!' He stretched his arms out as he turned from side to side. 'Father would be impressed! What marvellous work you must do! Perhaps, after you finish with your accounts, you could have a look over mine?' His tone suggested he was only partially jesting. Then his expression changed. He had exhausted his capacity for flattery. 'Still collecting old nails?' This riled Arthur a little because he had grown weary of being mocked by Andre when they were younger, but at the same time, he wasn't completely convinced that Andre had meant to cause offence.

'Well—'

'I'm only joking!' Andre interrupted. He burst into a short spurt of laughter that faded away, either upon sensing Arthur's offence or upon feeling silly for having given it. 'Work has been *steady* for me too! How about we get a drink together sometime? What do you say? Maybe we can fish Bauke out of that pond of parenthood, hey? I don't think I've seen him since . . .' His tone had changed. It seemed he may have been hiding . . . something – as if perhaps he knew, then and there, that he didn't have as much time left as he would have liked.

'Sure,' Arthur agreed. 'It's been too long. We really should.'

Andre looked around one last time, then clapped again and replastered the masquerade of contentment he had worn upon his entrance. 'Excellent! Well, I'll leave you to your work. All the best, brother. I can see myself out.'

And with that, he left again. They had had their differences, Arthur couldn't deny it, but they were brothers and they loved each other, and he sincerely had hoped to have that drink with him.

It wasn't until Andre's passing that Arthur learned two things he had never before known about his brother – for they were habits he had picked up later in life. The first was that he ate the exact same thing every day for lunch: a ham and cheese sandwich and an apple. Arthur wondered how he could keep his supply stocked year-round. The second was that he loved keeping lists. When Arthur was asked to sort through a few of his brother's things, he happened across several tattered old diaries. In them, Andre had lists of the places he had been, and the cars he had seen. He had lists of the books he had read and the funny things people had said. He had a list of the girls he had kissed, and he even had a list of his lists. But what Arthur found to be the saddest list of all was the list of things he had to do that he would never get to see through. He wouldn't book the plumber on Monday. He wouldn't visit the bank on Tuesday. He wouldn't wind the clock on Wednesday. He wouldn't call his client, or grease the gate, or fix the fence, or trim the hedge, or wash the car, or buy more tea, or return the hammer he had borrowed from his little brother. No. The list would always be unfin . . .

14

Dispute

Something had changed between them. Something had been lost. And it was his twenty-three-year-old daughter Maria who let him know. It was late when Arthur came home and so the house was asleep – all except for her. He had hardly locked the door before her angry voice kicked him in the back.

'I suppose work had to be done?' He turned to see Maria scowling. 'I suppose work was more important, right?'

He wasn't sure what he had done to warrant such a greeting, but he was wary of waking the house. 'Yes, work *is* important. And yes, work *must* be done,' he said, leading her into his study. He flicked a switch and the night of the room vanished into light. Maria closed the door behind her.

Arthur continued. 'You ought to know that by now. But maybe you'll never understand what it means to have responsibilities. Maybe you'll never learn what it means to—'

'And maybe one day *you* will learn that family is what matters most,' she shot back. She wasn't wearing her denture and the sight of her mouth and the sound of her speech made Arthur remorseful. 'Maybe *you* will learn that *we* matter. Not money. Not business. Us!'

'Am I missing something?'

'What haven't you missed these last few years? Do you even live here anymore? Do you remember our names?'

'And what expert are you on the subject? I have clients! Contracts! Deadlines! Timeframes!' Arthur defended, making a show of counting each item on his fingers.

'What you have is a wife. You have me.' Maria counted on her fingers as her father had done. 'You have Grietje, Bert, Maartje, Ingrid, and . . .?' She delayed while she pointed and left her last finger unassigned.

'Alida,' Arthur answered, but still it took him too long to understand.

'Yes . . . Alida. This time. But this isn't the *only* time. This isn't the only thing you've lost sight of. I hope you realise before it's too late. Goodnight, *Arthur.*' And with that, Maria turned away. She had said enough. She returned to the night beyond the room.

Her father remained alone and speechless in the light.

Her bedroom door slowly creaked open as Arthur stepped into the darkness of the room. He made his way to the side of his daughter's bed and knelt as if to pray. Her hand was palm-down upon the covers and he placed his over it. He searched her face for traces of resentment – if such a thing could show in her sleeping expression – and perhaps the peace she showed instead said it best. He swept her hair from her face.

'I'm sorry, Alida,' he said. 'I should have been home sooner. Happy birthday.'

Two years passed. For their eldest, it was well beyond time to start thinking about adult life. By 1959, out of his concern for her lack of direction, Arthur involved himself in what capacity he could as a father. Maria seemed to possess little scope for maintaining a serious and steady romance, and so he took it upon himself to arrange a suitable man for her to meet. And so, through a friend from church, he found the eldest son of the von Ahmon family – a young gentleman named Peter. Arthur set to work quickly and arranged a date for their supper. He planned to introduce Peter to his eldest and most fiercely stubborn daughter. The way he saw it, the two were of the same age and of similar social classes, and so he believed it was fitting that they too, should see the benefits of a marital union.

Peter was tall and athletic, clean cut and regally handsome, with thick, dark hair. He was from a well-known German family. He was well educated and had a promising future. Indeed, his credentials as an eligible bachelor were impeccable, but despite this, Maria had her own ideas. Arthur knew Maria was fussy – or rather, oddly selective – but he believed wholeheartedly that even she would see Peter's merits as a man and as a husband. It might have been because her personality resembled her father's too closely that the matter escalated the way it did, but whatever the reason might have been, it was clear that father and daughter were an even match when it came to being stubborn.

As per her father's arrangements, Maria's siblings and mother were out of the house. He had his housekeeper, a quiet, mouse-like lady named Nelleke, prepare several of her finest courses – indeed Arthur spared no expense on the meal. To that end, he tabled the most exclusive wines and spirits he could obtain on short notice. And after all the arrangements had been made, he knew the last thing he must do, for he had not contemplated her refusal, was to seek out

Maria. And so, just a few hours before the couple met, the news of her suitor's attendance at her home that evening was delivered to her.

When Arthur found her, she was slumped lengthways across his reading chair in the study, her back propped against the side and her knees folded over the armrest at the other end, like a cloth doll too flimsy, too careless, to sit upright. She was reading a book he had never seen before, but knowing it was likely foreign fiction, he dismissed its value in an instant. Indeed, her book was not one that she had found on his shelves – it was one she had collected on her travels many years earlier, and was written in English. Arthur guessed it to be vain, frivolous drivel. And besides, he believed his cause warranted the disruption. He had sought Maria out for something far more important than trivial travel tales told by some heretical drifter.

And so, Maria's indulgence in a foreign stranger's travels through lands more foreign still, was interrupted by her father's presence, and then by his blunt and peevish voice.

'You do realise you have your own room to read in?' His question fell on deaf ears. Her habits were too firmly established to change. 'Maria, stop reading. Give me your attention. You will meet someone at supper this evening and I won't have any of your usual nonsense. His name is Peter and he is studying to be a physician.'

At first Maria paid him no heed, and he wasn't sure if she had heard him for, in reply, she turned the page and maintained the book's position, making no sign of putting it down. Maria had hoped to continue her journey through its pages by demonstrating her disinterest in her father's campaign to control her life. She had been in a pleasant mood before his intrusion and really didn't feel like getting into an argument. Arthur was about to lower his guard, but then her reply came and they were once again embroiled in an all too familiar battle.

'Father, I'm really not interested in meeting anyone,' Maria replied curtly.

'Not interested? Don't be ridiculous!' He stepped further into the room as the door clapped shut behind him. 'Now, look!' he snapped sharply. 'He's a reputable young man from a wealthy, well-respected family. You'll want for nothing with him!' Arthur seemed to believe that speaking from a greater height would ensure his victory.

But Maria held firm against the full force of her father's tirade, and returned fire with fire. 'Well, I refuse to meet him,' she retorted, riled and reckless. She sat up from the chair, flouncing, snapping her book closed, crossing her arms and turning her face away from his. 'And you can't make me.'

Her father's face clenched in frustration. 'Stop acting like a spoilt child!' His temper had taken the helm and it handled his discourse in a wild and wayward fashion. 'You need a husband! You'll be thirty before you know it! You must stop being so darn fussy! How can you expect—'

'To hell with it!' Maria cried. 'I don't want any of it! I don't need *his* money! I don't want . . .' She lost her words for a moment, but they returned swiftly upon a new tack. 'I'd rather marry a penniless Englishman than anyone *you* find for me!' But her words, while they were empty at the time, suddenly moved beyond anger and started to take shape as some kind of fantasy – the kind of adventure she had always hoped for. She still clasped the book in her hands – its stories flowing through her, alive with the spirit of heartache and romance, of struggles and triumph, of villains and heroes. Her words were no longer a hollow threat or something spat out of spite; instead, they started to carry weight. They bore purpose. 'In fact, I think I will!'

'Don't be stupid . . .' said her father, his voice suddenly softened. The thought of his daughter following through with her plan riddled him with uneasiness.

'I will live with him in a land far away from here, and have lots of children, and you'll never get to see any of them . . . unless I send you a photo just to show you what you're missing out on . . .' She realised her words had become hurtful, and a part of her regretted it, but she was too riled up – too deep into her own threat – to apologise.

'So . . . where would this faraway land be?' Arthur challenged. 'How will you afford anything?' He watched his daughter's eyes dart about the room in search of a retort.

She settled suddenly upon nothing in particular, but her mind was still working as a sly smile bowed her mouth. 'Maybe I'll go live with Uncle Lance and Tante Tien in Australia. That's as far away from you as I can be! I'm sure they'll help me find a job too!'

'There's no way you'll be able to live in a place like that!' he mocked. 'It's too far away, for starters. And you'll miss your sisters too much. You won't have all the luxuries you rely on here.'

Maria stood firm. 'Well, I don't care. I'm going.'

Interchapter

Colin

The English winter repulsed Colin James Walker. When he returned home after three years abroad in Manama, Habbaniyah and Southern Rhodesia, he had lost his tolerance for the cold, wet weather that smothered London in grey misery. He wanted to be anywhere but where he was. The city had one feature, however, that helped it retain some residual interest for him and, of course, that determining factor was female.

Before Colin had left England in 1952, he had been boarding with Gert and Ernie Taylor. They were an old couple whose own children had left long ago, and they were happy to fill the void with young boarders who had nowhere else to call home. They were also, by convenient happenstance, the surrogate grandparents, or some kind of acting aunt and uncle, to a young girl named Anne Jones. She was only eleven when Colin first met her and he was fourteen, and yet she fawned over him the way any child does for an older person he or she admires. But, having lived a hard life, Colin had been made especially mature for his age, for he had never had a childhood in the conventional sense. For three years, Colin felt at home at the Taylors', but shortly after his eighteenth birthday, he enlisted with the Royal Air Force and left Dagenham.

When he quit the care of his landlords, he did so with nothing but the clothes he wore and a set of darts. The sun was veiled by a dense morning fog that enshrouded the street and the city. As he walked, the smart click of his footfall on the pavement sounded to him like the locking clink of a winch, winding him fixedly towards his future. Even so, he knew he would miss the Taylors. They were more like a mother and father to him than his biological parents ever were. They were still standing in the doorway, arm around one another, by the time Colin had crossed to the other side of the street. He took one last look at them . . . and waved . . . and waited . . . and watched . . . as they waved and waited. Finally, they were sent indoors by the cold and by way of courtesy to Colin's privacy. However, it seemed that the second he had farewelled them, an obscure, almost childlike figure, emerged. It flailed in a clumsy fashion, waving arms about without pattern or rhythm. Colin knew immediately that it was Anne and he could tell, even from a distance, that she was panting. Her breath billowed in the frosty air like the white smoke puffed from an old man at his pipe. Soon he could hear her raspy wheezing as she struggled to suck in the icy air that scorched her throat. The tap of her shoes echoed louder as she grew nearer, and he could perceive by the rhythm of it that her speed wasn't abating. Colin braced himself for the impact. Suddenly, all of her smallness slammed into him with a dull, full-bodied, thump. Her fair copper-coloured hair escaped from beneath her black beanie and stuck itself to the moisture on her cheeks. And she stretched her arms around and held him. Her pert nose pressed against his chest. Colin waited for her to catch her breath, hoping the encounter wouldn't delay him for too long. A moment passed and when she finally pulled herself from against his body, her young face was a mess of sadness and distress.

'Why do you have to leave?' she asked, clinging to the sleeve of Colin's coat. 'Do you hate me?'

The truth was that he liked her company but he couldn't return the affections she had for him. 'Hate you? No, Anne, of course not,' he started, full of brotherly patience and affection. 'You know full well that I can't stay here forever. How will I ever make any money?'

Anne slumped, her shoulders dropping the hope that had held her upright. He saw the injured look on her face and couldn't help but pity her a little.

'I might be back one day though,' he assured her, hoping to win a more pleasant farewell from his sisterly friend. 'But it won't be for many years.' His voice had adopted a more serious tone. He never liked standing still for too long and he felt his feet getting itchy for adventure. Even so, he knew he could spare her at least a moment's consolation.

'I would like it if you could write to me,' she suggested, but Colin's thoughts were growing distant. The wide world beyond this grey city beckoned him. 'Could you do that, please?' she pleaded again, hoping he would succumb to her desperate request.

'I'll be very busy,' he started, trying to shrug free of her gaze and the guilt it stocked. He knew he couldn't look her too long in the eye; his head was filled with ambition and he was cautious of letting his past get in the way of his future. He needed no distractions and he was anxious to commence the journey ahead. Everything was possible, but he knew he had to avoid the shackles of his history. He turned it over in his head for a while before giving her his reply. 'Well, sure,' he finally agreed.

Her face erupted into a smile and he was glad he had given her the answer she wanted to hear.

'But it won't be right away, mind you,' he added, hoping to dull the nature of the promise he made her. 'It might take me a while to find the time.'

'That's fine. I understand,' she replied, though she still couldn't wipe the smile from her face.

He was twenty, and in his three years abroad, Colin had seen more sun than he had in all his years beforehand. He had felt the dry heat of foreign lands and it had made him disinclined to be subjected, yet again, to the dreary English January. He was sent to West Mailing in Kent to finish his last nine weeks of service with the Royal Air Force, but there was one other reason for him to return.

Six months into his travels, Colin had found himself struck by the sudden dutiful thought to write to Anne. He hadn't completely forgotten about his promise, but the distance had made it easier to neglect it. He was inevitably compelled however, without realising it, by a subtle homesickness that quietly afflicted him. All he knew was that he felt like writing to someone, and that Anne was the only person that came to mind. Even the process of writing in itself helped him feel connected to the first place he had called home. What was more pertinent however, was that each reply he received helped him to feel remembered, and as a result, far less alone.

Through their correspondence, Colin and Anne developed a steady interest in one another, so it seemed natural that he should visit her as soon as he could. She was still living in London, in East Ham, and so Colin made the most of every opportunity he got to see her. They went dancing on weekends and saw a number of comedy shows – Max Bygraves and the like – for Colin never had a mind for anything particularly serious. Despite this, he quickly realised that he could no longer consider Anne the child he once knew. She was seventeen and had matured significantly. Colin had acknowledged this, and with his service drawing to a close, he knew he had to think ahead to which direction his journey would take him next.

The two had just left the Hackney Empire, a theatre on Mare Street, when Anne said she was in the mood for dancing. The delay in Colin's reply, and the fact that he had been unusually quiet throughout the evening, gave her the feeling that something was wrong. Not being the type to press people, Anne ignored it, hoping her happiness might encourage him to forget whatever unpleasant thought was on his mind.

Before they arrived, Colin pulled Anne to one side and led her away from the crowd gathered along the footpaths. Clusters of human shapes congregated and flittered about like moths beneath the blaze of lamplights. The night was crude and chill, yet the humming of life seemed to kill the cold. The city lights sparkled around them.

He placed a hand at her hip, as if in a position to glide across a ballroom, yet the other remained by his side and his feet were planted to the spot. He held her eyes with his. He wanted to keep the mood cheerful. He steadied his tone and spoke softly. 'So, Anne . . . what would you say to making our relationship a more serious one?' Colin was pleasantly surprised at how calm and collected he sounded.

But his relief was short-lived, for Anne almost immediately withdrew into herself and hesitated before answering. 'I don't know, Col,' she started, 'I could probably be more certain in a year or two . . . after I graduate and find work. It's not that I don't want to be with you, it's just that I think it would be in my best interest to focus on my career.'

Despite feeling dejected, Colin couldn't help but respect her choice. It was, after all, surprisingly sensible. 'I'll be honest,' he confessed, his voice low and weak. 'All this time, I've only stayed in London because of you.'

'I know,' Anne admitted. She knew all too well that Colin would never be truly happy if he were to be chained to the city he hated. She also knew that if her reason was not sound, that if she had admitted to him that she was declining his offer so that he could be happy, then he might grow to regret it one day. 'But I want you to be happy . . . and I'm just not ready,' she added, lost for what to say, for she had forgotten her lies and confused them for truths.

'Very well, that's your choice and I'll leave you to it,' Colin concluded with false pleasantry as he released his hand from her hip and turned to walk away.

'Col . . .'

He was halted momentarily when he heard Anne's soft voice call his name, but Anne had nothing more to say, and if she did, she couldn't find the words. An agonising silence stretched the ever-increasing distance between them and, when he couldn't take it any longer, Colin disappeared into the crowd.

Anne stood a while longer. Alone. Still trying to find the words . . .

In April 1955, shortly after his service was completed, Colin left for Australia from Tilbury Docks on the RMS *Otranto*. Before boarding, he farewelled Anne's mother, Edie, who attended on her behalf.

'Goodbye, Colin,' she said cheerily. Her mouth was like Anne's, but that's where the similarities stopped; her complexion was far from fair, her hair was dark and wavy, and her nose was round and masculine. She was often loud and opinionated, but Colin and Edie had always gotten along exceptionally well. In many ways, she cared for him as though he were her adopted son. For this reason, she was saddened by his departure. 'I hope you have a pleasant journey,' she added, smiling and reaching, wide-armed for a hug. She pulled him to her bosom and, as she held him there, she wept. 'And thank you for being such a good companion to Anne all this time. I'm so sorry she isn't here to see you off.' She wiped away her tears and tried a brave smile. 'You can rest assured I have made my disappointment well known to her.'

'Thanks, Mam,' Colin replied. 'Thanks for being so kind, and thanks for being here now, too. I could have happily stayed here, I think. But maybe I'll come back one day and things will be different.' His false optimism only fooled himself.

'Yes, I'm sure they will be,' Edie assured him. 'One way or another, things will be different.'

Neither of them truly knew where Anne was and why she had chosen not to say her farewells. It may have been because there was no real reason for her to – after all, it was she who had put an end to things. That might have been one reason. But, more likely was a second version of the truth: the situation was too painful and she, quite simply, couldn't bring herself to say goodbye to him for a second time.

Riet

Two sisters farewelled one another from outside the gates of the boarding platform. They had to raise their voices to be heard above the rain. The downpour was unexpected, and neither was dressed appropriately for the cold, let alone equipped to shelter themselves, or the luggage, from the pouring rain.

'Vaarwel, sister! I will miss you dreadfully!' the first declared in an overly dramatic fashion.

'Vaarwel, my sweet Maria! Your absence will agonise me!' said the second, echoing the sentiment of the first. 'So please, don't stay away too long – I don't know how I could ever live without you! I shall be eagerly awaiting your return!'

In truth, they jested to mask their sincerity – exaggerated truth to hide their heartache. One didn't want the other to feel guilty for leaving, and the other, for staying.

'And I will miss you too! But I must get aboard the ship, and you must get out of the rain before you catch a cold! I'll write to you as soon as I can!' The impending departure time and the increasing severity of the weather compelled her to secure herself aboard the ship.

'Please do! Bon voyage!' the second cried, and despite the deluge, the two hugged each other tightly, one last time, before parting.

In 1962, two years since her departure, and at twenty-nine years of age, Maria, whose name had by that time evolved from Maria to Mareecha, then to Reecha, before finally arriving at Riet, decided to visit her friends and family in the Netherlands. She had been living with her aunt and uncle in Esperance, Western Australia, for two years. In that time, she felt she had conquered something within herself. She had challenged and overcome her presumed limits, and had arrived at a revised state of mind. To add to her tales of adventure, and to ensure she was not going home empty-handed, she had met a sheep farmer named Philip Robinson and they were engaged.

After having to first travel north to deliver something important to a cousin in Coolgardie, his truck finally sped towards Fremantle. The two passengers sat in the stench of stale sweat, livestock and motor oil that clung to the cabin. A powdery residue of grey clay had formed a skin upon the glass of the passenger-side window like dried milk, and through it and the other windows, nothing but hot, red dirt seemed to stretch on in every direction, as flat and endless as the sky. The country was baked reddish-brown: ochre, for miles and miles upon miles and miles, like one huge space paved with terracotta tiles. Overhead, a single thread of cotton cloud, anchored to a sheet of pale blue, was being slowly plucked apart by the heat. Wind had raked the dirt into furrows that ribbed the land like wrinkly skin upon the back of an old man's hand.

The searing sun stung her eyes as she stared out at the scrubland. A sudden gust spiralled the sand into a frenzy that swirled dry weeds and dirt into a dusty, rusty, wriggling, gyrating pillar that fell apart as it hit the highway. There was a time when a place like this would have intimidated her. It was a land for leathered skin, cracked lips and hardened hearts – not for a pampered and pale European woman. The outback was an ocean of land. It was vast, and barren, and wild, and dry, and hot, and flat, and the flies and insects were fierce – but still, she found beauty in it. She had fallen in love with the ruggedness of it all, and while she was eager to return to her home country, she was far more excited about being in Australia. It was while she was battling this dilemma that her fiancé's blunt baritone broke her muse.

'Hey, hey! Look who's back with us! Sorry to interrupt ya thoughts, but I need to know whatchya thinkin' about,' he asked, without phrasing a question. He spoke in a rudimentary and drawn-out way that churned his words through the mill of local dialect, stretching vowels and dropping consonants.

'Thinking about?' she asked, lost for the contextual information needed to solve his cryptic expression.

'Well, do you wanna stop in for a bite somewhere before ya leave or are ya happy to eat on the boat?' She let the question linger a little longer, for food was not on her mind. She was too full of conflict to allow her stomach to add to the equation.

Her initial motivation for moving to Australia had not been to find a husband. It wasn't to reconnect with family or to explore new places and cultures. The primary objective was much simpler – she wanted, above all, to prove her father wrong. He didn't think she could do it. He believed she was far too accustomed to the lavish lifestyle she had known all her life. In fact, Phil's question, still unanswered, dissolved into the white noise of the roaring highway and the monotonous play-by-play of the cricket broadcaster that came through the radio. Riet drifted into the memory of the argument she'd had with her father before leaving her home in the Netherlands.

Her recollections were interrupted yet again, this time by the soft grip of her fiancé's hand landing with a clap on her thigh. 'So how about we make our own plans for supper then?' Phil suggested.

At first Riet thought she might be amused by the way the vibrant corn-coloured fabric of her clothes contrasted with Phil's brown hand, but instead she found that the colour she remembered no longer existed – it had been faded by the harsh sun and worn thin by the gritty water. For a moment she wondered whether she too might have been withered by the weather in much the same way – though she knew her change would not be visible on the outside. She had discovered that nothing new keeps its lustre long – especially not in this country. Eventually, a thick film of dust smothers everything. A person must be kept busy maintaining their shine, or they risked losing it for good.

She looked at the big hand that softly gripped the skirt-covered portion of her upper leg. The nails were gnawed short and grime burrowed itself into the crevices where the nails met the skin. She followed the hand up the length of an arm that seemed as thick as a pine post. She tracked it to where it met the faded navy-blue sleeve of Phil's best work shirt. From there she was led to a floppy fabric that collared a sun-scorched neck and a chest that sprouted a bushel of thin dark hairs like ravaged wires. She finished at an unshaved face, a crooked smile and a set of twinkling brown eyes.

'Yeah, sure,' she agreed apathetically.

'Well, bloody hooray for that!' Phil exclaimed, relieved to have finally received an answer.

They hurried a farewell kiss outside the terminal building, Phil having to arch his back quite a way and Riet having to stretch herself up onto her toes, to let their faces meet.

'I'll see you again in Vlijmen,' she started arbitrarily.

'You know it'd be much quicker if you'd just fly there with me,' he pointed out.

'But there's no rush, is there? Flying skips the most important part. It's not just about arriving at a destination. Besides, I love the ocean. I'd much rather go by ship.'

'I guess I'm just a bit worried about what might happen if I'm not with you,' he admitted. 'When they're at sea, people can get a bit . . .' he paused. 'Frisky,' he added, for want of a better word.

'Well,' she replied, quietly offended. 'I'll try to control myself.'

'You know what I mean,' he asserted, backpedalling. 'It's not *you* that I don't trust, it's . . . the other passengers.'

'Well, I'll keep an eye out, shall I? If anyone makes a "frisky" move on me, I'll run right away. Don't you worry. I'll be under lock and key, and only you can free me.'

'Well, okay . . .' he said, testing the air. 'Have a safe trip . . .' Then his brown cheeks turned radish-red as he mustered the courage to complete his sentence. 'I . . . love you,' he said, scared that he might not hear her say the same words back to him.

His awkwardness unfixed her shell of hostility at its hinges, and a smile stretched across her face. Still, she took a revengeful pleasure in drawing out his torture a little longer before she eventually replied, 'I love you too, dear.' And with that, she pulled his face to hers for one last kiss.

Colin

In 1962, at twenty-nine, Colin decided to visit his friends and family in England. The taxi door grated open to the grind and screech of steel on steel. He peeled himself from the plastic seat his skin had stuck to and climbed out of the car. He was immediately struck by a hot, dry wind that dried his sweat-glossed arms and back and made him feel a little cooler. He inhaled the arid air deeply through his nostrils, held it, savoured it, and let it out again. He smiled. He had grown a certain affection for the climate – perhaps because it was so distinctly different from the one he had escaped, and he knew he was going to miss it. He hoped – in fact, he swore to himself – that his travels would see him return to this place again one day. He had been in Australia for seven years, finding his way into new jobs with new people in new places but, having no particular reason to stay, he booked himself passage aboard the Lloyd Triestino cruise ship *Oceania*, and left from Sydney.

By the time the morning sun crept through his cabin window, he had arrived in Melbourne. His resolve was wavering, and he knew that any incentive to stay in the country he loved would have been enough for him to instantly change his mind about leaving. He pondered awhile, staring from his bed as the ocean rolled on under the traffic of floury clouds that seemed in no hurry to move onto their next destination. He had been to Melbourne before, and after a moment of sifting through his memories of the city, he recollected meeting a lady named Sally Willing, with whom he had gotten along rather well. They had parted on amiable terms, and he knew that if she were able to do so, she would see him – if only for a casual conversation. He watched the water for a minute more and without warning, a sudden resolve wrested his wondering mind – he would remain in Australia a little longer if he could reconnect with Sally. And so, alive with repurposed plans and self-made promises, Colin rose from his bed and readied himself to go ashore.

After getting dressed and combing his hair, Colin made for the landing platform, leaving his luggage to the security and convenience of his cabin for the time being. He had decided he had best call Sally to let her know he was in town and that he would like to see her. The thought that she might not want to see him, or might otherwise be indisposed or unable to do so, had not crossed his mind. Instead of rushing headlong to the nearest pub, he found himself at a phone in the terminal, calling the only number he knew to reach her at.

'Hello, you're speaking with John, how may I help you?' a rather regular and rectangular male voice recited.

'Hello, John. I'm wondering if I could speak to Sal, please?' Colin phrased sloppily, realising he hadn't completely thought the conversation through.

'Who?' John asked, expressing irritation at the nature of the phone call.

'Sally,' Colin said, more loudly and clearly.

'Sally who?' John challenged.

Colin's complete lack of foresight rendered him temporarily unable to think a single rational thought and the simplicity of the question seemed to make his disorientation worse. He thought he must have never known her last name. But then, from some abstract place in the depths of his memory, he was struck by the answer. 'Willing! Sally Willing. She's an employee. I thought she might be working today,'

There was a slight pause on the other end before the disobliging voice returned. 'One moment, please.'

With a soft and sudden clunk, the receiver was placed on what Colin imagined to be a desk or counter. He listened to a muffled conversation on the other end.

John picked up the receiver again. 'I'm sorry, sir. Miss Willing is not at work today.'

'Could you—' Colin started.

'Have a good day, sir.'

The receiver clicked in Colin's ear before snapping into a droning hum. He scratched his head a moment before hanging the phone back on its hook. He knew it was a rare and unlikely event for Sally to not be at work, but his inclination to see her died away as quickly as it had blossomed. He was too impatient to hang around on the idea of 'maybe', and so he returned to his cabin where he resolved to remain until he had arrived in Italy.

His self-imposed containment lasted five days.

Dance

After enjoying a light supper, Colin sought to stimulate his mind or, at the very least, to occupy it in some way. He swiftly realised, however, that he had expended every source of amusement he could find within the walls of both his cabin and the contents of his suitcase. This fact, coupled with the prospect of going ashore in Singapore the next day, fortified Colin's growing inclination to be among people. Social deprivation aside, he couldn't help but acknowledge that the boat was ferrying a score of attractive women his age. He had only ventured out of his cabin on a few occasions, but each time he did so, he found himself admiring the beauty of the women. He thought it might have been a trick of the mind – that perhaps his solitude had awoken some primal appetite in him and diminished the immunity he had developed while living in a society where such women were commonplace. There was one woman he recalled in particular, and who he figured would have been about his age. She had been standing outside the purser's office a few mornings earlier, when he had made a currency exchange from Australian pounds to British pounds. In that moment, he stopped himself from speaking to her and he didn't know why. Soon he felt he had made a mistake – that he had missed an important opportunity, and it kindled a flame in him to seek companionship. It had been gaining momentum ever since. His mind was made up. He would leave his cabin for the evening, and he would find someone new to talk to.

After pecking at her evening meal, Riet readied herself to spend the night in a social fashion. She wasn't the kind of person to sit around when there was a party to enjoy, and so preparations took precedence over dining, and her food remained relatively untouched on the

plate. She was excited to be landing in Singapore on the morrow –
albeit only briefly – and further thrilled by the thought of immersing
herself among an assortment of interesting people – all of whom she
anticipated having their fair share of fascinating stories to tell. And
though she was engaged to be married, she saw no harm in seeking
company and conversation and laughter, whether it be male or female.
And while she would never admit it to Phil, she could no longer deny
that her freedoms at sea had ignited a certain primal yearning that
she knew demanded a physical, human, connection. But waiting was
a test. There were handsome men aboard the ship – she had observed
them at every instant – but there was one man she had only spied
once. It was on the morning she had visited the purser's office, and
though her glance was fleeting, his shape and style, his shade and
smile, caught her eye and catalysed a rare reaction in her that, even
as she selected her evening attire and styled her hair and fitted and
fixed her teeth, made her consider her appearance from that unknown
man's perspective.

Colin was half-sitting, half-leaning on a stool, quietly sampling
a quarter-filled tumbler of whisky that rattled to the clink of ice.
Unfortunately, the only epiphany the drink served him was that he
didn't want to drink it. Instead, he measured his mood against that
of the room. The night was still young, so the crowd was quite small.
Music, and the unremitting hum of life, ebbed around him. He was
wearing a white open-necked shirt with a cut-away collar, and black
strides specked with small rice-like flecks. He wondered if perhaps a
drink or two might be enough to alter his frame of mind, from what
it was and what it had been since leaving Melbourne, to one better
suited for dancing, conversing with strangers and partaking in other
frivolous fun. Riet soon arrived at the same bar and took up a position

on a stool several spaces away from him. She hadn't yet made up her mind whether she would order a drink or dive straight into the crowd of dancers, but not being particularly fond of the song, she rested on her indecision a moment longer. Colin recognised her immediately. She was wearing a navy-blue dress that fell a little below her knees, and a distinctive floral blouse. The two sat in isolation. After a minute or two of fruitless stalling, Colin thought he would take a second, third and fourth look at her. His feet were getting itchy yet again and he couldn't rest on unanswered questions any longer. He was nervous, but he realised that never knowing would be worse than any other outcome. He started to feel inclined to speak to her. His heart trebled its beat.

Colin's trimly clad figure had caught Riet's eye, and she thought she might look his way to study him a little more closely. When their eyes met, Riet suddenly shied away, to feign interest in the dancing. But Colin did not release his gaze. Instead, he abandoned his drink and sprang to his feet impulsively. The unfamiliar song had finished and the next one would be playing shortly.

In the space between songs, he took the seven or so steps required to close the distance between them, and though she could see the outline of his form moving towards her, she dared not acknowledge him too soon. She didn't want to assume his advance was made for her, but before she knew it he had stopped in front of her.

He didn't know what to say. He wanted to come across as fun, suave. He wanted to match the mood of the occasion. He promised himself that he would make a good impression. He extended his hand in a gentlemanly fashion and, before any introductions were made, he found all the words he needed. 'Good evening, milady. Would you like to dance?'

For a moment she kept her hands on her lap. Phil's words of warning replayed in her mind, but a sudden, wild impetuousness – the very same that had driven her to travel and to seek new adventures, one she had let guide and misguide her on many occasions – made her hand take his as she rose to her feet.

'Sure . . .' She paused a moment and shook her head as if to retract her words. Part of her thought to decline the invitation. She would hate to prove that Phil's Theory of the Sea held merit. But she knew that her intentions were innocent. She was hardly going to fall in love; it was just one dance. She was free to frolic as she pleased. With that logic leading her, she beamed at him and added, 'I'd love to.'

Together, the two made their way hand in hand to the dance floor as the next song started to play.

It was after midnight by the time Colin and Riet tired from dancing, but seeing no point in sleeping when the boat would be arriving in Singapore in four hours, the two decided to find a secluded place to talk and learn more about one another.

Colin led Riet out onto the deck on the starboard side. The ship's lights made it difficult to see the stars, and the wind had a strength to it that twanged the cables overhead like guitar strings. At first, the couple appreciated the whip and wail of the wind; the force of it seemed to suit their wild and wilful behaviour. A storm was battling an invisible enemy on the horizon, sending spear after spear of lightning to the sea, yet from where they stood they could not hear the resounding canon-crack, for the wind and the waves roared above all other sound. The gust was much stronger than the daytime breeze, and much cooler without the sun to warm it. The sound of the swelling sea and of the ship slicing through the waves roared like a ceaseless choir of radio static, or the nautical snore of some deep-breathing behemoth.

They stared out at the moonlit ocean that crawled below them, rolling and rippling like bodies writhing and tumbling beneath a black satin sheet. To one unacquainted with such a spectacle, it might be likened to a field of felt, the lumps and hills of which had come to life to move about in the shadow of night.

And while the couple sank into one another's warmth, and waded through their unchaste affections, they halted a moment to talk.

'I love the ocean,' Riet said dreamily. 'The smell . . . yes, and the sway and spray . . . there's something so magical and mystical about it . . . don't you think?' She revelled in the realisation that she was at sea and free. But there was another, more greatly unexpected feeling welling inside her. She was falling in love. She couldn't deny it. In her heart she knew it was true, but it was far too soon to let herself say it aloud. She couldn't possibly. She wouldn't. At least not yet.

'That's kind of like this night, you know? It's a little like you and me,' Colin replied, confused by what he had said but confident in what he meant by it.

'This is just so special,' she spoke softly to herself. The sound of the ocean flowed freely between them as they drifted blissfully above it. They bowed their bodies together – snuggling into every nook to share their warmth.

'So, how did you come to be in Australia?' Colin asked in a sudden but tender digression. 'You're clearly not from there.'

'That's right, and neither are you I'd wager,' she replied, to ricochet the riddle.

Colin felt inclined to disclose at least something of his story to her, but he kept it simple. He grinned and said, 'Well, to answer *my* question . . . I'm from England originally. I came to Australia for work, and to escape the horrid weather.' Colin thought he had said enough, but the look on Riet's face urged him to divulge a little more. 'I've all but lost my ties to the people of my own country.'

'If there's nothing for you in England,' Riet began after a moment's hesitation, 'why is it that you're going there?'

Colin thought about it, but he already knew the answer. 'Well, sometimes I move on to the next place purely because it's not the same as the last. I suppose I simply need to keep moving. It seems to be the way I'm wired. Maybe a part of me just wants to take one last look at it. What about you? What's *your* story?'

'Perhaps another time . . .' she deflected. 'It's getting quite cold . . .' Her tone had lost the energy it had before.

In his years abroad, Colin had learned to recognise when and when not to press people, and so he dropped the topic. 'Shall I see you to your cabin, my dear?' he asked as chivalrously as possible.

Then her face regained its fervour, as if she suddenly held the winning hand of a poker game. 'No, how about we go to yours instead? You can show me all the treasures you've collected on your travels.'

'Very well,' he grinned and, taking her by the hand, steered her back into the heart of the ship.

They staggered down the narrow corridor, falling over one another and laughing like children as they went – a little due to fatigue, but a lot due to the ship's pitching and heaving, as well as the wayward nature of the hour.

Although Riet had asked to see what he had collected, Colin felt it was merely her way of learning more about him. He didn't mind, though. In truth, he was overjoyed to have female company in his cabin, so naturally he obliged.

After almost forgetting the excuse they had fabricated for her being in his room, Colin suddenly slung a big brown suitcase onto the bed. He unlatched the two leather belt straps that kept it closed, and slid a silver zipper along the equator. When the lid was folded back, Riet gazed upon an assortment of ornate wooden figures carved and curved and crudely painted into small animals and replicas of native artefacts. There were fabrics of various colours and textures, and all manner of souvenirs one might expect from foreign lands. She even found a case containing a set of well-travelled darts with rusted tips and tattered flights. Her hands and eyes went from thing to thing until she suddenly plucked a stuffed koala from among the knick-knacks. She looked over its plump grey body, its short limbs, glass eyes and furry ears. Of all the things in the suitcase, this toy seemed to intrigue her most.

She held it to the light for a moment, looked at Colin, and suspecting it was a gift for some lady he knew in his homeland, put the question to him. 'And who is this bear for, I wonder?' she urged, teasing him with a presumptuous smirk.

'This one . . .' Colin began, almost letting her think she had caught him in her trap. 'This is for my daughter.'

The information stunned Riet, and she couldn't help but think of him in a new light. She knew she had her own secrets to keep, but she didn't expect his to trump hers. The notion grew on her and instead of repelling her, the idea of him having a child had quite the opposite effect – it intrigued her. He suddenly appeared more handsome in her eyes, more mature and mysterious.

'You have a daughter?' she asked, oddly surprised that she didn't know everything about a man she had only met several hours ago.

Colin's growing grin nearly betrayed him, for he had set a trap of his own and she had walked right into it. 'No, not yet. But I will one day, and that's for her. She'll have beautiful blue eyes and long, blonde hair, and her name will be Marilyn.'

And that was all he needed to say for Riet to drop the bear back into the case, shake a scolding finger, and let Colin revel in his victory over her.

She flung her arms around his neck and pressed her mouth to his. He worked his hands down to her hips. They were close, and their falling bodies were caught by Colin's bed. In an instant, shirt and pants and dress and more were kicked to the floor, and two bodies beat together in a fury of carnal yearning.

The boat rocked and yawed as it rode the waves. Through the foggy chamber window, he could see little else but the infinite rising and falling of water. The ocean slapped the side of the ship – saltwater on steel. Colin watched as the ship shot its golden gaze upon the water, melting the obsidian crests into polished metallic light that trembled like fire. He had wedged both their pillows behind his back, for Riet's head was rested upon his chest. She stared out the same sea-sprinkled porthole.

Riet felt compelled to tell him something more about herself. She knew she had delayed long enough. She had finally decided that he deserved to know the truth. 'Mmm . . .' she moaned dreamily. 'The wide, wide endless sky.' She stirred the words and they wept like an open wound. 'That's what I always wanted . . . to travel and to see the world and to meet new and interesting people . . .' She paused. 'I'm originally from the Netherlands.'

Colin had heard her clearly, but made no sign of it. He decided to let her speak freely. He had resolved to listen.

'I moved to Australia to live with my aunt and uncle because my father didn't think I could. He's a businessman, my father. He owns a company. He says he wants what's best for me, but I don't want to marry someone for their money or for their family name. Anyway, there's something you really should know . . .'

Colin had maintained his unyielding gaze through the cabin window, but when she stopped, and he thought she might cry, he made to rise and Riet did the same. They shuffled to the edge of the bed, and sat side by side.

Colin placed his hand on her shoulder and it seemed to soothe her apprehensions. 'Whatever it is, you can tell me,' he assured her.

When Riet resumed, she fought for every syllable. 'Well, you see . . . I'm . . . engaged.'

They spoke at times to see if the other was still awake, and to update themselves on the hours and minutes remaining until their arrival in Singapore. All the while, Colin quietly considered the news that the woman he had suddenly become so enamoured with was, in fact, already claimed by another man. In a similar fashion, Riet had a number of conflicting emotions rising in her too: guilt, but also the early stages of a new infatuation. The two were in this state of remorseful, recalcitrant rapture, when they met the first series of islands that popped out of the oil-black ocean like mossy mountains bulging a barren field. However, the promise of land did nothing to sober them from their ocean-induced state of romantic intoxication. A new adventure had presented itself on the ever-unobtainable horizon.

In due time, they felt the boat slow, and when they caught the first glimpse of the shimmering shore of Singapore, they dressed and raced to the deck to join a small party of people who also wished to witness their own arrival.

It was still as dark as pitch when the captain's call was given, and Colin and Riet were among the first passengers to go ashore. Anything that could be seen was illuminated by the ship's lights that beamed its wrinkled glow upon the curling waves. To the casual onlooker – of which there weren't many – the couple might easily be deemed to be honeymooners. All severity of thought, any iota of regret or hesitation, had been left far behind in the recesses of their minds, where they would wait and be dealt with at a much later date. For the time being, they laughed and smiled together – their sleep-deprived minds fuelled by passion and adventure. For the duration of the short trip from ship to port, one always had a hand resting somewhere on the other – too frightened, perhaps, to let go of what they had finally found. And too riddled with romance to let the feeling lapse.

The ship towered over them like a massive metallic mountain, casting its colossal presence across the wharf and beyond – stretching as far as the twinkling city streets swathed in sequins, but patched by the light that broke from every conceivable point. The dock-stalls were a carnival of colour, lit by little electric lights, and painted like an eclectic basket of fruit; the women wore clothing dyed in reds, yellows, blues and greens. Further inland, the few men that were bustling about mainly wore white business shirts. The scene was like a resplendent children's playset – a land littered with all manner of human activity and shiny new cars scuttling from place to place like a line of ants. In the early morning light, Riet's eyes opened wide in wonder as she scoped the waking city.

Singapore was a buzzing metropolis – more modern than what tourists see of London and certainly more crowded than the busiest parts of Sydney. In fact, there didn't seem to be a space that wasn't occupied by human activity, yet it was impeccably clean. Police in white helmets, white short-sleeved shirts and black pants patrolled the area with hands held neatly behind their backs. At the busier intersections, similarly dressed officers directed traffic with large white gloves. The city was far more westernised than either had anticipated, and only the discerning eye could perceive that the modern façade masked the traditional Asian architecture it was built around. Colin had no particular plan for what they might see or do, but Riet needed no time at all to make up her mind.

'Oh, Colin, will you please come and look at the marketplace with me,' Riet implored with a need that he found both endearing and irresistible. 'I absolutely must find souvenirs for my sisters.'

Colin's reply came without hesitation. 'I'd love to.'

By approximately 5:30 am, after taking a scenic shortcut down several suburban streets, they found themselves back on a main road outside the Raffles Hotel. It was a grand old building – far more colonial than the other buildings they had seen. Out the front border was a line of large palm trees with limbs that stretched out like the ribs of giant hand-fans. Riet was about to step onto the road to cross when she was halted by a firm and sudden grip on her wrist. Her initial thought was that she had been saved from stepping in front of a vehicle, but when she observed that the road was clear, she was perplexed. She turned to see Colin with a peculiar look etched on his face. It was a look Riet immediately recognised, one of conviction.

'We should get married,' Colin said. His tone didn't falter. He had never felt surer of anything in his life.

Riet let him hold her arm as he had grabbed it – fixed in an almost horizontal position. She entertained no concept of doubt, her engagement overlooked, the threats she'd made to her father forgotten. Indeed all reason may very well have abandoned her. She gave her reply all but instantly. 'Okay.'

After the ship had set sail from Singapore, Colin and Riet were riding the fresh and fanciful waves of a new euphoria. They were so surprised and pleased with themselves that at any point when one of them felt their joy waning, they simply looked at the other and it returned fortified, more potent than before. They knew they didn't want to delay the inevitable wedding unnecessarily, and while they agreed to keep things simple, the matters that had been formerly neglected finally loomed upon them.

'I should probably let my family know,' Riet said.

'Of course,' Colin replied. 'That won't be easy to do ahead of time, though.'

'That's true.' And while she worked on solving the dilemma, Riet was struck with a sudden realisation. 'Phil.' She said his name aloud to herself, accidentally exhaling the consonant in a wide-mouthed whisper. Her mind had finally freed itself to roam among the weeds of her wild, often incoherent imagination, and the further into the brambles she dived, the more they scratched and itched, until her conscience was a red, raw rash.

'Is something the matter?' Colin asked, noticing the shock that had come over her.

'I just remembered . . . I should probably write to Phil. I'll have to let him know the wedding's off.' A silly smile grew on her face.

'I suppose I should probably write to Sal as well, then,' Colin added, returning the beguiling smile. And with that, the pair sat down together as they each prepared to pen letters to their jilted partners.

After a day or two of wandering the boat together, Riet eventually conceded to showing Colin her cabin. As they made their way towards the door, she stopped in the passageway and pulled him aside.

'I think I ought to give you fair warning . . . the girls are almost always in the cabin during the day . . . and they are far more . . .' she searched for the right word. 'Comfortable . . .' she added after a slight pause, 'than what you are probably used to.' Colin was a little perplexed by what she meant. But knowing he wouldn't be getting any more hints, he decided to wait and see for himself.

'Okay . . .' he said. 'I'm not here to judge.'

When they arrived at her door, Riet gave it two successive knocks and spoke to it in a voice loud enough to ensure that anyone inside could hear her.

'It's Riet. Is everyone . . . decent? I have company.' Colin thought it was a little odd to go to such lengths to initiate a man into the damsels' den, but the reasons for Riet's precautions were soon brought to light.

'Yes! Yes! Yes!' a perky voice trilled from within. 'Bring him in! It's only me!' But when Riet opened the door, and Colin's eyes roamed the room, he couldn't find a place to set them. It looked as if a lingerie store had been hit by a hurricane. He had never seen so many feminine undergarments in his life, and in the middle, lounged on her bed like the queen of it all, was a heavy-set, short-haired lady in nought but her underwear.

'This is Colin,' Riet introduced.

'Hello, Colin,' the lady started with a lecherous smile. 'Lovely to meet you. My name's Erica.' She finished by having the four fingers on her raised hand fall towards the palm, pointer to pinkie, in quick domino-succession to produce a short kind of effortless wave. Colin's head spun as it swam through the thick, lavender-infused air. It was a fragrance that he knew and usually enjoyed. In fact, he often found a peaceful pleasure in being fanned by the aromatic air breeze brushed his skin as women skipped by in summer frocks. But never before had it been so stifling, so smothering.

Still a little stunned and struggling to come to grips with his sensory discomfort, Colin formed his response. 'Hi . . . nice to meet you, too,' he replied, wishing for help, and hoping Riet could read his mind.

'We won't stay long,' Riet said casually, as though it were normal for there to be a large, half-naked, hungover German lady lying about.

'You really should have come with us to the officers' cabin last night,' Erica said to Riet. 'They really know how to treat a woman.' She ran her free hand through her hair.

'I don't think so,' Riet replied politely.

'No . . .' Erica drawled playfully. 'It looks like you might have been having plenty of fun of your own, eh?' She winked.

Riet's face flushed red at this. She gave Erica a sheepish smile. 'Shush, you!'

After several more uncomfortable minutes of Colin not knowing where to stand or look, or what to think or say, Riet had collected a few of her things and he could leave the land of lilac, lace and lavender, and breathe easy again in the open air.

When *Oceania* finally returned to her home port of Genova, Colin and Riet left what had felt like their first home together. They rather reluctantly lugged their luggage to Genova Piazza Principe and boarded the train that would take them, together, as far as Basel.

Though their tickets found them assigned to cabins at opposite ends of the train, they were never apart for longer than they had to be. They spent most of the journey in each other's cabins, or being social together in the bar car. However, the closer Colin came to England, the more disinclined to continue the journey he became. Riet had first noticed this when they had arrived at Massawa on the Red Sea several days earlier and Colin declared that it was as far as he could go.

'I think we could make a life here together, you know?' Colin said several hours after they had made port. They were ambling about the ship's top deck, for neither of them felt like going ashore.

'Are you kidding?' Riet asked in earnest, for she often found it difficult to distinguish where Colin's humour began and where it ended.

'No, I'm not,' he said. 'I really don't think I can go any further than this. It seems like the closer I get to England, the worse I feel.'

The salt-scented breeze fell still and the sultry air took hold.

Riet let him gather himself for a moment before she shared her opinion on the topic. 'Well . . . there's no way I'm going to live here. And besides . . . you'll have me with you this time. Not right away, of course, but I'll be with you as soon as I can. Perhaps I can make life there a little more bearable for you.' She knew that the offer she had made could not be turned down. His silence was her first clue. She gave him a charming smile and a kiss on the cheek.

Colin looked at Riet and knew that he could survive anything if he had her by his side. He returned her smile and took her by the hand. Those two signs were her second and third hints. Then the answer came. 'Yes, I'm sure you will.'

The train finally arrived in Basel and their journey together had come to its inevitable junction. They meandered around the station, making small talk and avoiding – with stilted denial – the ever-nearing hiatus in their time together. Colin's misgivings, allayed so tenderly by Riet in Massawa, had returned. They both feared the farewell. They were quite confident in the certainty of their reunion, but quietly concerned that the powers that be might find a way to keep them apart. All apprehensions aside, they were, in that moment, far more concerned with the present. They had shirked the subject for long enough, and it was Riet who first found the resolve to tackle it.

'Colin,' she started, breaking a heavy silence, 'it's time to go.' Her tone was flat, her volume low. He knew it did not matter how greatly he dreaded being away from her. The time had come when they must go in different directions.

'No,' was his first response, though he hadn't meant to say it aloud. 'Sorry . . . I really don't want to say goodbye.'

'Neither do I. But it won't be for long. And when we get together again, it'll be the last time we'll ever have to be apart.'

'I'll call you every night,' Colin said.

'I would hope so,' Riet responded with a smile, regaining an optimistic tone of voice that set his nerves at ease.

'Thanks,' Colin replied, though he didn't know why.

She gave him a reassuring nod. 'I'll see you again soon,' she promised. 'But I expect that I'll hear from you before that.'

'You will!' Colin rebounded.

They locked eyes for a second then wrapped their arms around one another and focussed on preserving as much of the moment in their memories as possible. The percussion of pedestrians, the buzz of the station, and the rumble of trains all faded. All that existed for him was her. All she knew, felt and thought was him. She pressed her lips to his, placed a hand on his cheek. And then, as their kiss ended, the obnoxious roar of the world returned. Riet slipped from his grip. She took several strides in the direction of where she needed to go.

Then Colin slowly snapped from his daze. 'Riet!' he called. 'Darl!'

She stopped and was about to look back when he spoke again, more softly than before. 'I love you, you know.'

Riet completed her turn and looked at Colin who stood a little awkwardly – arms out from his side as if he had asked a question. 'I know,' she said. 'But guess what? I love you more.'

Home

When Riet awoke in her bed one morning, several days after her return to Vlijmen, she had an uneasy feeling that someone was watching her. Her room retained the soft hue of night a little after day had broken, for the curtains had not yet been drawn – and even if they had been, the grey morning sky would have done little to illuminate it. She waded a practised hand through the dark and flicked the switch on the lamp beside her bed. Just beyond her toes, a vague human shape seemed to form itself in the dark. Panicked and confused, she lifted her glasses from where they had been placed beside the lamp and fitted them on her face. And, failing to allay her anxiety, Riet was mortified to find a man sitting at the foot of her bed. In that instant, he looked to her like the ghost of one who had been scorned by his lover and who had returned to haunt her and drive her mad with guilt. And while the image was true in many ways, Phil was very much alive. After her eyes adjusted to being awake she could discern that he had been crying, but she could also see that he had wiped away the evidence. She knew he was sensitive at heart but, being the type of man he was, he felt he had a certain masculine appearance to uphold. He didn't want her to know how much she had hurt him. He had hoped to preserve a modicum of pride.

The silence was disconcerting, and so, trying to come across as calm and casual, Riet's tender tone tore the tension. 'Oh, hi Phil,' she said, unsure of where to start. His arrival was unexpected – or rather, it had completely slipped her mind. She also couldn't piece together how he had found his way into her bedroom. 'What are you doing here?'

Phil's posture remained unchanged, and for a while he did nothing but stare at her. Riet found his expression difficult to read. It was simultaneously disgusted, confused, sad, yet still somehow blank. He was despondent but refused to admit it. And while she floundered through several futile plans to escape the situation, there came a tortured, human sound.

'So . . . it's true then, is it?' His voice was made small by the heartache lodged in his throat, with a huskiness that ought to have belonged to a man three times his age. Despite the vagueness of his phrasing, Riet knew what he meant. She knew that what he wanted to ask was *why*. But she also knew that she didn't know that herself. How could she explain it to someone else – to *him*, of all people? For her, all she knew was that it had happened.

'What can I say, Phil?' She knew an apology could not mend the damage she had done to him. She was also desperate to find a way to make him leave as quickly as possible. She was growing more uncomfortable by the second. Then – she knew she shouldn't, but she couldn't help herself – she let the words spill out, from whatever well her mind drew them from. 'I can't say I'm sorry. I want you to know that. I know I must own it – I must wear the hurt I've caused you. I have to bear it. But you must know that I did not mean for it to happen. It wasn't planned. It was a thoughtless impulse at first. So thoughtless, in fact, that my promise to you was truly forgotten. I can't blame anyone or anything else for it . . . I can't . . . and certainly not the ocean, as your theory would have you believe. There is really no excuse for what I did. And I know this is stupid of me to say, but I don't regret it, Phil. I think, perhaps, we weren't really a perfect match for one another. I truly hope you find someone else – and I'm certain you will. I don't expect you to forgive me.' And at that, Riet felt she had said all she could.

Phil had received her letter only a few days before leaving Australia, but he had resolved to continue with his journey to the Netherlands in the hope that it had all been some kind of mistake, and that perhaps she would see reason if he could be brought face to face with her. A part of him also wanted to hear the news from her mouth. Reading it was too much for him, yet he made himself. Time after time. Night after night. And each time, the agony never lessened. He visualised the words burning red on the page, each one corrupted by the whisperings of another man – as though he'd penned them for her. Each word struck a blow as hard as the last, until he finally knew he had to hear it from the woman he thought he knew, who he thought he loved and who he thought loved him. But when he had – even after travelling farther than he'd ever travelled before, only to catch her sleeping so deeply, ignorant of his heartache, and instead so peacefully – he realised that he only felt worse for it.

'Right . . .' he resumed, knowing he had to leave before embarrassing himself with some frivolous and fruitless confession. 'Well, I suppose there's no point in hanging around here. I'll see myself out.' He sprang to his feet and made for the door without looking back. Slowly, steadily, scuff for scuff, the flak of his footfall faded. She heard the front door open. Then she heard it click closed again. And Riet remained, still a little dumbstruck, in the bruised darkness of her room.

The moment he arrived in London, Colin found a phone. He thought about the time difference, but he was only an hour behind her. Still, he factored it into his calculations in order to avoid interrupting dinner. Night had fallen swiftly upon the city. The soft electric hum of the streetlights seemed to swell in the damp air like the buzz of mosquitoes that had so often found his ear in the more tropical places he had been. Even though he had been away for so long, Colin had lived in England long enough to know when it was going to rain. It was a sense that had been finely honed through experience. And so, believing he would soon be soaked, he quickened his pace for the phone booth. He was only twenty or so metres shy of the shelter when the rain began to fall thick and fast. It rebounded from the road, from the tops of cars, and from the roofs of shops and homes in an all-engulfing, rhythmic rumble. Any warmth that may have been radiating from the pavement and from the buildings was quickly dispelled by the deluge.

Colin flung the door open and hurled himself inside. Dripping wet, he lifted the phone from the receiver and dropped several coins into the slot. The clang of coins rattled around the booth and then he heard the phone come to life. The roar of rain persisted, yet in his mind it lost all relevance. His clothes were damp, and cold air crept through some unseen fault in the seal. He shivered, but as he withdrew his wallet, and from within it a folded piece of paper, he grew a little warmer. He dialled the number she had scrawled for him, and listened anxiously as the soft purr of technology connected his call. He imagined himself, transformed into an electrical current, rapidly tracing the lines, his course predetermined by the code that he had entered. He was a light-speed surge of passion pulsing through wires, racing towards his destination. Then he arrived. And a soft voice spoke. And, in an instant, two people who were countries apart, were brought together.

'Van Hessel.'

'Hello?' Colin reeled a little in confusion, for he was unprepared to be greeted in a language other than the one he knew.

'Goedenavond, u spreekt met Maria,' the female voice replied in a rather monotone manner.

'Hello, my name is Colin. Can I speak with Riet, please?' he enunciated as clearly as possible. There was a slight delay at the other end. Although it may have only been a brief second's pause, to him it felt significantly more – as if time was grinding against itself. A chorus of abrupt and incoherent thoughts paraded before him in that instant, each one a little self-mocking and completely irrational. Then the same small and distant voice returned, only it sounded much more familiar this time.

'Hello, Colin,' said Riet, smiling on the other end. 'I knew you'd call.'

And while their words arrived in one another, they were together in a place that was nowhere either had ever been. They were in a place between places, a place where they wanted to be, and could be together. They were wishing Time away. Yet their tears, laughter and expressions of affection were mixed with an air of waiting and wanting. For each of them, the voice that crackled under the strain of distance worked to remedy their loneliness a little, but it also made their longing grow greater.

They held each other with sentiment and kissed through distant lips with words that brought comfort and courage. But the call had to end and so, as the wintry wind whipped them again, they knew that they must release their grip on the phone. The conversation could be carried on no longer and they were forced, with a suffocating reluctance, to return to the realities from whence they came.

Wedding

As it swung left at an intersection, the top-heavy vehicle swayed like a grand old galleon riding a sudden swell. To the pedestrians wading along the shores of the footpath, it looked like it might indeed topple over. It was the ninth of February 1963, and Colin stood behind the bus driver – a jovial middle-aged man with a black, brush-like moustache. He was realising, with every shopfront they passed, that he was in fact, quite unprepared. Among other things, his attire was still to be completely assembled. And so, through his elation – for he was beyond excitement – and seeing that they were approaching a greengrocer's, he put in a bold request with the driver.

'Could you stop here a moment for me, my good man?' Colin asked. 'It's our wedding day, you see,' he added, gesturing towards Riet who was seated nearby, 'and, believe it or not, I need to buy a sack of potatoes for our meal at the reception.'

The driver shifted to a more upright position in his seat. His face seemed to suddenly come to life with colour and purpose. 'Right you are,' the driver exulted. 'I'll give you that chance.'

And sure enough, the driver left the bus idling in its lane as Colin jumped through the open door. Riet waited where she was, her hands held neatly upon her lap. The driver watched Colin disappear among Acton's bustling Saturday crowd of shoppers, and then – almost too quick to have been possible – return from the shop with a pillow-sized bag of potatoes, gripped firmly at the bag's knot. He bounded back aboard and smiled at Riet as he lifted the sack triumphantly into the air. He then placed them carefully upright on the seat beside her before turning back to the driver to make his second request, having spotted a men's clothing store a little further up the street.

'I have another favour to ask of you, if that's alright?'

'Anything to help a young couple on their special day,' the driver replied cheerily. 'How can I be of service?'

'Well, I think I had best buy a tie,' Colin reasoned.

'Yes, quite. Right you are,' the driver agreed, still aglow with stilted pleasantry. 'Off you hop, then. I won't leave without you.' And for a second time, the bus halted – this time outside the fashion retailer.

The other passengers seemed impressively indifferent to Colin's frenetic behaviour. In fact, they seemed almost entirely non-existent. To Riet it was as if they weren't there at all. But of course, in a universal sense, they were there. Passengers had been getting on and off at regular intervals, but their presence was inconsequential.

It only took a moment for Colin to hop to the pavement and stride purposefully into the store. The bus driver turned to Riet. He had thought to say something – possibly a friendly joke about their apparent lack of preparation for such a significant event – but when he looked at her, he appeared in that instant to decide against saying anything that might tarnish the occasion. Instead, he gave her an agreeable smile and, in acknowledgment, she returned it tenfold. Shortly after this friendly exchange, Colin sprang back aboard with his shirt collar upturned and a ribbon of shimmering black silk looped around his neck. He quickly flicked one end over the other and weaved the fabric into a knot before folding his collar down again.

'Thanks again, my friend,' Colin said clapping his hand on the driver's shoulder.

'Not a problem at all. I'm happy to help,' replied the driver with a friendly nod. 'Is there anything else you might still need? A set of two gold rings, perhaps?'

The pair finally arrived at their destination. They were later than anticipated, so when they stepped into the registry office, they were met by Colin's mother – a tall, unsmiling and slightly agitated woman. She had been kept waiting for longer than was due. Indeed, she had felt her patience dwindle with every minute she had lost to the hideous plastic clock she'd been watching. She wore a fitted white blouse with flowing sleeves that extended to her wrists. It was pulled tight, buttoned to the neck, and tucked into a high-waisted navy-blue skirt that stopped neatly above a pair of low-cut boots that glistened with polish like the black backs of beetles. A second woman beside the first looked no less irritable, albeit far shorter and stouter. Her fashion was much bolder – more colourful and contemporary – but her countenance appeared ironically hardened by the fact that she stood as an unannounced guest at the wedding of two people who she had never met.

Prior to their meeting, Riet had only been given a vague and rather unpleasant account of Colin's mother, and even in this brief initial encounter she found her a little frightening. She was a thin woman, but her resolute posture made her quite imposing. Her hair was rather commonly brown, but styled faultlessly into curls that kept away from her impeccable complexion. It may have been this very feature that Riet found most disconcerting. Her face projected very little expression. She didn't appear to be capable of emotion belonging to the most natural order of happiness – yet she wasn't particularly morbid. She was as stern as stone. She had a face like the ones men fought for in the war, and whose photographs from magazines they would pin above their bunks. Except, unlike them, she didn't seem capable of smiling. And in the rare occasions when she did, it never brought Colin any sense of comfort.

It was this very woman who saw to it that no more time was wasted. Perfunctory greetings were exchanged between the four.

'Hello, I'm Colin's mother, Elizabeth,' she said succinctly, extending an effeminate hand that seemed at odds with her callous personality. 'And this is my friend, Vera.'

'How do you do?' Vera smiled, tilting her head slightly forward in a singular, half-nodding gesture.

'You're quite late,' Elizabeth added abruptly, casting scorn upon her son. Colin considered apologising, but decided against it. Riet stood firmly, trying not to appear uncomfortable. She maintained a politely impassive smile as Colin introduced her.

'Hello, mother. And Vera, was it? Thanks for coming. I'd like you to meet Riet.'

'Hello, Mam,' Riet said on cue.

Elizabeth nodded curtly and reverted her attention to her son. 'Well, let's not dawdle. How about we get started with whatever it is we must do?'

Knowing it all too well, Colin was unperturbed by her single-mindedness. He obliged her with a cursory nod, and led the ladies further into the building.

After the necessary forms were completed, the newlyweds, with their witnesses still in tow, made for the closest Catholic church they could find. As they stepped from the registry building and out into the busy square they were met with a rather lovely summer's day. They strolled along, two by two, as the sun slowly warmed their backs. Colin held in his left hand the sack of potatoes he had bought earlier in the day, and in his right, his wife's hand. Elizabeth and Vera followed behind them. One spoke very little, the other – considering herself an expert on the history of the area – quite a lot. They continued in this fashion until they arrived at a Gothic church with a spire that stabbed the sky like an upturned tack. They followed the bordering hedgerow until it gave way to a steep set of steps.

'How does this place look to you, darl?' Colin checked with Riet.

'I think it will suit us perfectly,' she decided – rather indifferent to the church's appearance.

'I thought you'd find it to your liking,' Vera verified, to validate her attendance.

Elizabeth expressed no opinion on the matter. 'Well let us not dally. We can't have this take all day,' she said before ushering the others towards the steps.

The priest was a dishevelled homage to antiquity. His unkempt beard was the colour of cigarette ash, and he smelled of it too. Wiry grey hairs sprouted from his dry, blotchy flesh in the parts his habit didn't hide, namely the wrinkly skin beneath his chin that shook like a rooster's wattle as he spoke. His blood-red vestment painted him as the very picture of Catholicism, and indeed he looked it in many ways. Before him, standing face to face, were Colin and Riet, all set to receive his blessings upon their recent marriage.

Given the time of day, the church was occupied by only a handful of parishioners, who were scattered around the room. They kept to themselves in silent prayer, confession or reminiscence, which meant that Elizabeth and her friend were the only two on the front pew. Even seated, Colin's mother maintained impeccable posture.

Heedless of the small crowd, the priest's voice reverberated around the hall in a glorious monotone. Colin found himself temporarily distracted by a second bearded man, more refined than the first. He was fixed in his frame, backlit by the sunlight. He was ruby-robed and also wore a turquoise cloak that covered his shoulders and partially concealed his arms. He was holding against his hip a magenta-fronted book. In his other hand was a golden chalice, positioned on his chest like a pendant. Behind the man was a wall – a translucent tapestry of clover-coloured vines that twisted and spiralled to cover all but a plate-shaped sun that was the same creamy yellow of an egg yolk, through which the real sun shone brightest. Colin contemplated the meaning of the man for a while – what part he played in what parable – but more than anything, he stared at the stained glass window rather absentmindedly.

Eventually the mind-numbing mumbling stopped, and Colin regained his focus. He looked at Riet, who had been watching him bemusedly while he roved around in his own mind, quite lost. Then the voice returned briefly, this time in a more direct tone.

'That'll be two pound ten,' the priest pronounced.

After a short delay, Colin registered the request and dug his hand into his pants' pocket. As he did so, the priest turned towards Riet. 'Could you not have found a man of your own faith?' he chided, coupling pity and angst to produce a tone of voice not unlike her father's. Riet readied herself in retaliation, for nothing irked her quite so much as being scolded for her choices. Colin heard the man's contempt too, but having a cooler disposition, knew that the best way to win the contest was not to show offence. He calmly dropped the coins into the priest's cupped hands and gave him a menacing wink as if to say *Our love is stronger than your faith.*

The priest took his fee, yet felt he'd lost something more than he'd gained. He watched bitterly as the newlywed couple, and their rather peculiar company, left – taking their sack of potatoes with them.

Part IV

January 1988

Two gold rings gleamed amid the tranquil thrum of motors and machines and movement. Then the shrill shriek of a siren collided with the air like an axe swung upon a log, and its incessant echo triggered a slow unwinding of the tight-stringed noise that had filled him. Arthur suffered a strange dizzying sense of shifting between places and, as he tried to walk, he almost lost both his balance and his consciousness. The hum of machines and the rabble of workers seemed to be the very energy that had driven him. He had been like a puppet that danced to the piper's song, steered in constant, mindless, routine. That was when he realised he had made his way back to the factory floor after having lunch and robotically resumed working.

His recollections were incomplete, but one could hardly blame an old man for skipping over the boring bits. Some things in life simply seem to be remembered better than others – sometimes for no apparent reason at all. All Arthur knew was that these were the moments, meaningful or mundane, that mattered most to him in the end.

The unscheduled siren must have signalled a necessary stop in production. Some error, either human or machine, needed to be corrected. Recalibrated. Reset. Restarted. Instead of jumping to the helm, Arthur took the opportunity to rest. He would let someone else resolve the issue for a change. It was a test of their initiative and, in a way, of his detachment. As he rested, he watched two workers walk by carrying a large sheet of damaged glass. For whatever reason, it had splintered yet, oddly, it held itself together – maintaining its general form. The pattern printed upon it – or rather, chiselled into it – was like lightning preserved in crystal, frozen in time. The zigzag cracks tracked from end to end, tracing random faults to look like the stripped branches of an ancient tree. As the glass passed by him, Arthur couldn't help but see his shattered visage within it. His white tie and hair were lost – scattered and transparent in the fluorescent light that shone through the glass in a thousand fractured directions. The deeper he looked, the more he reflected on his life. *Have I achieved anything worthwhile? Has my life had purpose? Will people miss me, remember me, mourn me when I'm gone?* It was unusual for him to think like that, but questions such as these often arise without reason.

Defective glass rarely remains intact – there is no fixing it, no salvaging that feeble mess. In his experience, Arthur had found that people were not like that. People were not as fragile as a pane of glass. People could persist. People could conceal their hurt and imperfections beneath their immaculately maintained surface, and still be beautiful and brave and broken and brilliant.

Then the shattering crash of metallic thunder, like a tray of a thousand steel utensils dropped upon a kitchen floor, smashed his thoughts into oblivion. Arthur regained his grip on the broom and sought to escape reality. Time had lost all meaning to him. Then, now, soon, all existing as one – and none of it mattered. Arthur knew the answer was close at hand. He had known it once – he was sure of it. And he would know it again. He simply had to reach out and take it. Rake. Check. Map. Name.

Shortly, to the scuff and scratch and chafe of nylon bristles, Arthur found that he had departed from the present once more and had let his mind wander back into the past, lulled by the pull of nostalgia and contentment.

15

Return

Time passed and passed and passed. Arthur realised that the ambition that tunnelled under and towered over him had made room for a more practical and logical approach to business. He found that the company had become less about success and profit margins, and more about innovation and keeping up with a growing demand. Most of the town, which had grown quite large and more modern, had his glass in it. And Arthur thought that made the world a little better. The elderly, vulnerable to the cold, could still see snow fall; the boy too young to leave his home after dark could still gaze at the stars. The sun could still warm the nurseries of newborn babies. That thought brought him solace.

It was 1962. Bert sat at his father's desk and his father stood near him as they tallied their workers' wages and balanced the week's accounts. The tranquil night seemed to seep into the room through the window the way light creeps and stretches through the dark, only in an inverted fashion. A banker's lamp cast a yellow glow that bronzed the walls and threw strange shapes across the ceiling. Arthur looked at Bert and realised how much his son had grown – not only in body and face, but in wisdom and intellect, too. He had expressed an interest in inheriting the company since he was a young boy, and had developed a sound mind for business. He presented with an optimistic and gentlemanly charm that made people like him, but behind his smile and beguiling laughter was a mind that had been honed for profit and industry. He never hurried over his words when he spoke, and his deep voice demanded attention. These qualities, paired with a mathematical yet entrepreneurial mind, meant that Arthur could entrust the future of ARVAH to him.

They worked in silence, and while Bert busied himself with the ledger, Arthur decided to sift through correspondence. He gathered a pile of papers and flicked through the envelopes until he found one that was distinctly out of place. The foreign stamp was the first clue and the return address on the reverse side was the second. It was from Australia. The handwriting was familiar, yet the identity of the author eluded him, at least momentarily. Then he realised there was only one person it could have been. He collected the letter opener from the desk's top drawer, slid its blade into the envelope's edge and then withdrew the folded letter. Tucked between the folds was a wallet-sized photograph that depicted a strange stone wall or wave, and little else. He put the photograph aside for the time being and looked to the letter. As he had deduced, it was from his firstborn daughter. This made him a little apprehensive, but he knew the reality was probably less cruel than his speculations made it out to be. In many ways, he felt fortunate to have received any word from her at all. He knew, at least, that if she had put pen to paper, it meant she had been thinking of him, and that in some small way, he existed in her thoughts, for better or worse. As he read, time and place seemed to melt away.

Dear Father,

Much to your disappointment, I have thoroughly enjoyed my time in Australia. I know you were convinced that I couldn't handle the heat and the isolation, but it turns out I wasn't lonely at all and I have grown rather fond of the weather. Even so, I am bound for Vlijmen to collect a few important personal belongings. I plan to be with you all for Christmas. I will admit that I do miss my mother and sisters, but I won't be staying.

I have met a man named Philip Robinson. He has a cattle farm here in Western Australia, near Hyden, and we are to be married when I return from Europe.

I will travel by sea. Phil also has plans to come to Vlijmen to visit me and to meet you all. But we won't be travelling together. Instead, he has booked flights for a later date and should arrive shortly after I do.

I know you probably won't approve of my decision, but I want you to know that I am very happy. Please try to be happy for me.

Your loving daughter,
Maria

Bert had given as much attention to reading his father's face as his father had applied to reading the letter. Arthur let his hand hang limp at his side. The two exchanged a look wherein they each tried to read the other's thoughts, but recognising the futility in it, Bert was first to speak.

'What is it, Father? Is everything alright?'

Arthur thought for a moment, but it was only for a moment. He later reflected that, if he had delayed a little longer – detached himself and taken a minute to compose himself – perhaps he could have responded with less pessimism. But his response was not measured – it spilled from him in a state of rawness. 'In short, no. No, not quite *everything*. No. Everything is not alright . . . not quite right at all,' he said, as much to himself as to Bert. But his wishful denial did nothing to change the fact of the matter. He knew that it couldn't. 'It's an affront to me . . . and to you. To our family. Bert, my son, I'm afraid your sister has made a huge mistake. If this is what she meant by making a life for herself, then I won't accept it.'

Arthur could tell that Bert was worried – more than likely he was concerned about the wellbeing of his eldest sister. Thinking it best to allay any further unease, Arthur resumed his rant in all its remorseful rudeness. 'Your sister is coming home, but she won't be staying. She says she has met an Australian man to whom she has resolved to return.' He paused on that point to allow Bert to come to grips with what he was saying. While Arthur did so, he tried to determine what it was exactly that had made him so furious. He knew, only too well, that every young heart is made love's fool, himself included, but in no way could he find it in himself to accept his daughter's actions. As far as he was concerned, she was as good as married to Peter. It was just a matter of time. She could have had herself a good man, but she abandoned him for a foreigner who, he imagined, had seduced her with his silvery tongue, flashy smile and wayward charm. Maria had tainted the family name and Arthur couldn't, on the very principle of it, even lie to her in reply and say that he gave his consent to her elopement.

Bert interrupted his father's caustic cogitation. 'Do you suppose Mother would know?'

Jo always kept in close contact with Maria, even after her self-imposed estrangement, so Arthur didn't require long to reach an initial conjecture. This, however, gave rise to a second supposition: Jo, likely knowing what the letter said, had slipped it into the stack for him to find.

'Yes, I believe so, son. In fact, of all people, I feel your mother may have known it first.' He didn't mean for it to sound so bitter, and Bert knew it. Jo would have had her reasons.

The rest of that evening was not well occupied. Arthur thought that, perhaps after a minute or even an hour had passed, and with hindsight's clarity of mind, his anger might abate. Instead, it lingered. It never grew worse, but nor did it get any better – it simply turned in different directions, offering new ways for him to regret his daughter's failings.

Late in 1962, as she had forewarned, Maria came home. Her father was at work when she arrived and so, before he even got to the front gate, he heard the animated gossip of girls echoing intermittently through the still wintry twilight. To him, the sound palpitating from his home was like that of a healthy human heartbeat, rhythmic and full of life. The subtle scent of smoke from the hunk of oak he posited to be ablaze in the fireplace smelled to Arthur like season after season of peaceful, precious family time, and it made him long to be inside with his. But he knew his arrival would cause tension, so he stole in through the back door instead of the front – all with a firm focus upon his stealth. It felt peculiar to Arthur to infiltrate his own home like a common burglar, but there was something of value in there that he wished to indulge in – without permission if he must. He wanted, quite plainly, to witness a joyous family reunion. He knew that this would only be possible prior to the inevitable and regrettable disruption his presence would cause.

He slipped off his shoes as he stepped onto the inner door mat and put all manner of effort into the agonising slowness with which he closed the door, ensuring that its hinges would not squeak. Then, with the door safely shut, Arthur sneaked on socked feet to the edge of the wall that opened into the drawing room. He remained there for a minute, out of sight. And, in that stolen moment, he listened to his daughters' laughter – peppered at regular intervals with words of admiration, amazement and amusement – as Maria shared with them and their mother tales of her adventures in distant lands. They were spread across two chesterfield couches set perpendicular to one another while a tender fire embraced the room. And as he skulked, hidden and alone in the half-dark, his back pressed to the wall like a shadow, Arthur let their elation fill him. He imagined what it would have been like to be among their company in that very instant, chatting, chuckling, nodding, smiling and applauding. And he wished, wished and wished that he was.

Before the fantasy became more bitter than sweet, he forced his hostilities back in place. He had to think about what he was going to say. He knew he wanted to make amends for the harsh way he had dismissed his daughter in their last confrontation, but he knew he couldn't do it – he couldn't concede, not unless she met him halfway.

Maria had always been stubborn to a fault. When she set her mind to something, there was no changing it. Arthur was convinced Peter was her perfect match, but she wouldn't listen to a thing he told her. In the end, she said she would rather marry a poor foreigner than a wealthy and respectable man – if her father had any part in it. And her threat to run away and elope hadn't proved as empty as Arthur had initially believed it to be. She left. She said she was leaving and she left. She was leaving, and they all knew it, but he never truly accepted it. But she was going, and then she was gone. She left and her father was left without her. She went to Australia, as she said she would, and she met a foreign man with no remarkable reputation to speak of, as she said she would, a man her family had never met and to whom she was to be wed.

Setting aside the anguish of the past, Arthur emerged from the shadows and stepped casually in as though he had just that moment arrived home. As an essential part of the ruse, he acted as though he had no knowledge as to why they were carousing. Yet, in his reconnaissance, he had used several auditory clues to make an informed estimate as to where Maria was seated. So he directed his attention first to whoever was positioned at the greatest distance from where he expected to find her.

'Goedenavond, Jo,' he began.

'Goedenavond, dear,' she replied. 'And welcome home.' Jo was hoping that her husband would get the hint and acknowledge their eldest daughter, who was sitting suddenly mute, at the other end of the room.

'Hallo, Alida . . .' Arthur resumed, starting with the youngest. 'Ingrid . . . Maartje . . . Grietje . . .' He followed in that sequence, nodding to each of them until he arrived at the first born.

'Hallo, Father,' they greeted in grinning unison, for they were all bystanders, ready and eager to see how the long-awaited encounter would unfold.

Maria waited with an air of uncertainty.

Her father paused a moment to ensure his greeting was not missed or dismissed. 'And hallo to you too, Maria. Welcome home.'

To celebrate Maria's return, Jo ensured everyone's favourites were on the menu. Regrettably, Bert was out of town on business. Jo had hoped that catering to everyone's palate would promote pleasant dinner conversation that dallied more in the present than in the tarnished aspects of the past and the disconcerting future. She wanted her family to discuss trivial things like work, Ingrid's and Maartje's studies, Alida's friends from school, Grietje's family affairs; perhaps it might even afford her the opportunity to share the noteworthy parts from her day at home. Unfortunately, her efforts were in vain. Despite the festival of flavours in their mouths and the complete contentment of their stomachs, the past was not forgotten – not at all, and not for a moment. It hung on hushed lips and floated, like a noxious fume, in the suffocating silence.

The atmosphere was thick and sticky and odorous, almost edible. The intermittent clatter of knives and forks was all that cut and stabbed the otherwise prevailing silence. They sat in company, yet in isolation from one another. Arthur imagined that, like him, the others were carrying out conversations in their minds but were unable to phrase what they wanted to say. No one dared to try. At times, he would raise his eyes from his food, but they were never met by his fellow diners. It wasn't until the plates were cleared that this strange game of gaze evasion came to an end. Jo's ears had caught the clink of their cutlery one too many times, and she yielded. Their meals and their distractions were finite. This obstinacy could last no longer and Jo's patience could stretch no further. The family finally found a voice.

'Well,' Jo began, suddenly standing and making no effort to mask her frustration. 'I hope you have all enjoyed your meals.' With that – but not with the words themselves, and whether it was her intention or not – she had said just what she needed to say. And it only worked because it was she who said it. They had all stewed in a simmering pot of their own conceit and cowardice and stupidity, and Jo lifted them from the stove with mitted hands. All could recognise her disappointment, and it catalysed a collective inward reflection. They were made to swallow their pride, and it was lumpy and sour and curdled like spoiled milk. But born from this bitter rumination was an unuttered truce that transformed the very colour of the air in which they steeped. And their eyes rose from the table, hesitantly at first, but then with more freedom and with more purpose.

'Oh! It was yummy!' applauded Alida, the room's youngest voice.

'I enjoyed mine too,' seconded Ingrid.

'It was wonderful, thank you,' agreed Maartje.

'It was perfectly delightful,' added Grietje, keeping her thanks as succinct as those who went before her.

'I never knew how much I could miss the taste of your cooking,' complimented Maria, knowing that her gratitude would have to be made doubly known. She had a full mouth of teeth, but she still bore the trace of a lisp and it made Arthur think it must be hard for a person to chew when their bite isn't completely their own. 'I loved it, Mother. Dank je,' Maria concluded.

All eyes were now on Arthur. It was his turn to play the part his position demanded. It was his turn to put his thanks on a plate and serve it seasoned and seared and rested and garnished to perfection.

'It was a lovely supper, dear. But what's more is that . . .' he paused. He cradled a glass in his upturned palm, the stem between his middle fingers. 'I'm truly and deeply grateful that we can all sit together tonight. That we can eat and be here as a family.'

It was enough to satisfy his daughters. They knew it and he knew it. So they turned their eager and unified gaze upon Jo.

She locked eyes with each of them in turn. Then she sat back down. She placed her hands on her lap and smiled. 'I'm pleased to hear it. Now let us enjoy the last course to the pleasant tune of a happy family discourse.'

Dessert was an enlightening affair. For the most part, Arthur was surprised to feel a trite and trivial pleasure in hearing the fifth-hand gossip affecting his friends and neighbours, with whatever merit it warranted by that stage. With any news passed from mouth to ear, mouth to ear, and on and on, the end product often bears little resemblance to the first. But like all things of its kind, it would be readily forgotten and replaced by newer, wilder and equally inconsequential news tomorrow. So while they supped on the sweet, sugary confectionaries of conversation, and while Maria's engagement was undoubtedly on everyone's minds, all parties steered clear of that topic. Her contribution to table talk, beyond the reciprocal, comprised primarily of infrequent remarks regarding carefully censored details from her life in Australia: the weather, the kind of work she did and such like, but she made no mention of men, nor of marriage.

'You would have loved the colour of a tree I saw,' she started excitedly. They all knew she meant that she had seen it in Australia, but at the same time they were glad she didn't say it. 'They had been in full bloom a month or so ago. It's difficult to describe, I think. But it's my favourite colour now . . . the colour of the leaves, I mean. I think it's the leaves. Or the flowers. I don't know. But the whole tree is wonderful. The colour most certainly is. I think it's like purple, but I've been told it's blue. I guess it's a shade of bluish purple. Either way, it is the prettiest tree I have ever seen. Try to imagine the colour of lavender or a violet tulip, only a little different, and the tree is full-sized, and the petals, or whatever they are, are so tiny and they dye the roads and lawns and footpaths like a lilac snow.'

'It sounds so pretty!' remarked Alida.

'Do you know what it's called?' asked Grietje, fascinated.

Maria had to search her mind a moment – thinking back to what Phil or some other such person must have told her. 'It's called a jacaranda, I think.'

'Do you think we could get them here?' Ingrid asked her father.

'I don't know. You might need to ask Klaas at the garden shop,' Arthur suggested, in full support of the idea. And with that, the family's first successful sortie into the world of Maria's travels abroad was accomplished.

After they had finally eaten their fill, they returned to the drawing room for tea and coffee. They were making up for lost time – but for missed affection more so – and each of them wanted to wring the evening for all it had. They had hoped to carry the dialogue with them and drown out any remaining hostilities. Arthur had the secondary objective of draining the bottle of shiraz he had uncorked, and hoped to do so in company. He took the time to read the room and noted first that Grietje, who always feared a loss of sleep, was growing apprehensive, possibly due to the lateness of the hour; it was the relentless twitching of her leg that gave her away. Maartje was loosely and mindlessly twirling a lock of hair around her finger, so he knew she was bored but enjoying the familial peace. Ingrid was biting her nails, as she was inclined to do when she was daydreaming. Alida was animated, clearly tired, but still excited about being allowed to sit up with everyone. And Jo, like her husband, was taking it all in and enjoying every sip and syllable.

But the evening's pleasantry took a turn for the worse when Maria couldn't keep her secret from her father any longer. She figured it was better for it to be out in the open than kept from him indefinitely. They were about to delve into a discussion on Bert's new business endeavour when Maria suddenly spoke over everyone with clueless indifference to that topic.

'By the way, Father,' she interrupted. 'I imagine you'll be happy to hear that I will *not* be marrying Phil – the Australian man I met . . .' She waited on that point.

Arthur had to admit he was relieved. He did his best not to show it. He was, at the same time, a little vexed as to why she had left it so late to tell him, but his short-sighted jubilation swiftly outweighed his confusion. 'Oh really?' he asked, and in his wisdom, looked to Jo for guidance. She did little besides give him a gentle look that conveyed her trust in him to handle it. But there was something more to her look as well. Her face seemed to tell him to wait, and that he had only heard the good news.

Maria didn't reply right away, so her father knew he had to speak a little more. 'Well, I hope—' he started, before she cut him off.

'And I know this must sound to you like some horrible and ridiculous ruse, but I want you to know that I *am* still getting married. I have met another man. An Englishman.'

Silence squeezed them in its slipless grip once more: their parade brought to a halt, their plans uprooted, their progress undone.

Arthur spoke without thinking – without restraint – and his fury chose words that left a nasty taste in his mouth. 'You haven't changed at all, have you? Still the same foolish girl you were before you left.' A number of things about what she said bothered him, but what annoyed him most was that she could so easily break her promise to another man – a man who probably loved her, and had likely been assured of her love for him.

'No! You're wrong! I have changed!' Maria insisted, her voice quavering as she spoke through her anguish. 'Even if *you* can't see it! I'm not a little girl anymore . . . There's more to life . . . there's more to the world . . . there's more to *me* than you think!'

'If you really think you have it all figured out, why bother coming home at all?' Arthur shot back. The instant he said it he knew he would not and could not rightly recant it. He had spoken with stupidity, not with the level-headed judgement he ought to have, and each of his daughters rallied in turn.

'Oh Father, you can't be serious?' warned Grietje.

'How insensitive!' scolded Maartje.

'Really, Father? You ought to know better,' chided Ingrid.

And he was in the wrong. Maria debated her point at length, but Arthur refused to accept that words alone could compensate for her actions. She insisted that it was not for this Englishman alone that she would not be returning home again, but Arthur couldn't help but believe he had manipulated her in some way – made some promise of fulfilling a fantasy that no human could ever hope to make possible. She was impulsive before, but this engagement – this endeavour – was beyond whimsical. It was ludicrous! He snarled, he growled and he howled. And his carefully constructed argument collapsed under the weight of its own idiotic ambition.

A few days passed and in that time Maria and her father saw very little of each other. They existed in the same house but at different times, and if one had staked a claim upon a room, the other would avoid it at all costs. Maria moped about like a fog and simply sighed her days away, while Arthur brooded like a black cloud, waiting for his chance to burst. Fortunately, their normal routines ensured that they ate their meals at different times, which certainly helped them evade each other and avoid disrupting the usual household hush.

On one of these days, when Arthur was set to occupy his study, he discovered a book he didn't recognise. Something about the cover seemed familiar. It was slotted between titles he knew well, but its spine was out of place. He thought briefly that he had happened across the book by chance, but then guessed coincidence played no role in its reappearance. His next thought was that it could have been Jo who had planted it for him to find, but whatever the case might have been, he slid it from its neighbours. The cover was creased and had lost its lustre. It had clearly been read many times over, and its age made the pages compliant to turning. Arthur couldn't make much sense of the writing, though he could read a little English, but even if he were to have it all translated, he wasn't sure that he would find the appeal. That was no matter, though, he reasoned. It wasn't his book. He put it back where it had been, so that it might be found again one day.

The next morning, Arthur enjoyed a quick, quiet breakfast alone before he left for work. He had only travelled as far as three or four houses beyond his own when he saw a peculiar man plodding along in the opposite direction. His clothes were mismatched, and certainly not warm enough for the weather. To top it all, they were far too loose and altogether tattered. But what struck Arthur as most bizarre was the vacancy of the man's expression. He was like a lost and senescent dog, flea-ridden, half-blind and stiff-jointed. The same purposelessness was evident in the language of his body as well. His posture, his movements all drooped. His shoulders sloped forward as if he'd spent a week in the stocks and each stride of his tottering gait seemed to jolt his spine with agony. In many ways, he looked like the soldiers Arthur had seen returned from battles – beaten but alive, a shell, haunted by the things seen or done. But this man's injuries seemed less severe, and beyond those initial impressions, Arthur gave him no further thought. It wasn't until Arthur came home that evening that the identity of this mysterious, misplaced man was made known to him.

He and Jo were sitting quietly in his study – for Maria had occupied the drawing room with Alida, who had become something of her shadow. Arthur was hopeful that Maria's influence on Alida would not be a negative one.

The evening sun broke briefly through the clouds as if a giant trident was splitting the sky with its silver-tipped tines. The room was bathed in a tepid bronze patina. Arthur was at his desk while Jo was at his side, a little beyond arm's reach. It had become something of a fancy of theirs to sit together in the evening so that they had some measure of time before bed to enjoy each other's company. While Arthur was polishing his glasses in the transition between studying work correspondence and reading the *Brabants Dagblad*, and while Jo folded, fitted and sealed the letters she had been writing into envelopes, she thought to raise a topic she knew was sensitive.

'You might remember that Maria was engaged to that Australian man, Phil?' she began in all nonchalance.

'Uh,' Arthur grunted reactively. 'Of course.' Then, for an instant, the image of that man from the morning suddenly flashed into his thoughts.

'Well, he came by today – can you believe it?'

'Really?' Arthur returned, reeling in the reins to carefully scrutinise a mark on his lens that he couldn't seem to shift. 'Why?' he asked, giving Jo no time to answer before he added, 'Did he stay long?'

He could tell Jo was disappointed by his response, even though she had been the first to act casually. The situation was clearly not an everyday event; it wasn't as if the man had cycled across town – he had flown thousands of kilometres. To express his disdain for the whole debacle, Arthur played it down, as he would if he had noticed a spelling mistake in a magazine or had been told that there was a lost cat in the neighbourhood. The entire business was folly, in his opinion, and everyone knew it. As he honed his attention again to the spot on his lens, a cloud smothered the sun and a frigid pewter shade dimmed the room.

Jo still hadn't answered her husband's questions and her silence urged him to ask yet one more, and it was one that he asked with more weight than the others. 'Is Maria . . . alright?' He had removed the spot as the need to ask the question was conceived. Then, a moment after it had met the air and Arthur had repositioned his glasses, he caught a glimpse of Jo fighting back a smile.

She readied herself to answer the question she had hoped he would ask sooner. 'She's a little lost for how to feel right now. But, with time, she will be fine.'

Arthur knew he couldn't have expected anything more than what Jo had told him, yet her words brought him comfort. The light and colour of the sun suddenly filled the room once more, and it was clear to him what he needed to do next.

When he found his daughter, she was in her room. She sat at the foot of her bed, her hands resting on her belly and her gaze fixed through the window. Rain ran down the pane like tears. Arthur stood awhile in the doorway just watching her watch the world. He tried to guess where her thoughts were, but he knew they were further away than he could ever hope to reach. He edged closer, stooping lower with each step until he could follow her gaze. He tried to train his eyes in the same direction as hers, to share her line of sight. He wanted to see the world as she saw it. But it was, of course, not possible. He sat behind her, no longer trying to gain her perspective. His view was perpendicular to hers and he knew it always would be. There was no point in forcing it. His weight on the bed made her rise an inch and she spoke without breaking her focus.

'What do you want?' she asked. Her anger had turned to indifference, and Arthur wasn't sure which was worse.

'I really don't know,' he admitted, surprising himself by the truth of it.

For several minutes, neither of them spoke. Strangely, the silence seemed to bring them closer. Their proximity had a healing property of its own, and they both felt it. It was enough just to be close. He didn't move and she didn't tell him to leave. Something was working, and they let it mend what it could. They let the meter fill, and as it neared capacity, Arthur made ready to stand.

'Thanks,' he said, glad that he and his daughter had found, incomplete as it was, some form of peaceful compromise in their mutual solitude. 'I know we didn't talk much today . . . but I hope we can sit together again some time . . . without the fighting.' He stood and placed his hand upon her head before turning and making for the door.

On his way, halfway across the room, his daughter's voice tapped him gently on the shoulder. 'Dad, wait . . .' He turned, and she was looking at him. 'Come here. I want to show you something.'

He made his way back to her, only this time Maria had moved across and twice patted the place she wanted him to sit. They sat side by side. She pointed through the glass and bade her father follow the line of her finger. 'Can you see it?' she asked.

He fixed his eyes forward and traced the track. As best he could, he followed. One straight route from A to B. He strained. He squinted. Then he saw beyond the blur. And he realised that he saw nothing – nothing he hadn't seen a hundred times before. All he saw, beyond the fence and the street and the rooftops, was the edge of town and the endless horizon beyond it. And, yes, he *saw* it.

'I think so,' he answered. 'Yes, I believe I see it.'

Maria left again. It was inevitable – they all knew it, and they also knew better than to try stopping her. Before she left, Arthur told her, in no uncertain terms, that she shouldn't expect him to ever accept her new husband as part of the family, but he knew he couldn't stop her having him as a part of hers. All things come around, though. It was many years after their wedding that Arthur heard the story of how Maria had met Colin. Whether it was a profound love that developed in all but an instant, or an impulsive act carried out on a fanciful whim, the two had only known each other for a matter of hours when they committed to spending the rest of their lives together – leaving behind their countries, friends and families, all to start anew in a foreign country where they knew very few people besides each other. It shouldn't have really come as a surprise to him – after all, once upon a time he too had felt compelled to deviate from the path laid out before him.

Arthur didn't speak to Colin for twelve and a half years. Not for any *good* reason, but not for any particularly *bad* reason either. It was for no reason, really – no reason other than his own stubborn pride – that he maintained the farce. Arthur had made it well known to them, and everyone else, that he didn't think Colin was good enough for his daughter. She had tried to introduce him to her father on more than one occasion, but on each visit Arthur feigned a sudden, all-consuming interest in reading the newspaper, or was completely absorbed in any other menial distraction at hand. And though she tried, he wouldn't have him on the telephone and he certainly wouldn't write to either of them – though he read their letters when the opportunity arose for him to do so in secret. And it was in this way, and through what information Jo shared that, in August 1963, Arthur learned of his granddaughter's birth in England, Marilyn, who came 'a little earlier than expected', and of the subsequent grandchildren that followed. Jo deeply wished to meet them. Arthur could see it in her eyes when she read the letters and looked at photographs. He heard it in her voice when she spoke about them on the phone. And he heard it, every night, in the tender, loving whispers of her bedside prayers.

16

Widowed

On a Tuesday morning, early in July 1965, Doctor Henk Peeters died. He had always been the picture of health and his habits were no more harmful than any other man's, so it came as a shock to everyone, especially Maria, when his heart gave out as he made breakfast. It was a horrible time for her. She first heard the clatter of the counter clutter rattling and crashing, and almost immediately after that, the thud of a human body hitting the floor.

She rushed downstairs in her bathrobe, for she was fresh out the shower, and when she arrived at the scene she had to quickly make sense of the mess sprawled across the parquetry, even up to several metres from the kitchen. Chunks and shards of a shattered mug were scattered across the room. Maria's eyes followed them across splashed streaks to a widening coffee-coloured pool. Several sheets of paper with his handwriting on them were being dyed brown by the aromatic water that spread across the floor. All lay in disarray around her husband who was lying, half-curled, on his side, with his hand clutched to his heart. She had none of the skills for resuscitation that he did, but he was in no condition to teach her. And so, unable to be revived, Henk died. If the roles had been reversed, the couple could have perhaps lived many more years together, but fate did not work in their favour. All she could do was call for help, hope it arrived swiftly, and wait, wailing and whimpering on the floor with her husband's non-responsive body.

It was Henk and Maria's son, Basile, who called to tell Arthur what had happened. As he was at work, it was Jo who was informed. Despite the nature of the news, she managed to stay composed and receive it as well as anyone could be expected to. She offered her sincerest condolences and did everything a compassionate person could think of to comfort Basile.

Jo called Arthur on his office phone and passed on the news. Arthur was in shock; the reality was difficult for him to grasp.

He and Jo were invited to attend Henk's funeral. Arthur was certainly affected by his sudden passing, but he also wanted to provide what support he could for the widowed Maria. Henk's death made Arthur contemplate what he would do – and how he would feel and react – if he were plunged into the same position.

At intervals throughout the church service, and later at the burial, Maria was a tragic mix of hysterics and stone-faced confusion. The heart that had throbbed in her chest, tender with affection and adoration, the heart that had once made her giddy, as if in every moment Henk and she spent together she drew a measure of the world's finest wine, was now deflated. The glass was empty and could not be refilled and Maria was left to suffer the withdrawal and the hangover by herself. When Henk was still alive, it was clear that she was deeply in love with him. Her love was broadcast to others like a glorious autumn moon, glowing in amber hues, full and ripe and large like a bloated pumpkin that took two hands to hold. But now her heart was a shrivelled husk, a wilted weed. A blackened match. A shapeless stone misshaped further still by the crust of ice, the fog of the glass, and the torrent of rain upon the pane.

Arthur and Jo extended their condolences, but words can only do so much; they can only reach so far and can only offer so much sympathy. Maria's husband had died and so too had a part of her.

Several slow weeks had staggered by since Henk's funeral and so, at Jo's suggestion, Arthur went to visit Maria. They hoped Time might have mended some portion – some corner – of the gaping hole formed from where her heart had been ripped from her chest. But they had no measure for the depths of her loss, for none can know another's pain until they know their own.

Shortly after Arthur arrived and had been invited indoors, the two of them sat at a table in a small white room that echoed the soft, yet stifling silence that separated them. The only interruption was the steady *tikke takke* of the clock that stood like a curious guard in the corner – as though in that small clock was the sorrowful, scowling spirit of Doctor Henk Peeters. Maria sat upright, still as a statue, eyes downcast. Arthur's tie felt tight around his neck. He tugged at his collar and cleared his throat with a constricted cough. Maria's eyes, wide, darted upwards, at him and into him. Her mouth was pressed tight and Arthur knew she took it as a prelude to him speaking. He couldn't tell for sure if she wanted him to. But he figured it was as good a time as any, and so he opened, recklessly, into cliché.

'How have you been, Maria?' he started, sounding instantly silly to himself. He watched her awhile and realised she wasn't going to answer. In fact, she acted like she hadn't heard the question at all. An awkward silence passed as Arthur thought and thought about what he needed to say. Eventually, his labours and logic arrived at a new approach. 'I know I can't begin to comprehend how you must be feeling. I imagine the agony is too much to bear at times. And I know the world probably seems like a dark place right now, but time will pass and things might become a little easier to manage. Remember, you still have a lot of good in your life.' He rested a moment – more to ensure his rambling didn't become too insensitive than for any other reason. He wished he had brought Jo along. She would have known exactly what to do. But perhaps therein was the lesson and the test. *He* had to figure it out on his own. So, after silence had steeped between them for long enough, Arthur spoke again. 'I've heard it said that parting hurts because it reminds us of what we've lost. And I guess, with that in mind, the absence isn't so bad – as premature and as unexpected as the doctor's . . . as Henk's passing was. What I'm trying to say is that it's the time together that matters – I think that's what is important to remember.'

Maria stared at him, and he was worried that she had found his tone too tactless. But she simply looked away and out the window. Arthur watched her slip into indifference – a pantomime of etiquette and autonomy.

'Will it never cease?' she muttered in a broken voice. 'This weather . . . it's too much.' But she didn't seem to realise she had said anything at all. Arthur thought it best to politely continue to pretend – to act as if he hadn't heard her heart cry aloud, and that it didn't make his heart ache. 'It is simple enough to say it, I know, but it doesn't make the pain or the loneliness any easier to manage.'

Arthur could see that the shock of her husband's death had taken an immeasurable toll on her. Her blank calmness concerned him. Behind her mask, she had likely lost a deal of sleep. She had probably not been eating well. She seemed broken on the inside, like a bell that had lost its chime; she looked the picture but her spirit was gone. Arthur mused on the consequences of life – how it changes people. He thought of the young and naïve Maria he had known so long ago – too ignorant of the pain of life and death and love and loss to fear any of it: simply excited for it. He wished that he had thought to watch her more. He wished he had looked closer, stared longer, if only so that he might recall that picture more clearly. The Maria before him seemed helpless, listless, purposeless. She had been stripped of meaning: sapped of her vitality like a lonely conifer that had lost its leaves in spring. All he could do was hope that she would bloom again when the dark season passed.

Daylight's marigold glow gleamed and winked on polished floorboards and furnishings. The myriad sounds of birds and insects, of people and traffic, life and movement, blew in on the breeze from an open window, its lace curtains braiding sunlight and shadow into loose lines on the opposing wall. Then, into the red-orange tea, Arthur stared. It leapt and lapped when it landed and fell flat as a lake, tranquil and tamed and contained within a teacup. In his and in hers. Two steaming cups of auburn tea on their saucers aside a tray of sugar-dusted sweets and windmill speculaas sat between them. Aniseed, cinnamon, nutmeg and cloves scented the air. Arthur watched several renegade tea leaves swirl to the bottom – to the shallow depths of the cup. He crunched on a koekje, and each crumbling chomp echoed in his head to shatter the suffocating silence.

When the treat was finished, though he fancied more of the flavour, he decided not to have another. And after sip-slurping stingily at his tea for several minutes, it too was finished. The stagnant silence reigned once more. When he felt enough time had swept soundlessly by, Arthur again took up his efforts to console his friend, with a little more composure and compassion.

'How are your children?' He paused. 'Basile, Leo, Elena?' He had hoped their names might invite a positive response. Maria stirred a little and parted her lips as if to speak – but only silence spilled from her mouth, a hollow sigh of cool air. Arthur let it fill the room a while, to surround them in its intimacy, then cautiously resumed. 'This might sound strange, and a little out of place . . . and forgive me if this sounds selfish . . . but I know I don't see you as much as I would like to, and I'm quite fine with it . . . and would you like to know why I like to miss you?'

She looked at him with a confused, yet intrigued expression. The sculptor had reworked the stone. Arthur was happy to see that she had, at least, heard what he said. 'It's because . . . if I miss you, I am reminded that I have known you and we have shared many important moments in our lives. It means you occupy an important place in my heart.'

There was a pause. Arthur watched Maria turning the thought over in her mind, or at least that was his guess. Then he could see her face start to change and liven a little. He was hoping he hadn't overstepped the bounds of what was appropriate to say. She seemed to be rolling doubt, hope, fear and courage about in her mouth, not knowing whether to spit them out or to swallow.

'I see,' Maria said at last. Arthur had planted a seed of fresh perspective in her mind – but it would be up to her to nurture it and let it grow, or to forget about it and leave it to wither.

To seize upon the momentary lapse in her mourning, Arthur offered a practical solution to deal with at least a few of the many things she needed remedies for. 'Perhaps you could do something to keep yourself busy,' he said, picking up the trail of a grand idea, tracing the slippery silvery thread back through time. 'A productive distraction. Is there anything in particular you would fancy doing?'

'Well, nothing comes to mind. But I suppose I could consider doing something . . . if I could ever find the motivation,' she said in slow convalescence. 'I haven't been sleeping well,' she confessed, shrinking into her stupor.

Arthur fell silent too, as he concentrated on the elusive idea that he couldn't seem to follow through the mazy woods. They sat again in thought, until, finally, the answer presented itself. It was something he recalled Maria mentioning many, many years ago. 'How about that shop you spoke of?'

'Sorry? What shop was that?'

'At dinner once. We were all together, you and I, and Henk and Jo. I think your drink had done your bidding, for it spoke your silent ambition aloud for us all to hear quite plainly. We laughed at the idea, as you may recall, but it wasn't to disparage you. No, not at all. I'm confident we were dreaming along with you. I remember how Henk thought it would do you good to have a project. And Jo said she would love to volunteer her time. And while I held my reservations mutely, I sang of the benefits with conviction. All those years ago, you said to us that you might like to own a shop. So why not? It would keep you busy. It might bring in a little money. And I can help you to get everything set up. I'm sure Henk would have approved. He just wanted you to be happy, after all.'

'I don't know . . . I wouldn't know where to start. It sounds like a lot of work.'

'Well, sometimes, acknowledging the problem is the first step in its solution.'

Maria nodded softly in agreement. Arthur thought she had lost herself in the rekindling of an old ambition, but it wasn't the case.

'I miss him,' Maria eventually repined. Her face trembled as she fought its compulsion to cry. She had more to say, more she wished to share with someone. Arthur knew she felt the world had cheated her – given her hope and promise, let her know love and matrimony, then, without notice, taken it all away. But at the same time, she knew to appreciate the memory of those things. And it was at that thought that she, at least momentarily, managed to climb above despair. She blinked, and when her eyes reopened, a tear slid down her face, like a rain drop racing down a windowpane, gathering momentum as it went. It hung, as clear and as pure as crystal. He waited for it to fall. At any moment the pain and sadness, the frustration and confusion, would burst in silence. Splashed. Splintered. Shattered. Nothing but a damp dot upon the table would remain. But before it fell, she wiped it away. She smeared it across her cheek and across the back of her hand. 'But I'm glad I have you to rely on, Thurke.' A small smile bowed her mouth and glazed her teary eyes. And her mind was suddenly moving – he could see it, somehow. Her face was alive, glossed with a sheen of indulgence and newly coloured by delight. Her eyes fixed on him and she leaned in closer. Her mouth was pursed as though she were about to burst into laughter. 'You know what?' she asked with widened eyes. 'I've had this dream all these years . . .' Her smile brightened. 'And yet . . .' She started to whisper. 'I never even thought of a name for it!'

And suddenly the laughter stacked between them, growing louder and louder and louder, until it had climbed above reason. It erupted in an explosive exchange. Slow at first, then quicker and quicker. It was hot and abrupt and free. Swelling. Pulsing. It spurted and collided and multiplied until they were short of breath and their jaws were sore and their bellies ached, and they were, at least momentarily, happy.

17

Chocolate

A small set of bells above the door bounced in surprise as he entered the store. Escaping the wind's icy reach, Arthur was instantly welcomed by a wave of warm, chocolate-coated air. It was 1968, but sudden nostalgia brought thoughts of Hestana to his mind, and with it came a memory from childhood. He was cast back to a day when he had watched through the window as the streets were stippled by the first snow of winter. The world was grey, the wind had died and the snow floated to the ground like light leaves on a gentle breeze. He stared out contentedly as his father watched him from behind the counter where he worked, his shirt sleeves folded tidily above his elbows. Arthur was wrapped in the blanket of a bristling fire and the warm smell of roasting coffee. It was an uneventful day, but for some reason, and in all its pleasantness, the memory of it persisted.

Then the memory faded and Arthur returned to this time and place. But the sense of peace remained for several minutes after the memory had fled. The store was alive with the excited chatter of customers, all dressed in their winter best. Small children, their older siblings and parents, men in cloaks, women in shawls, tourists and locals, were all pointing and perusing, eyes wide in awe, as they made their selections. Mirror-backed cabinets with glass doors lined the two side walls, and a long glass-topped table was positioned in the centre. At the far end of the room was a counter that housed a display of the most exquisite specimens. Each mahogany-framed cabinet contained an assortment of chocolates in different sizes, shapes and shades. Half a dozen incandescent bulbs hung overhead like glowing orbs at the end of a hypnotist's thread. Their tranquil yellow light threw soft human shadows to the wax-blackened floorboards.

Arthur decided to act as just another casual chocolate connoisseur and resolved to wait until the last customer had left before he approached the store's proprietor. While he waited, he read the handwritten cards that had been folded in half lengthways and placed like A-frame tents ahead of each battalion of sweets. He steered himself towards unoccupied spaces and observed, in the displays, ranks that had suffered significant losses at the hands of hungry humans. Their gap-filled rows had opened vacancies for new stock – a pleasing sign of a hard-fought victory for their maker.

Though Arthur had been sauntering about the store for close to an hour, time seemed to pass by quite quickly. The streetlights flickered on outside as darkness settled in, and it was a quarter of an hour past closing time before the last patron left the store to the simultaneous knock of timber on timber, the click of a catch and the echo of bells. Maria had met his eyes moments after he had walked in, but they had communicated, in that stolen second, the plan to temporarily suspend their reunion.

After hanging her apron on a hook on the wall behind her, Maria came out from behind the counter and they hugged in greeting. When they pulled their bodies back to smile at one another, Arthur recognised a discernible glint in her eye, a pretty and familiar pattern that formed the expression on her face. He knew right away that it was the pride she had in herself – and in her accomplishments. He could tell it had been a long day for her; it had probably been a busy number of days, but Maria insisted on fighting fatigue with enthusiasm and conversation.

'It's so nice to see you. You're looking well.' A small sigh escaped with the words.

'Dank je, Maria. It's nice to see you too,' Arthur returned. 'And your shop appears to be going well.'

'Oh, yes! Dank je! It really is so much fun, Thurke. I'm so grateful to have it in my life. It gives me such a sense of purpose, and I love seeing the smiles on my customers' faces. It makes me feel good to know I can bring some sweetness and a tiny bite of happiness to their lives. I don't know if I'll ever be able to thank you enough for helping me get the place up and running, though . . .' she trailed off as a sudden idea derailed her train of thought. The two had released each other from their embrace, and without realising it, they had gradually made their way to the front of the store. Arthur kept quietly to himself. He didn't feel it was his place to interrupt what must have been a private meditation. After a moment standing still and silent, Maria slowly lowered herself until she was seated on a bench at the window. Arthur took up the spot next to her as she turned to look outside.

After a few seconds, Maria freed herself from the thought she had been following and turned back to him. She seemed to remember where she was. Arthur had been so fixed on watching her that he hadn't thought of what to say. He quickly clambered through dialogue and where each conversation might be taken, but before he could think of what to say, Maria's voice entreated him.

'Arthur? Arthur . . .' She repeated his name several times before she knew he had heard her. 'Arthur, could you close your eyes for me? Just for a moment.' She was smiling with self-mocking humour.

'Of course,' Arthur replied without second-guessing her request. Her voice, her expression and the invitation itself filled him with anticipation. He didn't know what to expect, but he had his hopes – though these carried their fair share of inhibitions, and he wouldn't let them get the best of him. He closed his eyes. Without sight, he found himself relying on his other senses. His heart was beating more distinctly, and he could hear the crackle of the fire beyond that. He could smell the sweetness of chocolate and feel the soft push of the warm, cindery air as Maria shuffled a little closer. He inhaled the flavoursome scent of the room, slowly and deeply. He held it a moment, then let it spill slowly out of his narrowly parted lips. On his third breath, he felt something smooth and firm press against his mouth. It crept inside. The weight of it dropped on his tongue as it passed the boundary of his teeth. At the same time, Maria's soft fingertip landed on his lips. Taste was delayed by touch. Then his tongue reacted and triggered a reflex to bite, to suck, to chew. His mouth swam in the rich, sweet, sticky flavour of chocolate. With eyes still closed, Arthur concentrated entirely on the subtle snap of the outer shell, and the firm meaty texture of a nougat centre. He cradled it in his cheek, mauled it with his molars, and swallowed a section of it. And another. He went on in this fashion until nothing but its lingering flavour remained. Then he realised Maria's finger had moved, but couldn't determine at what point it had left. He opened his eyes and expected to see Maria looking back at him, but her attention had been caught by something outside. A little abashedly, Arthur followed her gaze through the glass.

She must have felt his eyes awaken, for she suddenly faced him and smiled. 'Look at that, Thurke. It's snowing,' she declared with an almost childlike wonder.

'So it is,' he confirmed, and together they watched through the window as the lamplit streets were stippled by the first snow of winter. The night was grey, the wind had died, and the snow softly floated to the ground like light leaves on a gentle breeze. It was just like his earlier memory of being a child on such a day. They were wrapped in the blanket of a bristling fire, the warm smell of roasting coffee, and the comfort of each other's company.

18

Expansion

It was 1972. A sense of accomplishment filled him, like air in a balloon, lungful after lungful, as over the hill's crest and between the buildings and traffic, his factory came into view. It sat, glass glistening and shimmering, like a glorious golden trophy in the mid-morning sun. On a pole at its peak, the Dutch flag flapped in the breeze and immediately below it, adorning the column that cut the façade in half, were the capital letters A R V A H vertically signed in a brilliant bold white font. Several visitors' bicycles and a moped were parked against the front wall. Something about the scene made Arthur reposeful, or rather sentimental, about the past.

Like Arthur, like everything and everyone everywhere, Vlijmen had changed – indeed developed – rapidly under the influence of industry. The streets he had walked as a child were not the same as those he had walked only a decade later, or those he walked a decade after that. It seemed every year brought new changes to the scenery. Dirt disappeared under layers of paving and concrete. Roads widened and rumbled with the heavy flow of cars. In all directions, the landscape had been transformed by man. Even the seemingly ageless skyline was, at sunset, filtered through the silhouettes of towers and antennas – through glass, brick and steel. And, inevitably, Arthur evolved with it.

Through the cool darkness, Arthur navigated the map in his mind to where the corridor opened up into the workshop. He let three fingers slide down the wall to flip all six switches on the panel and as he walked onto the factory floor, he scanned the ceiling as the buzz of electricity zapped white light through the fluorescent tubes as they popped and sizzled to life. In the space between flashes, Arthur studied the steel that supported the roof above everything, like the innards of a giant beast of his own creation. He was thriving in a skeleton of steel and concrete. He remembered scouting the premises with Bert a few months before they bought the place, and how they planned the whole layout as they had walked around. They did the maths, tallied expenditure against profits, balanced capital over cost and knew what they had to do. They knew they needed to upscale – to lay claim to the progress that was theirs, the expansion made possible by this facility – and so they had set to work making it happen.

As the click and squeak of his shoes echoed and returned to him from every sleek surface, from every wall and window, Arthur thought back on his journey to this point – to this place and time. But something seemed amiss. He couldn't be sure of it, couldn't convince himself with any degree of certainty that he was satisfied, so he went back in time to 1958. ARVAH had outgrown its little shed in Vlijmen and Arthur moved its operation to a larger facility in Orthenstraat. He knew – felt – remembered that, at first, he was hesitant to leave the birthplace of his ambition, but he found some comfort in the thought that he would be making room for the next generation, that perhaps another future could be built there – another aspiration brought to fruition. Besides, Arthur knew he couldn't let sentimentality stand in the way of progress. He kept finding himself with bigger contracts to wealthier clientele who had loftier projects. Then he jumped forward, eight years later, the first of October, to when ARVAH moved to a factory on the outskirts of Den Bosch, in Koenendelseweg. By this time the company had grown significantly, and Arthur had thirty-five employees. Then he wound the clock hands forward as far as they could go and he arrived in 1972, to only several months before, when ARVAH had moved again, to a larger facility – this one, which he dubbed 'De Herven'. Arthur had chosen it as the new site of operation as it had its own rail connection from the station, which meant that shipments could be delivered to him directly – he remembered that now. But still, Arthur felt haunted by the feeling of something missing or out of place or overlooked.

After work, Arthur returned home. The same strange, bothersome feeling followed him. He and Jo had sold their first house. Because the last of their children had moved out and there was no longer any need for them to maintain such a large residence, they bought a much smaller home and found that it brought them a greater sense of closeness. They felt they owed it to themselves, and to each other, to finally enjoy the other's company – completely, as they had once done when they were young and free. They were free again. In the edifying light of hindsight, Arthur found that he and Jo had fallen into several lonely habits. All too often, at close of day, they would say their goodnights and turn away from one another. They were content to simply feel the familiar human warmth they had grown accustomed to. They were happy though, happy to know that the bed they shared was theirs, and that they were together and each had the other sleeping nearby.

As he showered and dressed for supper, Arthur daydreamed about his old house. He could navigate it in his mind as though it were right there before him. Many nights, in his dreams, he would be in that house, living there once again, and he would awaken from his sleep believing he still was. He had been a little reluctant to leave. The house had always felt like home. Leaving was like abandoning a member of the family – a feeling he knew too well. So quickly, it seemed to him, they had packed their lives into boxes and labelled them. And everything was moved from one place to the next. Before he left, Arthur walked through the hollow shell of the house, and in a way, he felt just as empty. He was saddened to be leaving, but he knew he wouldn't be leaving the memories behind – they would be with him, always. That was, he thought, what contented him.

A few days passed, and Arthur and Jo hosted a small family gathering to help make their new house feel more like a home. Children and grandchildren, parents and grandparents, siblings and cousins and aunts and uncles, all stood and sat, scattered about in the porous shade of the garden and in the light of the open house where they chatted and laughed and drank and ate and played.

An hour after lunch, when the young ones grew tired, they went inside to watch television together. They sat together, all watching some program none could later remember the name of. After it finished, Arthur switched the television off and watched the characters, the settings, the action and the drama, the song and the dance, all vanish behind a grey glass veil. He stared into that opaque mirror for a while and noticed the way it caught their reflections. He saw them – generations of them, staring back at themselves – all happily mindless, all blissfully vacant, all together and apart. They had welcomingly surrendered to that world of flashing lights, of singing and dancing, of exotic lands and beautiful people. They were together, but not as they were before. They were happy, but not as they were before. Not when they were talking and walking and staying and interacting with one another. Arthur's life had been a testament to the truth that through windows, people are guilty of watching the world pass them by – and television was really no different. Still, Arthur and Jo enjoyed the company – they hadn't always had so much of it, even before they moved. There had been a stretch of several years when their children rarely visited. They were, understandably, preoccupied with work and with tending to the needs of their own families. But that phase passed, as all things do, and they started visiting more regularly.

Throughout that time, Jo spent many hours of the day on the phone. She would call each of them every other day, and ask that she be caught up on every little detail of their lives. Arthur was sure that she even spoke to Maria on a number of occasions. And when she spoke to them, she spoke as if they were right there in the room with her. She was happy to have their company on the phone, and she would laugh and smile and frown and ponder deeply with them, and her face would flush with concern and sadness and angst at times too. And when she had her first and furthest on the phone, Arthur knew. He knew because every so often, while she spoke, and while she listened, she seemed affected more heavily than usual. She hushed her tone and guarded her words, but Arthur knew. Her laughter brought tears of joy. Her seriousness was stilted. And she seemed to no longer exist in the room in the same way. She stared further out into the world – gazing long and longer and longingly into the unknown distances, travelling over land and sea and time and weather to be there alongside her. Here and there, from time to time, he caught a word or two, a name or a place, that let him know they were speaking of things that only they could speak about. Arthur knew . . . all along and every time . . . Arthur knew.

Then one morning, hoping it might mend the matter of his melancholy, Arthur visited Bert. Because he worked with Bert most days, Arthur had never had much cause to visit his son at his home. The same was true for Bert. Arthur was sixty-six. Bert was half that, and yet older than Arthur had been when his son was born. They rarely saw one another outside of work, so Bert found it strange to see his father at his door.

'This is unusual. What's happened?' Bert asked, turning pale.

'Everything is fine. I've just come for a quick visit,' Arthur explained, though it didn't put his son much at ease. Bert welcomed his father into his drawing room, but they soon made themselves comfortable at a small breakfast table just out from the kitchen. He made a pot and poured them each a tea. But Arthur soon discovered that business was a wall between them. The bridge that had once connected them had, in fact, somehow kept them apart, for without it, they could speak of little else. It wasn't time for numbers. What they needed was words. But they couldn't speak. They didn't know the language. So they waited. They sipped.

'Son, I don't regret much about my life,' Arthur heard himself say. He had blurted it out without meaning to, and with nowhere to go, he said no more.

'I'm glad to hear that,' Bert nodded, puzzled.

'What about you? Do you have any . . . regrets in your life, my boy?' Arthur could see his son think about it. Neither of these men were particularly adept at the subject or, moreover, the nature of it.

'Yes, I think. A few . . .' Bert admitted with a sort of slow, shameful nod.

Arthur had no intention of prying into his son's personal affairs, but he thought that merely recognising them – bringing them to the surface – was enough. 'Newness. And oldness. I've seen so much of both that I can be no expert on either, and yet I . . .' Arthur tried to explain. 'I . . .' he started again, but then hesitated again. 'For me, as you know, Andre, and my mother and father, have passed . . . I know there is no way for me to right the wrongs – to reclaim the time lost between us. It's a mistake that can't be undone and a regret that I must take with me when I die.' His heart stuttered but his words did not. It hurt but it helped. 'But you . . .' he said, looking at Bert, holding him without touching. 'You're still young, far too young to let regret destroy you. You must be careful to not make an enemy of yourself.'

Bert nodded again, not in shame but rather in acknowledgement.

Arthur continued. 'For so long – forever, it feels – I have regretted not having had it within my power to prevent the damage done to your sister at the hands of those . . . cruel, cruel men. That day often replays in my mind, and I wish I could have somehow been granted the foresight to find a way to protect her.' Arthur stopped to breathe. 'Beyond that, and in many respects, I'm happy with the way things have worked out. I feel truly blessed for what I have: a beautiful wife, children, home. I've never wanted for anything . . . but regret has a funny way of working its way into your thoughts . . . I regret, as many do, not travelling more – beyond the usual places, I mean. For one, I think I would have very much liked to go to Australia. I think . . . no, I certainly should have gone. I can say, though it is difficult even now to admit, that my biggest regret was losing your sister. I know Colin isn't to blame, and neither is she, or the country. I don't think I could even blame fate. No, son, I realise now – albeit too late – that I was the one at fault. The only person who has control over how we respond to a situation is ourselves. Not knowing this sooner – that is my biggest regret.'

Arthur felt Bert's eyes on him and he knew his son was listening. Then Arthur fixed his gaze upon the tea. The shuddering shade of a drifting cloud swept over them and then the light returned – brighter, it seemed.

'Son, you'll make mistakes too, I'm sure, but remember, mistakes are part of the process. Just make sure you learn something from them so that, next time, you'll know better.' Arthur was surprised to be speaking his mind so naturally. 'Talk. But you must listen too. Keep your promises. Never make a stranger of family. Ensure you never leave a kind word unsaid. And never leave anything important undone.'

In the ensuing silence, father and son each turned back into their tea. It was cold, but that was no matter. They drank it all the same. Then they had only the empty cups . . . the empty cups and the taste of tea on their tongues.

'Thanks for visiting,' Bert said suddenly, but he didn't mean it as farewell.

'No, not at all. Sorry for not calling ahead.'

Bert merely shook his head and smiled with a droll expression Arthur hadn't seen him wear before. 'It's a good thing I was home.'

'A very good thing indeed,' his father agreed. And in an instant, they both knew something had changed between them. A wall had shifted, a new bridge had been built, and they were closer than ever before.

19

Grandchildren

Early in 1973, Arthur received a letter. It was addressed not to Jo, but to him exclusively, from his daughter Maria. In the envelope was a photograph of five blond-haired children: three girls who looked almost identical but for their height, and two boys, again, separated only by age. All five wore very few clothes, and he could tell from the photo that their skin was darker than most children he knew (though he knew very few), clearly bronzed by a fiercer sun than theirs. Arthur instinctively flipped the photo over and saw five names written there: Marilyn, Dennis, Lucy, Nicole, Paul. As well as the letter and photograph, there was a postcard tucked inside, from a place in Western Australia called Broome. It showed a line of brown-specked greenery, some sort of native grass or reed, and in stark contrast, a white sweeping beach of sun-bleached sand and a flat belt of ocean as blue as the naked summer sky above it. Putting the pictures aside, Arthur willed himself to turn his attention to the words.

Hallo Father,

I'm really not too sure where to begin! I've been on such amazing adventures – the likes of which no book could have ever prepared me for. I love the life Colin and I have made for ourselves out here. We have bought a double-decker bus – one that was sent to enjoy its retirement under our hot Australian sun, far from the grey skies of London, where it had been formerly employed. Colin is a clever man and he has converted the bus into a mobile home. We sleep on the upper levels, and the lower part is the living quarters – a kitchen and dining area. It suits us perfectly because neither of us likes being planted in one spot for too long. Australia is a vast country. There's so much to see and the people are almost always friendly.

We're just doing what we can to get by. Even though I've always wanted to spend most of my life travelling the world on ships, Colin says that he's sure we will face a lot of 'hardships' together!

Oh Father, I really hope you will get the chance to get to know him one day. I don't expect much, but I would like you to try. What I want, above all else, is for you to be happy for me. I know it isn't the life you imagined for me, but it's the life I've chosen.

Your daughter,
Maria
P.S. I'm coming to visit everyone soon and I'm bringing the whole family with me.

Her letter filled him with a kind of remorse that was at least one part apprehension and another part envy. And while he sat stewing in his bitterness, he felt, at the same time, a certain fatherly affection. A precious memory, mined from the archives, presented itself. Hot coals on the hearth. An unlidded shoebox on the mantel. A frail, blue-eyed baby lying within. His daughter. His pale and feeble and beautiful daughter. Were they truly one and the same? Was this mother of five really his weak, strong, stubborn, impetuous daughter from all those years ago? Warmed by the fire of fatherhood, Arthur grew excited by the prospect of finally meeting his grandchildren, and in his fancy, he drafted a letter that he knew would never be penned.

Dear daughter,

Please know I am excited to have the opportunity to meet my grandchildren. I only wish I could have been a more positive presence in their lives. I hope they won't hold my mistakes against me.

As your father, I want for nothing but your happiness. But I would like to ask one thing of you. If you can bear the burden, please heed my selfish request. While you travel these strange and foreign lands, can you please do so for me as well? When you find yourself marvelling at what the world has to offer, could you pause a moment to see it through my eyes? Even if you can only spare a glimpse, I'll take it.

Perhaps if I had been a little less stubborn, a little more open-minded and a lot more like you, I could have done it myself. But I never knew that the path you chose existed. I guess I never appreciated the freedom afforded to me. So instead, I must accept this consolation. Can you let me live the way you live, through you? Can you permit me to visit the places you visit, to meet the people you meet and to see the things you see?

With love from,
The man who always was,
And the man who always will be,
Your father

And as she said they would, they visited. It was many years after their first trip to the Netherlands together that they made their second. Only this time, Maria and Colin brought five children in tow.

After lunch on the day after their arrival, they all went to a nearby park. The grass was wet and thick with clover, yet the leaves on the trees, and those that littered the lawn, were the roasted colour of toast, and as crisp. Silver clouds crowned the peaks of the city's buildings as the sun scaled the sky where it was glazed gold like a coin that had been tossed with promise into a fountain, where it sits on the bottom, blurred by the rippling pond above. While the children ran about and played, and their parents and grandparents stopped to rest and digest, Arthur couldn't bring himself to utter a word to the man seated merely metres away. On the bench, Colin and Arthur sat like crusts cut from different loaves of bread at either end, with Maria and Jo together in the middle. The women spoke a little, but for the most part the four simply watched on. A cluster of leaves not yet raked up suddenly surged to life. They tumbled together on the lawn in dizzying circles, like children chasing one another. Several lazy leaves watched on, too stuck to move without the wind to peel them from the damp.

Then one of the girls ran over to her parents while the others stopped to watch her. 'Hey, Dad, can you come and play? We want to show you the game we've invented.' An eager and hopeful expression brightened her young, freckled face.

'I'll be right there, Nic,' Colin said.

Then, from where he knelt, the youngest boy called out. 'Dad! Hey, Dad! Watch this!' And when he knew his father was watching, the boy somersaulted into a pile of leaves he had prepared for the job.

'Wow, Paul! That's very impressive,' Colin called back.

And while Arthur watched and listened, one fact was made abundantly clear: these children loved their father. It was much the same for the remainder of their trip. They loved their mother too, that was obvious, but the way they asked for their father when they were hungry or tired or bored or fed up proved to Arthur that Colin was a good father.

Then it happened, partway through their stay, on a perfectly ordinary morning while they breakfasted together. 'Would you care for another cup of tea, Colin?' Arthur asked without a second thought. He had noticed over his son-in-law's stay that Colin wasn't one for coffee, and that he was rather partial to tea. Maria and Jo were dumbfounded. They stopped mid-chew and Maria nearly coughed up her toast.

And to add to their bewilderment, Colin's reply came just as naturally as the question. 'Yes, I think I will. Three sugars and a dash of milk, please.'

It took Arthur longer than the others to put the pieces together, but he soon realised that he had spoken to Colin, acknowledged him and offered to fix him a drink, and he wasn't immediately sure why. Arthur nodded and made for the kettle. And while it boiled, and as he set the tea leaves in their sieve, he reflected on the change. Colin had his faults, but he was a good man and an acceptable role model for his children. Although he wasn't the husband Arthur had hoped she'd choose, he had to accept that that man was giving his daughter the life she had always wanted. He made her happy. He loved and provided for her. And while Arthur poured hot water into Colin's cup, and tea-scented steam rose into his face, he finally knew, in his heart, that he was a man worthy of her. He was good enough for his daughter.

20

Together

In 1978, on the eve of no particular occasion, except for what he felt would be a warm summer Saturday, Arthur resolved to conceive of a romantic venture that would enable him and Jo to bask a little in life's simple pleasures. Pushing thoughts of work aside, Arthur sat up in bed across from his wife, whose feminine form slept soundlessly. He decided to do something special for her. Jo shivered as he brushed several strands of hair from the back of her neck. She shivered again as he softly pressed his lips to the skin above her collar. Then he let her rest while he put his mind to work. Arthur knew the riddle's answer from the start, but all the same he let himself muse over the alternatives.

He wondered, at one point, what it might be like to take a tour by water. In doing so, he pictured Jo sitting at the stern of a rowboat, her face laced by the shade of her parasol, her bodice and gown of baby-blue untouched, unruffled by the cool summer breeze. They were seated on flat timber slats. Arthur was in the middle, facing back towards the stern listening to the knock, squeak and groan of the oars rubbing and rolling in their tholes. He could feel the weight – the thickness of them in his hands. The paddles roiled – dipping, softly splish-splashing, and sending ripples that faded flat before reaching the bank where a mother duck led her line of ducklings through the reeds. He could see the slippery, silky surface of the glass-faced river glide beneath them. And in that image made of pencil, paint or pastel, they looked the perfect picture of every whimsical romantic fancy.

Arthur then thought that he might take her on a trot through the countryside, but was deterred when he considered how horses made Jo nervous. She had told him once that their size worried her, that they could easily startle and trample her by mistake. But she said that, logic aside, there existed another quality in them that was more difficult to explain. It was their eyes, she said: they were too intelligent. It was as if they knew secrets not yet learned by man, and it was this detail that she found most disconcerting. Then, Arthur thought back to the first moment they met, and jumped randomly between memories from the varying pages of their past. That was when he knew where he wanted to take her and, most decidedly, how.

Arthur was already dressed for departure when he woke her.

'Geliefde, get dressed and pack your suitcase, we're going to Australia!'

'But I'm already dressed,' she replied, whipping back the sheets and flapping them into the air like a sail at full stretch, pulled taut in the breeze. 'And I'm already packed,' she added, revealing that, indeed she was. Shoes and all! 'My suitcase is already in the taxi!'

And yet, even in Arthur's fancy, they shook their heads. It was a conversation that never took place. The sheet fell flat back to the bed where it had always been. Arthur could imagine it. He could stage the play in his mind, but it would never happen. He knew it. Jo probably knew it, too. He could not be so wayward. Even the thought of it made him uneasy. Besides, he had plans that were much closer to home.

The recollection of his scheme shook him from his sleep. Jo was awake first and so Arthur sought her out with a kind of frenzied haste. It was midway to noon by the time they left the house, for owing to the short notice, they were quite unprepared. It meant however, that the weather was in their favour. So, with a floral sun well in bloom, they were set to return to a place they had been once before, what seemed like many lifetimes ago.

Their bikes hissed across sand and stone. The road was certainly less rugged than they remembered. Modern vehicles had smoothed the surface, and their bikes were better designed. Eventually they found what felt like a familiar spot beneath a shady chestnut tree and there they lay out the blanket. They settled in the underbrush and gazed out into the grassy glade. To Arthur, the clearing seemed less clear, the space less spacious, but perhaps it was simply that he had outgrown it.

While Jo arrayed a tray of snacks from the basket she had hastily thrown together, Arthur did some arranging of his own. Upon the drawing board of his mind, he laid out every conceivable topic of conversation. Odds and ends, bits and pieces, this and that. But nothing important; it all seemed ornamental. There was nothing to say of substance. So, he abandoned words for the time being and set about simply sitting. He sat and shared the sun with Jo, who sat beside him. She pulled him towards her with nothing but a look. She may have said his name or tapped his shoulder, but he was senseless to it all. He was oblivious to everything except the unnamed feeling that told him that this woman, his wife, wanted his attention. Arthur surrendered himself to her. She fixed him with her eyes, but held him with a charm that was more than a face alone could achieve. It was the work of memories, of the love that had lasted so long and was still alive and thriving. And, drawn slowly closer, their lips – their older and thinner, yet still affectionate lips – touched.

On this spot, in the shade and in the sun, they spent their Saturday. Reminiscing, laughing, eating, sipping and chatting the day away. They were happy and together – *really* together, and time and place and age were all irrelevant.

21

Mass

Eventually and inevitably, Arthur officially handed ARVAH over to Bert. Not only because he was his only son, but because he was fit for the job. Yet, despite his retirement, Arthur continued to busy himself at the factory. In this way – with Arthur regularly visiting ARVAH – several months and years passed, until, one day, his body insisted he do so no longer. He knew it wasn't that Bert's interest in the business had waned, but rather that Bert wished to fulfil other, long-held ambitions. He saw the potential for new ventures in selling ARVAH, and Arthur knew that he would do so after his passing. Arthur understood it well, and while he was sad to know the future that awaited his life's work, he accepted it and found himself thankful that his son had the decency to delay the deed. Bert told him that Gompel's glass company had expressed an interest in buying it. Arthur found solace in the circular nature of that – in the fact that it would be sold to the very same company he had purchased his first crate of glass from so, so long ago. Arthur's only abiding hope was that his legacy could linger and, in some way, help his children and their children, and theirs.

Arthur thought how, over the course of his life, he had bought and sold and cut and carried and fit and polished countless sheets of glass. He had seen his business suffer and thrive, wilt and blossom, and grow and grow and grow. He had spent thousands upon thousands of hours sweeping. Every day. Day after day. Just sweeping and sweeping and sweeping the dust away. And knowing, believing, that it helped someone, in some way, kept him going.

Nails upon nails upon nails. Generations of twisted steel crashed to the bench like a chain collapsing in on itself in a chaotic coil. A thorny shrub of short, jagged needles sat like an upturned nest, a dozen shades of orange and brown and deteriorating stages of chrome. Beside the pile of scrap metal was a beaten old paint tin, emptied, split at the sides where its waistline bulged. Its first life had been brief. Its second was painfully prolonged. It probably wished the former had lasted a little longer. A belly of cream traded for a gutful of salvaged steel that stabbed and battered it from the inside out. This old bucket had been made to bear the burden of years. It travelled from site to site – flung upon bench after bench, dropped in a corner, kicked under a desk or thrust on a shelf. It was made to suffer Arthur's habits, his stubborn nature, and the weight and load of his lesser ambition. It served a secondary, peripheral purpose. And as it sat there, its contents spilled out across the bench, it was finally freed of its function.

He selected a nail at random and untangled one that had been given an elbow, and whose otherwise flat hat had been folded down on one edge. The second was a little straighter but stained orange, like a dirt-caked carrot pulled from the earth. The third was brown, gnawed by rust and bowed like a dog's hind leg. He lay them down beside each other, forming a queue where each waited their turn, like people politely biding their time in line at a bank. Then he pinched the first between his fingers, picked it up and tightened it into the table vice. He gripped the mallet and struck the spine against the bend to force it straight. Then, from the vice he positioned it on the anvil's face. His mallet mashed it. And again. And again. And every echoing slap shook away the flaking, powdery skin.

While he worked to the peal of bangs and clangs and smacks and cracks, he noticed Bert send him a certain look. It was hard to know exactly what he was thinking. He probably thought his father was old and foolish – that he was wasting his time. But Arthur wasn't sure. His son's smile didn't seem at all condescending. If anything, he looked genuinely happy – intrigued and impressed. All he knew was that he had spent a good portion of his life collecting those nails, saving them from workshop floors and jobsite junk piles, to one day be repurposed, and that fateful day was finally upon them.

The stash of crudely straightened nails steadily increased, each one deposited into a blue plastic tray. A chalky orange residue dusted the anvil and stained Arthur's hands. Then, as he readied the mallet to hit another nail against its bend on the anvil's horn, he felt a finger softly pat his shoulder. He dropped the nail to the bench and lowered his striking hand. He turned from his work to see it was his daughter Maria. She was visiting for her parents' anniversary in a few days' time. She was with Colin. As he prepared to greet them, Arthur clapped his hands together and rubbed them with a rag that had been hanging below the bench. They had been watching him for some time, and like Bert, they were probably a little puzzled about the purpose of his project. From their perspective, he imagined that they saw a wealthy man doing a poor man's work. They may well have thought, therefore, that he had lost his mind, gone senile. Arthur knew that repairing old nails would make no difference to the company's overall profit margin. He knew it would have been quicker and easier to buy new ones. But it wasn't about that. He was fixed on the principle of it. And he was glad Maria had witnessed it. It made him hope that she could relate what he was doing to what she was doing – to understand that not all broken and damaged things need to be replaced. Sometimes, the old can be made new again. Things *can* be fixed.

With his hands a little cleaner, and with the ringing of metal still in his ears, Arthur acknowledged his guests.

In 1982, the year that marked fifty years of marriage, Arthur and Jo celebrated their anniversary with a high mass at the church of Saint John the Baptist. It was an evening to venerate and give thanks for their love and life together. The pews were packed with friends and family, all sitting together like herrings in a barrel. And as the priest spoke of their matrimony and honoured their holy union, Arthur looked upon his wife to try to find where half a century could have been spent. And though he searched, he knew no short or simple answer existed, but that their investment of that time was, without a doubt, more rewarding than anyone could ever hope anything to be.

On the morning of that same day, while he sat alone, Arthur had suddenly come close to tears. Not tears of sadness, nor tears of joy. Whatever the reason, no tears came, though they strained and stung. He kept himself composed by thinking of Jo. He thought of her long, long, long ago, with her sleeves bunched to her elbows while she bathed a baby in the sink. He thought of Jo sitting on her bergère, her face smiling through the phone pressed to her ear, her ankle rested across her knee. He thought of Jo exhausted at the end of a long day, wincing against lethargy. He thought of her in the summer, sipping white wine on a sunny Sunday. He thought of her in the winter, wearing warmth – a knitted scarf and rosy cheeks. He thought of her startled in the night by the clicks and creaks and groans and moans of the house. He thought of her holding a child's hand as they scurried across a street. He thought of her beside him . . . on the couch, in the car, as they supped, as they slept. He thought of her face. And he thought of her hands. He thought of her hair as it fell out of place. And he thought, and he thought, and he thought of her.

When midday came, Arthur felt he needed to get out of the house for a while, but as it was late November, the weather was not in his favour. The clouds threatened rain and the wind was brisk, though it was, for now, dry. Without delay, he shoved his feet into his shoes, donned his coat and hat, and was away down the path.

Everything seemed empty, stripped. Nothing made noise except for the wind that swept over it all. The trees were bare of leaves and birds, and the streets were free of people. Cars were parked without their drivers and houses slept soundly with curtains closed. He was a lone traveller in a vacant world, but he didn't feel alone.

As he walked further, leaves littered the pavement in piles, like a mess of shredded parchment cluttering a desk. But the morning dew had made them damp, and so they didn't crunch underfoot as one might have expected. Instead, they stuck like soggy stamps to the soles of his shoes. As he walked, Arthur heard a sudden rustling behind him. He turned to see what creature had made the sound but witnessed, instead, a sudden flurrying gust that lifted leaves into the air like the whiskery pappus blown from a dandelion. The breeze rushed at his back and he quickened his pace. Arthur had taken fewer than a dozen strides before realising his attempt to race nature was in vain. The leaves were set to overtake him on their journey to some other place, and would undoubtedly beat him there.

He had slowed his stroll and thought back to his first return journey from Mol, all the way back when. The season was similar, though his destination wasn't – or rather, it was the purpose that had changed most. Indeed, many things had changed in the space between that walk and this one. Arthur, for one, was not so green, though he was certainly just as stubborn. He was a little less sharp than he had been once. He was a little more crooked too. He no longer fancied himself much of a traveller, either. Setting those thoughts aside, he measured his stride. And while he endeavoured to maintain a uniform pace, he unexpectedly discerned a rhythmic and ominous pounding against the pavement, like a peg-legged pirate pacing his deck. He held his breath. He listened. The pounding grew a little louder, then faded completely away. He halted, and inhaled deeply. The musk of damp earth had dressed the air for autumn. Arthur looked around. A bending band of cerulean sky broke the tin-coloured armour of clouds that garbed the horizon, and he knew the last whip of summer would soon be snuffed out. Then, in the miraculous silence, a man he had not seen for millennia approached him.

Time had aged the man almost beyond recognition, but a closer inspection soon revealed the defining lines that could not be hidden, but rather were deeper set. The jaw flexed, the lines loosened – warped and widened – and a voice like an angel's harp stroked its strings in glissando.

'Mijn snelle paard! I knew you were a sure bet! Fast out of the gate with the stamina to finish the race like a champion! I've heard you're still in business. I think it might well be time we put you out to pasture!'

There was no mistaking the man. He was Arthur's first client and a man whose connections helped ARVAH begin. Frans Engelbrecht. There was no mishearing the way he sang his words, yet his euphony was at odds with his wilting appearance.

'Frans, is it really you?'

'Please, don't let me interrupt your gambol,' he replied. 'I implore you not to stop on my account. But I'll continue alongside you, if that's alright. I've aged some too, but I'm still sprightly. I'll do my best to match your pace.'

'Very well,' said Arthur, accepting his invitation. And on they walked. 'By the way, and please, I hope you don't misunderstand me,' he continued, thinking it best to make use of the silence, for knowing Frans it would have surely been short-lived, 'but it seems such an odd thing to call me, yet I never asked why you insist on doing so.'

Frans turned, his friendly face marred with concern. 'You mean "snelle paard"?'

'Indeed. Yes, that,' Arthur nodded. 'All these years, it's made me wonder.'

'O jee! I hope it hasn't upset you. I haven't meant to cause you any offence! I meant for quite the opposite effect, I assure you,' Frans said, plainly distressed.

'Well, I think I have it figured now . . . but could you clarify it for me all the same?'

Frans was clearly grateful to have the opportunity to redeem himself – though in truth, Arthur felt no defence was needed. 'It's quite obvious, don't you think, old friend?' he replied. Alas, their path was split by a road and they were made to wait while a car crawled by. While the pair waited, Frans suspended his speech, but Arthur could tell he had paused it at that point quite intentionally. He wanted to leave the air unfilled. He was setting a pace of his own, granting his friend the room to think. As they crossed the junction, he continued. 'I could see it straight away. Upon our first meeting, I could tell – you're a courser . . .' Frans started to pause more frequently, though it was less for effect and more for function. 'I knew you were a man ready to compete . . .' He caught his breath and went on. 'You were well equipped . . . you had your sights set . . . you know, not every horse has what it takes to win . . . but you . . .' A double pause for twice the recovery. 'If I were a gambling man, and you were the horse . . . I would have bet my wallet on you!'

The two men, quite an age older than at their first encounter, soon arrived together at the site of Arthur's first workshop. When he had first set his mind to the expedition, Arthur had expected to be alone, but having Frans with him gave him a second perspective to consider.

While Arthur stood and stared, Frans did the talking. 'Your old shed was demolished many years ago,' he said solemnly. 'I can't understand why no one has done anything with the land.'

Arthur's hands felt for a broom. All the time he had spent sweeping away the dust and dirt seemed pointless. In no time at all, Nature reclaimed what had been taken from her. She couldn't be outrun. A strange sense of sadness – a feeling of something lost – welled from the depths of remorse that had long lay dormant in him.

Bald tyres and crooked piping and splintered doors and broken bricks and frayed rope and a thorny briar sprouted through the clover-capped mounds of black earth. A ghostly chill washed over it all. Frans was silent. The sky was bleak. The sky was toxic. The sky was death.

'I suppose the past must stay in the past,' Arthur muttered. 'The shed that was here, in this place once . . . it served me well. I had hoped someone else – some young ambitious man, some upstart – might come along and let it see the best and worst of him, like it did for me. I had hoped it might make something of someone and do so again and again. But it's silly of me to be so sentimental about it . . . I made the decision to sell it, after all.'

The paint peeled from the sullen sky and sunlight tore its way down in golden bars, corroding the clouds like acid. The scene was painted anew. The briar had a rose of deep red. The harp was strummed and a voice sang.

'No, I understand,' comforted his old companion. 'You did what anyone would have done in your position. If it makes you feel any better, you can have my guarantee that it will not stay this way forever. Nothing does. Someone will do something with it one day, and I'm sure it will have meaning again.' They lingered a little longer, and when the moment passed, Arthur nodded. Then he spied, half buried, a nail. He crouched to the ground to be sure. He pinched at it and steadily uprooted it. He flicked away the soil and held, within his dirty fingertips, a mangled and crusty nail.

'You're right,' he said. Then, for no reason other than the fact it came to him, Arthur spoke a line of nonsense. 'Like cherry seeds and withered leaves . . . life goes on.'

Arthur had timed his walk well, for only moments after hanging his hat and coat back on their hooks by the door, the rain rushed upon his house with an almighty roar. He swapped shoes for slippers, and by the time he had stoked the fire, thawed his fingers, fixed himself a coffee and set himself in his chair to peruse the newspaper, the pouring stopped. Fortunately, as far as his mood was concerned, the day remained grey. Still determined to enjoy the flight into relaxation he had readied himself for, and while the gutters dealt with the water spilling from them, he read and retreated to the rapid *plens, plens, plens* of nature.

With the fire warming him from the outside and coffee at work on the inside, Arthur pressed his weight into the cushioning and apprised himself of current events. He was partway through the paper when he happened across an article about a local man who had made something of a name for himself in his own trade. Arthur recognised the name as one belonging to a former employee of his, and gradually drifted into a kind of daydream. The hero of the narrative was a meticulous and polite man, still young in Arthur's memory of him, and his name was Arjen.

On an ordinary day, several years ago, Arthur had arrived back at his factory after inspecting a job in town to find that something about the workshop was different. Something had changed in some way – but what it was, he could not place. To others, he looked quite lost, for he was stuck to the spot and couldn't compel himself to move until he had solved the puzzle. He closed his eyes and reimagined the room laid out in his mind. After he was sure he had the picture fixed in his memory, he opened his eyes to discern the disparity – yet no answer presented itself. He repeated the process as he scanned the room in sections from left to right, taking note of the positions of benches, machines, tools and stock. His investigation revealed nothing. After several minutes, he knew the need for an answer outweighed his desire to find it for himself. A young man named Arjen loped by and Arthur stopped him in his tracks.

'Hallo,' said Arthur.

'Oh goedendag, Meneer van Hessel. How can I help you?' Arjen replied, eager to attend to whatever task his boss might ask of him.

'It's a trite matter, but one that has me a little perplexed,' Arthur explained. 'Mind you, it might be nothing at all. Let me get to the point. Do you think you might be able to tell me what has changed here since I left this morning?'

Arjen's eyes sharpened as he hesitated before quickly turning his head away from Arthur's to look around the room. It was clear that his inability to supply his boss with an immediate answer pained him. 'I'm very sorry, meneer,' he fretted after a minute's contemplation. 'Everything appears to be as it always is. Although . . .' Suddenly his face was free of the grievance that had plagued it a second earlier.

'One of the new guys cleaned the clerestory windows. I overheard him tell Joris and Piet that there was one in particular that was almost impossible to reach. He said he managed to get to it and that he believes he was the first to ever do so. Said the grime was thick upon it. Maybe that's what has made the difference, do you think?'

Arthur had to think on it. Was the solution so simple?

'It sure seems that little bit brighter in here now,' Arjen added, inviting Arthur to verify it.

Arthur strained his neck towards the ceiling, where sunlight seeped in through the clerestory windows. Then he started to faintly recall that there was one pane in the uppermost corner that always seemed to exist in the shade of the roof above it. Yet he had never noticed how opaque it had become over the years. A blue sky, clearer than clear, now beamed through the frame, and it looked so close Arthur felt he could almost touch it. He turned his attention back to the ground and to the workshop around him and realised that everything did in fact seem a little brighter, cleaner, renewed and restored. Then he caught Arjen's face – anxiously awaiting to learn whether he was right or wrong. Arthur smiled and nodded approvingly and Arjen's face relaxed in turn.

'Thank you, Arjen. Yes, I believe that's what has made the difference.'

'I'm happy to have helped. Tot ziens!' He smiled before walking away and returning to work with a purposeful short-strided shuffle, leaving Arthur to reflect on his amusement at how he could get so accustomed to accepting things merely as they appeared, to seeing things as they are, that he never stopped to consider how they ought to be.

Arthur awoke to the snoozing cinders of a sleeping fire. How long he had been out for was difficult to gauge, but the room was quiet and the shade seemed a different hue of grey to earlier – dimmer, slower, older. He refolded the papers blanketed across his lap, stirred the embers, fed the fading fire and ascended the stairs. Jo was fixing herself at the dressing table in their bedroom when he found her.

'How was your rest, dear?' she asked, her eyes on her husband in the mirror.

'I must have needed it,' he answered, his head still half in a daze.

'I thought as much,' she said, smiling. Her attention turned back to herself and Arthur watched. He swayed and delayed. He dreamed without dreaming. Her process was peaceful and hypnotic. Then reality returned.

'I'd best get myself ready, too,' he suggested, and Jo gave a simple nod of patient agreement.

An hour later, their taxi arrived a minute ahead of the appointed time and they made their way downstairs, donned their coats and locked the door behind them. The glow thrown from the window lit their path. It was the light of a lamp they had set as their sentry, tasked with seeing them returned safely home again at the night's end. The sentry watched as the old married couple tucked themselves into the car. Then, strapped in their seats, they slipped down their street and away as their home dissolved into the distant dark behind them. And as they barged through the black night, and as Jo was illuminated by the light of passing cars, a faint memory stole into Arthur of a party long ago.

'So how do you know Arthur?' he had heard a nearby voice remark. Arthur tracked it back to a man he remembered as one who had met him with opposition in the early days of ARVAH. The man was sceptical that Arthur had any concept of the inner workings of business, and he let it be known to a small audience of his associates.

'It'll fall through,' he announced with a pompous air of certainty and a bloated sense of self-importance. 'Give it a few years, and when he learns that he's in over his head, he'll scamper back to his father and look to regain the inheritance he foolishly declined. He'll learn the hard way that naïve boys like him will never make it in this world of men.'

Perhaps Arthur mistook his own arrogance for confidence, or maybe his pride had made him foolish; either way, he thrust himself into the group to confront the slander head on. 'Good evening, gentlemen,' he said, interrupting their smoking, chuckling and chatter.

'And who might you be?' the first man asked contemptuously, piqued at Arthur's uninvited arrival.

'My apologies, I thought you must have known,' Arthur quipped.

'How could I possibly be expected to know?' the man scoffed, puffing up like a toad. 'These gentlemen and I were merely discussing little cows and little calves.'

'Very well,' Arthur said. 'You and your companions can call me Arthur – indeed, I am the very same man you mentioned merely a moment ago. I am the proprietor of ARVAH. I'm sure you've heard of it.' He paused on that point.

The man was clearly unprepared to be made the subject of his own ridicule, and retaliated in a haphazard attempt to save face.

'You own your own name? Well, I'll be . . .' joked the man, brandishing his chubby cigar. 'That's something, don't you think, gents?' His peers compelled themselves into a short round of laughter as each man relied on reassurance from the herd. He was quite proud and surprised by his own wit and made ready to laugh aloud with them when Arthur interrupted him again.

'No, you're quite right on both accounts.' Taken aback, the flock paused. Arthur went on. 'You see, my company's title is in fact derivative of my own. I ask you, gentlemen, what man can call himself a man who isn't willing to stake his name on the very entity he is known by?'

'How pretentious!' another of the men declared.

'Perhaps it is,' Arthur agreed, fixing his gaze on him. 'But I'm not the kind of man who is happy to hide behind a pseudonym. My reputation – my livelihood – indeed everything I am – hinges on my success. If my business fails, I'll go down with it. Gentlemen, I take pride in my name and what it represents. I'm running a risk – one I'm sure none of you could take, for it relies on establishing a brand that people will respect for its merits.'

In the ensuing silence, Arthur and the first man locked eyes. It was a battle of resolve. But Arthur knew he had won the very second it started, for his nemesis had never regained his composure from the moment Arthur had interrupted his campaign to malign his name. All Arthur had to do from that point was to stand his ground while the other man tripped and staggered. Arthur watched his foe's focus waver and break.

The man grimaced and looked to his feet. 'Come, let's go get another drink,' he said to his friends, his voice embittered by defeat.

One or two of them scoffed in agitation or embarrassment or because it was all the reply they could manage. And with that, they left.

Arthur revelled in his triumph. He felt confident and powerful. And it was while he was silently celebrating his victory that an anonymous spectator approached him.

'Tall trees catch much wind. Jealousy is such a terrible poison, Arthur,' he said without introduction. 'It affects the mind unlike anything else. And as we observed with those men, it will inevitably make a man lose his way. And it's because of this that I hope you harbour no ill feelings towards them – because that would make you no different, right?' This man smiled from the corner of his mouth as he spoke, and though he never rushed, nor did he give Arthur an opening sufficient to reciprocate conversation. He always resumed talking in the fraction of a second before a single syllable could escape Arthur's lips. 'In fact,' he continued sagely, 'I think they deserve no more than your pity. You might learn soon, if you haven't already, that the weak are weak because they are too often blind to their own imperfections. They don't recognise their own faults and can never correct them. Their dissent is born from their own failures and inhibitions. The man you met is Daan Visser, and he has no courage of his own. You saw how quickly he fell when you singled him out. I suggest you pay him no heed whatsoever. He has always been quick to temper – his insecurities make his ego sensitive, but I don't think he'll bother you again. And I'm sure he'll think twice before talking about you behind your back. It's as they say . . . a lion doesn't concern itself with the opinion of sheep.'

Then the man, with his advice served free and the receipt of purchase written clearly on Arthur's face, saluted him with the raising of his glass, a nod of his head and a self-assured smile.

For the umpteenth time, Arthur set himself to speak to him but in that same moment, someone tapped his shoulder. He turned to greet whoever it was that had sought his attention – but there was no one standing where someone ought to have been. He checked over his other shoulder to be sure he hadn't been pranked by that favourite game of children, but again he was met with an unfilled space. Arthur turned his attention back to the anonymous man but, instead, he found himself staring, once again, to an empty space where a person ought to have been.

Arthur and Jo arrived ahead of time and secured their usual place ahead of the transept and before the chancel. They met pairs and packs of other punctual people as they stole through the narthex, and those who they knew were equally early to extend their compliments. But they didn't dally more than etiquette demanded, for while they wished to stay in everyone's good graces, they wanted the evening's focus to remain on them.

The service commenced and the priest spoke well. He seemed especially energised, perhaps by the opportunity to address such a large crowd. He delivered a sentimental sermon that acknowledged the sanctity of family and made a special mention to Arthur and Jo's marriage. Arthur's eyes were drawn to Jo from time to time, catching her unguarded profile less often than she caught his gaze and returning it with one that playfully told him to behave. Arthur wanted to see, to understand, to accept the way she had changed – grown – aged – matured, without him ever seeming to notice. He wanted to look at her, and even after all this time, to learn more about her. He wanted to know every line, every mark, every detail. But, after being caught one too many times, he had to find consolation, for the time being, by returning upon the simple fact that she was his wife.

When people stood at the end of the service, Arthur and Jo smiled in silent celebration and rose with them. They spoke to the priest first, while their friends and family waited and chatted among themselves. After they had once more been blessed, they gave themselves to their guests. Congratulations were repeated and repeated, as were expressions of elation, exchanges of affection, and applause. People came forward in turn and among them was their daughter Maria. Since seeing her and Colin at ARVAH, Arthur had put them quite out of mind. He was content without their company – as far as it was normal routine for him to not see them. She didn't make a big show of her attendance and Arthur could see that she had changed in remarkable ways. Her presence spoke louder than words, and he was grateful for that.

'Hallo, Maria,' he said tenderly to her. 'And good evening to you too, Colin. I'm so glad that you could both be here with us tonight. It means a lot to Jo . . . and to me, too.'

And in the way their eyes replied, it was clear that they were glad to hear his sentiments shared aloud. 'Thanks, Dad,' said Maria, and he knew she meant it. Then her face changed from smiling to something a little more serious – though she still appeared in good humour. She lifted her hand to her face and removed her glasses. She looked at them, then looked at her father's. 'You know, Dad . . . I tried your glasses on once. I was just curious, I guess, to see if they suited me . . .' Arthur smiled reassuringly, a little unsure where the story was headed and why his daughter had decided to share it with him now. 'Well, they didn't fit my face, for starters, but also . . . if I thought my vision was bad before . . .. I couldn't see through them at all! They gave me quite a headache!' And as she finished her story, her smile returned brighter than before.

Arthur didn't know what to say, but felt he didn't need to speak. He simply leaned forward and kissed his daughter's forehead. Then he stepped back, and he and Colin shook hands. Then Colin found his wife's hand and they merged into the line of departing guests.

When the crowd had quite dispersed, and they had met with each and every one of their well-wishers, they readied themselves for home. Freed as they were from etiquette, Arthur could finally allow his attentions to return to Jo. And when he looked at her, and when she smiled when she caught him staring, he knew this was all that mattered.

The rain fell steadily on the journey home and the wipers worked full speed. The headlights cast their beam through the dark while it glistened through the cascading beads of white. As they drove, Arthur looked across to Jo and reached for her hand. They were linked in the back seat, in the dark, by their touch.

When they got home, Arthur and Jo dashed, hunched beneath his coat, to the door. Heaving the door shut behind them, they shed their outer layers, let their first sentry, the lamp, rest and lit a second to start its shift. Then, with Jo in the lead, they made their way upstairs. They washed and got into their pyjamas and into their bed, where, beneath and between layers of sheet and down, they nestled together, body into body, arm over arm, fingers through fingers, breath melding into breath, warmth warming warmth. They shared air and space and heat and touch. And in that way, folded and fitted together, they slept swiftly and soundly to the gentle, hushing rush of rain upon the roof.

22

Change

B y the start of 1986, Jo had been unwell for three months and it
didn't look as though she would recover. She was hospitalised in
Den Bosch, and Arthur stayed with her as often and for as long as he
could. It distressed him to see her in so much pain. She had breast
cancer, and on top of that, her veins were bad. When she slipped on
the steps and her leg was wounded, it would not heal. When it turned
septic, she had to have the leg amputated. But to no avail. Neither
her pain nor her fever subsided. Arthur was instructed by doctors
and nurses, and he was implored by his family and friends, and even
begged by Jo herself, to go home daily to rest. It was during one such
absence that, on a Friday, the third of January, her doctor called to tell
him that it was in his best interest to get to the hospital as soon as
possible. The situation was dire.

When they were face to face, Jo's doctor told Arthur that his wife
would pass away sometime over the weekend. Despite the prognosis
being bleak from the start, Arthur had managed up until that point
to manifest optimism in the strangest ways – though in truth, that
was wishful deception. Christmas had been spent between home and

hospital and their children did their best to visit. Arthur wanted so much to have his wife in the bed they had shared for so long together, warmed by the heat they exchanged beneath the covers on cold winter nights, and to have her lit by the gentle yellow glow of their lamps. They hadn't lived in their new house long, but Arthur wanted her there, cosy and safe, in a place that felt like home all the same. And he wanted to have her watched over by the faces of the friends and family in the photographs that stood on her nightstand and dresser and stared, shielded behind the glass of ornate frames, each one whispering its stories to them as they rested. But despite it all – despite man's medicines and a desperate man's prayers – Arthur had to accept that Jo was where she needed to be, where doctors and nurses could treat her and numb the pain. She could be kept comfortable. And so they endured. They compromised. They resolved that where they could be together was where they wanted to be.

In the company of a few close friends and family, and with Arthur holding her hand, Jo died on Saturday morning, the fourth of January. It felt surreal to Arthur – as though he would eventually wake to find it had all been a strange and horrible dream. He felt that an essential part of who he was had been permanently and irrevocably removed. The world seemed instantly and profoundly darker, colder, as if the pages of a children's colouring book were sapped of the life and colour they had been lovingly, tenderly, carefully, passionately given. It seemed as if her smile was the sun that had shone upon him, selflessly sharing its light and bathing him in soft warmth. He knew the world would never be the same again. How could it be? It had lost a truly beautiful part of what had made it special and worthwhile.

When Monday came, Arthur went to work. It was too much for him to be alone at home. There was an injured emptiness there that affirmed her absence. He had to escape it, at least for a little while.

When he arrived, he faltered. Outside, upon ARVAH's crown, the flag sagged lifeless and limp like a soggy rag set to drip-dry on the line, its red and blue stripes now two shades of grey. Everything was suspended. Everything floated in a fog that dulled the senses.

Given what had happened, the workers were a little surprised to see him. Arthur was half-aware of speech sent in his direction – of a hand upon his shoulder – of expressions of pity, but he couldn't make meaning out of any of it. He'd been told earlier that he should take at least a week's rest from work and spend time with family. Instead, he sought refuge in routine. He hoped that busying himself with work would provide some element of distraction, or at the very least, fill the void he felt consuming him. Arthur thought he knew himself best, but it seemed that while his own death was something he could accept as inevitable, the passing of his wife was one he could never be prepared for.

He remained at ARVAH all that day. Arthur recalled, only vaguely, that Bert came into the factory as well – though he couldn't say when or why. He may have been looking for his father. Or, perhaps, he too sought an alternative to stagnating in a house that was forever filled with the heartrending whimpering of women. Arthur could understand their pain, but the moaning and the sniffling and the jolted, spasmodic breathing, was too much for him to bear. It was like a leaking tap that drip . . . drip . . . drip . . . drips into a basin all night long.

But being at work did nothing for him, either. The day was an empty blur. It was as though his hearing and vision had diminished by half and everything existed in a mute state of perpetual grey. He wandered aimlessly about the floor, into his office and back out again. He picked up the broom. Swept. Put it down. Picked it up. Swept again. And, at one point, to the soothing sound of scuffing, he wept. He kept to himself and he swept and he wept, yet the dull numbness remained.

Days of nothingness passed until, in the place their vows had been sworn and their lives declared as one, and where their children were baptised and where their family was welcomed every Sunday and Catholic holiday, Jo's funeral was held. At two o'clock on Tuesday, they were nestled together, all in the dour colour of death. Even Arthur had traded his white tie for a black one. Between the hallowed walls and beneath the sacred roof of the church of Saint John the Baptist, people gathered from near and far – from across time and place – to remember the life of one wonderful person. Fathomless connections spanning a lifetime of interactions came together in mourning.

The sun did not light the leaden windows – it could not. The censers' scent did not reach his nose – it could not. Arthur sat with Bert beside him on one side, and no one on the other; a vacant space reserved for the void in his heart. Behind him sat his daughters and their families. The priest was perched on high at his pulpit. Arthur watched his mouth move, his finger glide along a line from his book, and his arms gesture upturned palms to the crowd, but he heard nothing – he could not. The priest was new. Arthur didn't know him.

Then, after time passed indiscernibly, they all filed outside and Arthur watched as Jo was lowered to her final resting place. His old friend, Maria, was there. He didn't notice. His daughters were there. They held him. They held each other. Tears were soaked into tissues. Soil was cast upon the casket. Flowers were strewn upon it. And all the while, Arthur longed, in some strange way, for the time to come when he would sleep alongside her once again and forever.

The morning's squall had abated, yet slowly, steadily, snow still fell. The whole place was floured like a baker's board. Arthur's focus had been on the sky until something caught his eye. It was a goudvink – puffed out like a furry pink peach, perched on a snow-capped picket. The little bird darted his black head in all directions as he kept a constant vigil for food and danger. Then, without so much as a chirrup and with remarkable efficiency, he fluttered his wings to the clapping of paper fanned in *subito accelerando*, and shot out of sight into the twitching, needle-like foliage of a snow-powdered pine. How he could have hidden himself so swiftly was beyond Arthur's reckoning – unless he could conceal his colour in a deep-set nest. Even still, he should have been as plain as day to see. It ought to have been like spotting an orange in its tree, its full weight bobbing against its leaves, deep and green. Or like the golden scales of a goldfish sparkling in the still green waters of a pond, its belly brushed by the wispy hair-like algae as it foraged through the shallows. And though Arthur could no longer see the goudvink, he no longer felt alone.

A full month had passed since the funeral, and though he saw little benefit in standing where he was, staring at a cold, grey slab of snow-speckled stone on the lawn lost beneath a crusty layer of ice, he couldn't deny that it brought him some sense of closure. Yet it afforded him no comfort. To Arthur, Jo was very much alive in his house and in his photographs and in his children and in his memories. He didn't need nor want an inscription, a date, a number telling him otherwise. He didn't need the weather and the stone and every other plaque and cross and rectangular rock in the vicinity to convince him that her body was buried beneath him. No. Not while her spirit was above him.

Not while he was alive and she was alive in him. Arthur had come because he was expected to come. It was what others wanted. But all he found was a fact – a certainty that assured him that he could find her here when he couldn't find her anywhere else. He'd known before, but was made to accept with greater persuasion, a logic that could not be ignored. And the case was such that upon every subsequent visit, she would be there. Waiting. As patiently as ever. And in the end, that fact brought him solace.

So he stood for an indeterminate time, staring at the solemn stone. And slowly it stirred something inside him. Like a wooden spoon dipped in a long-rested stew, it disturbed the untouched sediment at the bottom of the pot. It scooped and ladled loss across the earth somewhere at his feet. His body convulsed, as though tugged from the inside, with each sorrowful spoonful fished from him. Then an indefinite, furtive feeling stole over him. It was that same uncanny trick that earlier snapped the line that had tied his sight to the sky. A spherical fluff of red-crested feathers came to rest again, without resting, on the very spot on the fence, that its predecessor had found before. Whether they were one and the same, or if these two were known to each other, he could not tell. Though Arthur searched for some distinctive mark, he couldn't recall the image of the first clearly enough to make the comparison. As before, or like his companion, the little bird jittered and shuffled on the spot before zipping hastily away again into the snow-dusted brushes of the tree. Fleeting and flittering though the visit had been, Arthur mutely thanked him for his company.

Then Arthur was done. He made his way towards the gate. With his hands dug deep into his pockets, his focus turned upon the path and he strode between sculptures that rose in rows. He stepped across the frost, paced the path and pushed out an elbow. He summoned Jo to his mind and she accepted the invitation, and together they left, strolling, linked arm in arm.

Eight agonising months had crept by since Jo's death, and Arthur missed her every second of every day. He tried to help his children go through her things, but he was no help. Hardest of all were her clothes, which hung on their hangers in the wardrobe beside his. There were some that she had never worn, but that she had been excited to wear when the season changed. Some were worn well and would have been worn again. But none would get that chance now. They were all empty of her, though her scent still lingered on them. Memories were worn upon them, woven into the fabric, sewn into the seams. Some happy. Some sad. Some mundane. But every single one was precious. The shoes were the same. Hollow. They stood without feet. Paired together in a neat row. Vacant, throats gaping like the mouths of hungry fish. Bare. Never to walk again.

To pass the time, Arthur kept himself busy doing what work he could at ARVAH, but it was impossible to distract himself for long. He and Jo had been married for more than fifty years. He didn't know how to function as he did before. He didn't know how to talk and act around people or how to occupy himself when he was alone. Quite simply, he had forgotten how to exist, how to live, without her. He would find himself in odd places, not knowing when he had arrived, or how, or why. He felt lost in familiar rooms and spaces. Food had lost its taste. Sleep was sparse and broken. His bed was borrowed, his privy was public, his car and his couch were common. Nothing held the meaning it had held before.

It itched. He scratched, yet still it itched. For weeks, he had let the fur grow thick on his face and he looked like a wild man coated for the winter. And when he saw that same strange man – foreign and feral – in the mirror one morning, he knew he was a man who had given up. He was a lost and careless and lonely and bored and busy and suffering man. He was a tired and weary and old and scruffy shadow of his former self. His face was confused. *Is he me?* Arthur thought. His eyes narrowed and his eyebrows furrowed. *Am I in there somewhere?* He watched himself half-fill the sink with steaming water. His fingers pincered his chin. Then, with soap and dish, he gripped the brush and lathered it thick with cream. He lowered his hand and took a razor to his jaw. He shaved and dipped and rinsed the old Arthur away. And what was him, but wasn't really him, fell in foamy clumps. It floated and sank and mixed about in a sediment like drowned ants, black and grey. Then he pulled the plug and the old Arthur drained away. The tools were rinsed. His face was patted dry with a towel, royal blue, and he was near-new again: itchy-necked and bare-faced and smelling of soap.

He awoke in darkness. The darkness of nautical dawn. And in the near-dark, though his hands were mere shadows in the shade, Jo sparkled like a star – shining, twinkling and simply existing in the purple twilight sky – recasting the light she caught in the golden ring around his finger. And so, without delay, Arthur washed. He dressed. He left.

He caught the train to Mol. It was unlike him, but he knew his destination was fixed. Driving would have distracted him – given him too much room for doubt, too much time in a place that allowed his mind to wander, unrestricted, untethered, free to roam where it wished and where he hoped (though he had convinced himself) it wouldn't. His intention was trained upon its track. Arthur felt fate had waited long enough – *they* had waited long enough, and nothing and no one would steer him from this course.

He sat alone in a small compartment of the train's front carriage. The rear carriages were occupied by people who he assumed were either frequent travellers, families, or the otherwise financially deficient. Arthur favoured a seat with legroom and was happy to pay a little more for the peace and privacy – the teacart being the one exception to the latter. Gone were the days of steam and coal. They were accelerating through an electric age. All the way, the black line ran overhead like a shadow upcast – the catenary wire that invisibly sent surging energy to the engine that roared its gentle roar. The windows and walls rattled as they thrust their way out of the station like a toy pulled along on a string. Crawling, walking, striding, soaring. The koploper's silver belly glided over the rails, the blue sky reflected bluer still in its blue body.

There were only a few stops along the way but each pause allowed Arthur to catch his breath. He was not a well-practised passenger and the lack of rehearsal in the role rendered him unwell. The slick movement of the train felt unnatural. He had to close his eyes from time to time, and focus on objects fixed in the distance to combat the travel illness that made him feel hot and faint. Fortunately, as time passed so too did his discomfort.

Arthur wrapped a white ribbon loosely around his wrist and slowly wound it through his fingers. He thought of the girl who had once worn it in her hair. They were both much younger back then, and yet he had hidden it ever since – kept it boxed up and sealed away. He had thought to show it to her to prove that he had kept it all that time. Perhaps she would know what that meant. It wasn't until late the night before that Arthur had fished it from the shoebox which, among other things, contained every letter she had ever written him. But the ribbon – that singular strip of white fabric – was such a dainty thing for him to hold. It felt almost weightless. And it still smelled of her – at least as much as he wished it to. Soon unlooped, it sat like a scribble in his cupped hands. It felt to him like he was holding a baby bird. It was ready, at last, to stretch its wings, finally free to leave the nest.

The mid-morning sun cast the train's shifting silhouette along the floor outside his window where it flapped like a flag in the breeze – perforated by a shaft of light streaming through the carriage windows. Arthur was mesmerised by the way it slithered across the roadside flora like a speeding serpent. He could feel the same fixation consume him, and he felt driven by purpose. And yet he embraced the occasion to admire the scenery that he so often failed to appreciate when driving, with eyes fixed firmly on the road ahead. Arthur had caught a fresh breeze that quelled his unease and afforded him the opportunity to enjoy the ride. As a passenger, he could select some fixed point at random, like a tree, and focus on it, and watch it rotate on its axis as they approached, aligned front on, and left it behind, in the same place it always was and always would be. In this way he could watch everything pass him by. Fix on something new, then move on, with the scenery changing ever so slightly each time. Fix. Move. Change. Fix. Move. Change. Easy.

The carriage clicked and clacked and skated smoothly along the tracks. All the while, as was his habit, Arthur took to thinking vicariously via a series of conversations he could have with any fellow commuter or worker who happened to gain his company. Each was coupled with an array of conjectures as to the opinion of the people whose eyes he met.

'Hallo, meneer,' the first man might say.

'Good day,' would be Arthur's reply.

'Where are you travelling today?'

'I am on my way to visit an old friend,' Arthur might answer, hoping to avoid further inquiry. But in his mind, he fancied he might make a game of it. 'You see, I wish to fulfil a promise I made to her many lifetimes ago.'

'How interesting,' his interlocutor might respond. Arthur would revel in the mysterious character he had made of and for himself. 'What was the nature of the promise?' the man might add, for in Arthur's fiction he was not shy about prying into a stranger's affairs.

'I plan to make her an offer,' Arthur would say with perfect candour.

His acquaintance's eyes would likely widen at this and he might take a moment to reply – for fear of causing offence. It was in that delay that Arthur found his train of thought had been unexpectedly derailed. But it was no matter, for he could repeat the game with the next person who caught his eye. And if and when his fancy for speculation subsided, he would turn back to the vibrating windowpane, and squint through the rushing line of trees and the flower-flecked meadows, to the swelling skyline beyond and, at least for a little while, wonder what kind of life he could live out there, far from the world he knew. Then he would return to the train, borne once more on the track to his journey's terminus.

Arthur descended a short flight of five or so timeworn, shoe-stained steps, sliding his hand along the slippery smooth steel of the handrail. To the snap of his shoes on the pavement, he exited the station onto a soot-licked city street that teemed with grey-faced people wearing grey clothes under a grey sky. Silver smoke slowly spiralled and kinked from chimneys choked with soot, like pillars connecting Heaven and earth. He hailed a taxi and permitted the driver to carry him to the end of his journey.

Arthur firmly knocked on her door and waited. He straightened his shirt. Adjusted his tie. Felt for the ribbon in his pocket. And waited. He looked at his wristwatch but did not read the time. And waited. Then the world around him shifted. The door opened. And there she stood. There was no more time for waiting. Arthur found her hand and took it in his. Their touch was enough. The wait for it brought the weight of it. The weight of years and years of waiting. Arthur dropped to his knee. He looked at her hand, her fingers and her wrist, and up her arm to her face. His chest rose to his throat. Nerves quaked his hands. She stared back at him, and he spoke.

'Maria. My little kitten. We have known one another for all this time. You have been like a little sister to me. You have always been family. You have always been a friend . . . a dear and irreplaceable friend . . . and our love for one another has taken many forms, and has thrilled and confused us . . . and we still may not completely understand it . . . but for what it's worth . . . I don't think we need to understand it. We know how we feel and I know, without a doubt, that I would be a very happy man, if you would . . . I guess what I'm trying to say is . . . will you be my wife – for what time I have left of this life? Maria van Essen-Peeters, will you marry me?'

Love and loss can make people do crazy things. Throughout his life, from time to time, Arthur had often found himself wondering what Maria held in her heart during the beautiful days of their innocent youth. Arthur needed to know whether he would live to lament again if he didn't explore the possibility of the two of them marrying, should fate provide an opportunity. He needed to know if it was ever too late to love again – if he should withhold his love for her simply to maintain dignity or avoid the disapproval of his family and hers. Dust settles on old age like a lacquer of guilt. People become trapped by habit and forget how to overcome the social conformity they find themselves reliant on. But inside, they have nothing to do but think about every mistake they have ever made, every regret ever repressed, and they circle in a sea of negativity. Perhaps, if the path had been clearer – if the light had been brighter – if the years had been kinder – if he had been but a little wiser, the world would be a better place. Arthur had seen Maria through a haze of wooden light, smiling at Henk . . . and he had seen her devastated by his death. He had seen her in her shop, proud and peaceful, and he had heard the voices of his children singing for Bonma. He saw her in another life, standing as she had once stood before him, bare and brilliant in the blue hues of the moon. And he heard her voice . . . he heard her ask him once more if he could love her as he would love a woman. And he could finally answer her.

Maria had been married to Henk for two months shy of twenty-nine years. After that, she was widowed for a further twenty-one years. In that second life, she must have been lonely. She must have been envious of other married women whose husbands were alive despite their faults and falsehoods. She had served her sentence. She had waited long enough – indeed longer than any woman ought to wait – to let herself love again, to revel in romance, to permit herself to enjoy another man's affections. To know again the kind of love so longed for but always so worth the longing.

And so, in reply to his proposal, Maria spoke not in a feverish, childlike way, nor in a stern, adult way, but in a calm, clear, cheery way of her own. 'Oh, Thurke, I'm afraid I can't quite tell if you're being serious . . . but I suppose it's not like you to joke like this . . . I know you're an honest man . . . and I would love to marry you . . . but isn't it a little crazy? I don't know . . . I think it would be silly, wouldn't it? It would be completely foolish of me . . . to make such a mistake . . .

and I know I would regret it if I said . . . no. So, yes! Yes, Arthur van Hessel. Yes!'

Their words were superfluous, they knew that. They could just as easily have dispensed with the dialogue and forgotten the formalities. If anything, the words got in the way. But they went through the rigmarole nonetheless.

Upon his proposal, Arthur fancied he perceived, beyond its near imperceptibility, that Maria looked to the wedding band that was still on his finger. But he believed that, in that moment, she resolved to always accept it as a part of him, to think of it as something as permanent as his very heart. She never even hinted at the removal of it. She even confessed that she wanted it there. It helped her to honour her friendship with Jo; to serve as a reminder of the person she aspired to be, in her own way, for him and for herself.

On the twenty-sixth of September 1986, Arthur married Maria. It was a Friday, and the world was bathed in the hues of early autumn. Arthur was two months shy of eighty. Maria was seventy-four. They both knew there was an agreeable frame of age that they were both well beyond. The summer of their youth had already been spent and taken from them and Time, in all its selfishness, in its endless avarice, was not about to return it. Maria was no longer the child that scampered about the terrace, the wide-eyed kitten that played and purred and pressed itself against him. No, her eyes were the wise, grey eyes of a cat. Her manner was graceful, her nature far more mature.

But they were alone in the world. Whether through chance or fate, they were given the opportunity to live out their remaining days together. And in a way, and in the end, it seemed appropriate that their journeys apart could end where they had started, together.

After Jo died, Arthur had come to rely on Maria's counsel as she had once relied on his. He would call her and find comfort in her words. They were apart, but they could be brought together in the never-realm of technology's electric pulse – they existed, there and nowhere, in its cabled veins. It helped, but a phone call is no substitute for human contact. And in many ways, talking on the phone had seemed to make the longing stronger, the distance greater, the isolation lonelier.

Arthur stood at the altar, staring with a sense of strange familiarity into a sea of half-recognised faces. In his daze, he fancied seeing, several rows from the front, and at the centre of that pew, the face of a young girl he once knew – a girl who had occupied that very space at his wedding all those years ago. He thought back to the young Maria, the innocent and ignorant child he had once known. Their relationship had been different then. She would visit with her family and seek him out and beg and plead for him to tell her a story. She didn't want to hear one from a book. No, she said she could read one just as well herself. Arthur couldn't confirm, with any certainty, why that was the case. Maybe she wanted to hear something from him. Maybe she had hoped he could weave her into a world of their own – to have them exist there together. He was reluctant but she would persist and insist upon it. Even after her parents told her to stop bothering him, to go and play with her sisters or read a book on her own, she would implore, her hand on his knee. And Arthur would eventually give in and spin some silly tale of an adventurous girl facing the world alone, meeting strange creatures and overcoming frivolous challenges along the way.

Before he was permitted to relive any other old memory, the face in the crowd changed to some other girl. Some young person who was really there. And he remembered who he was waiting for. At any time, the girl, who had grown into a woman and whose careworn face he wouldn't allow himself to hold and to heal with silent stares of compassion, would soon be making her way towards him up the aisle, and he could watch her as much as he wanted, and as much as his old heart could bear.

Arthur had discussed it with Bert, but not to any great length. Over time, Bert had become something of Arthur's confidante, and so a few days before Arthur made his trip to Maria, he and Bert sat at the same small breakfast table that had seen them talk over tea so many years ago.

'I don't want to die without the world knowing that there is a second woman to whom my heart belongs,' Arthur said. 'I loved your mother, and *this* doesn't change *that*. But I will not break the promise I made to Maria. I will not falter now. I will not waver. I'm done with regrets. I won't have any more.'

'I know,' said Bert. 'After Mother died, I suspected you would want to spend as much time with Maria as possible. But I must admit . . . I didn't expect *marriage!*'

'It must be marriage,' Arthur replied. 'It simply must be.'

'Please know that I can't completely accept it,' Bert confessed. 'Not now, at least. Not so soon . . . I can't. And I'm not sure others will, either. But I can understand it. I know that wisdom has no bearing where love is involved. For now, the best I can do is respect it.'

And for Arthur, that was enough.

'It will take time for *everyone* to get used to it,' Bert added.

'Yes,' said Arthur. 'I know. All things do.'

Step-together, step-together. In that fashion Maria approached. Her stride was measured but she showed no hesitation. It was while she made her way up the aisle that, for a moment, Arthur permitted himself a second to recall the time when Jo had made the same journey. And in his mind's eye, as he glanced briefly to the unfamiliar girl at her spot in the centre of a pew, he saw Jo, almost the way one might mistake light and shadow for a ghost, only this apparition was far clearer and not at all frightening. On the contrary, Arthur found it to be of great comfort. It might have been simply a fabrication of the mind, but he could picture Jo's face and she seemed to be there to witness the wedding, just as Maria had been once upon a time. The two had merely traded places more than five decades apart. But in his dream's design, Jo didn't appear angry or upset – her posture was not limp with love's deficit. Instead, she smiled her enduring smile of acceptance, as if by that she was openly and wholeheartedly consenting to their marriage. She wasn't disappointed or envious – those traits never existed long in her nature – but rather she granted Arthur this expression of his and Maria's longstanding friendship. She had always known of the pact between them, and Arthur thought that, in some strange way, Jo would have found consolation in their marital union.

The music stopped. Maria had arrived. The veil was lifted and Arthur could finally stare into the kind eyes of his dearest friend. The priest placed her hands in his and he felt their coolness and frailness and nervousness. The priest spoke the words he had to speak and when the time came, Arthur slid the ring onto Maria's finger. Maria slid a ring onto his. And there, next to another, the ring gleamed gold against his skin.

Part V

January 1988

Two gold rings gleamed – yet one wore Time's passage more plainly. They should have been identical in size and shape, but the ring nearest the finger's base was scuffed and scratched, moulded seamlessly into its groove and altogether quite impossible to move – yet the skin beneath it was pure and pale like the white flesh beneath the peel of a potato. The second ring was clearly cleaner – newer – and belonged to the limb in a different way. It was made to be a perfect fit, yet the flesh of the finger, having not endured the years of wear needed to fill in around it, permitted the ring to slide from its spot with relative ease.

With that same hand, Arthur rested his weight on his broom and drew his attention from the past to the present. He had never noticed, or at least not with any deliberation, how naturally his hands seemed to curl around the timber handle – how it felt like an extension of his body. As he studied the broom, he saw, for the first time, how what was once blond pine had been stained grey with sweat where hands had held it. The broom's bristles had been ground down – far from stubble, but at the same time far from the thick, stiff, black brush it had originally been. He could tell many of its fibres had been lost over time, and those that remained had been bent, snapped, scraped and shortened. Arthur felt somehow proud of the broom and the condition it was in. It served as a reminder, or a symbol, of something greater than itself. All things wear out eventually, some quicker than others, and people are no exception.

The buzz and snap and whir of workers and machines that had been drowned out by thought suddenly thrilled Arthur to an awareness of the present. This awareness brought with it the sudden realisation that he was being watched. For a moment, Arthur caught a glimpse of a young Maria, watching him from behind a tree, but as she came into view, she transformed before his eyes into the kind lady he had come to know so well. She was on her way to the workshop floor and it took Arthur a moment longer to realise she was in the company of a young man and woman, both wearing what he had seen people of their age wearing: patterned jumpers and denim jeans and sneakers. It took him another moment still to realise that the man was carrying a baby. The three were smiling and the baby was gazing wide-eyed and stupefied by the strange new sights and sounds.

Maria introduced Arthur to the young couple, which immediately reminded him of the fact that he had been anticipating their visit and should have made the connection much sooner. It was his eldest daughter's youngest daughter, Nicole – his granddaughter – and her husband, an Englishman named Kevin. The baby was their son, Arthur's great grandson, and his name was also Kevin. Arthur couldn't help but look at him. His eyes were an endless blue and he felt he could see Jo's kindness in them. But it was how the baby reminded Arthur of his own children at that age that kindled a deep-seated familial affection.

Their visit was a pleasant one, but it made Arthur remember his daughter Maria. Having the company of youth managed momentarily to ebb the tidal regret that perpetually swelled and subsided in him. Arthur was bitterly disappointed in himself for being stubborn and for not spending more time with her, for not getting to know Colin better, and for not being involved in the lives of the children she raised – his own grandchildren. But even though he harboured regret for not finding forgiveness soon enough, and for delaying it time after time, simply because he couldn't approve of her elopement, Arthur knew, deep down, that he loved her. He loved her when she was born. He loved her when she started school. He loved her when she left home to travel. He even loved her when she told him that she had decided to live in a foreign country, thousands of miles away, with a man he had never met. He had always loved her and always would, and nothing could ever change that.

It was decided that they would continue to get to know each other at Arthur's house. The others went ahead of him as he tidied up. He swept the dross into a dustpan, dumped it into a bin, and gathered his things. As Arthur walked towards the front door, the inner lights made it impossible to see through the glass that had been made black by the night sky outside. The only exceptions were a few twinkling lights observable in the distance, yet they weren't what caught Arthur's eye. The reflection that had been obscured, fragmented and washed out was made vibrant. In it, his white tie and white hair beamed like beacons, their whiteness made bright by the night that swallowed the world outside the glass. The wrinkles of his face were deep and his age was made undeniable. He had thought about it. He had dreamed about it. But despite the way the feeling pained him, he knew there was no going back in time. He could not, would never, relive those days. He smiled. And as he readied himself to step out into the dark, he did not allow his mind to wander into the past. Not again. No. He resisted the pull of nostalgia and just remained, as he was, in the present.

They were seated on couches and armchairs around a coffee table. Coffee cups on coasters hid the windmills and sailboats and flowers printed upon them. The room was gently lit by two buffet lamps with tan-coloured shades. Arthur spoke a little with his company. They posed for photos. Nicole and Kevin fussed over their baby. Maria smiled warmly. Arthur sat amid it all. His English was not as good as it had once been. He wanted to speak with them some more, but somehow he knew that being in this room with them was enough. Being able to see his granddaughter, smiling and cheerful, was enough. And seeing his six-month-old great grandson was certainly enough. Perhaps, he thought, *that* was the answer.

Several weeks later, Arthur woke one morning with great difficulty. His health had deteriorated. He couldn't deny it. He couldn't resist it. He was cold. His body ached. His energy had been sapped – as though his sleep had worked in reverse. He could have lied and told himself that his fatigue would pass, but he knew that no degree of deception could fool his vigour into returning. Rest could not restore. Time could not be tricked so easily. Old age had finally found him and he was fixed in its firm and final hold. Arthur knew that his remaining days were few.

23

Time

I t is easy to change the truth in a painting. Even a photograph can be misleading. In fact, there is no way to ever truly know how we once felt, because even memories cannot be fully relied upon. The only real truth is the one we know now. In our mind, *we* are the painter. And often the subject. We control the weather of our past: the wind, the sky, the rain, the sun, the moon and the stars. We watch the world we make. We dismantle and rebuild. We recreate that which we cannot recall. And all the while, we sit at the precipice of everything.

Sapped of our childhood ambitions, too many of us become mindless vessels for industry. We operate without experiencing real human connection, and we wish away most of our lives, longing to reach that fleeting experience of what it means to be alive. We watch through windows as our lives pass us by. We wait to have a drink with a friend on a weekend, or travel to an exciting place, just so we can forget, for a little while, about the constructs that tell us that we should be working to meet a quota. We complicate things unnecessarily. We create systems, codes, laws and unwritten rules to follow simply, because it brings us comfort knowing that other people do the same.

The same structures for everyone to abide by. The same template to shape us. But at the same time, we thrive beyond our means. We hurtle forward with more sentience than we ought to possess – though not as much sense as we believe ourselves to have – through a world that is magnificent and vast. We shun our instincts, deny our compulsions, led by the belief that our true nature must remain hidden. We slink through the tawny veld, lulled by our desires and ambitions, yet too frightened by our dreams to pursue them. We track over the footsteps of those who came before us, wondering when and whether to stray. We lurk. We prowl. We chase. And then we reach the end. Crawling, walking, running, through the unknown world. We fumble, flail and fall, again and again. From sunrise to sunset, we stand, we climb, we rise. We survive.

As we grow old, life seems to flash by in a steady, incoherent blur, like cobblestones turned to a rushing grey streak beneath the humming wheels of a bicycle. Day. Night. Day. Night. Dawn. Noon. Dusk. Dawn. Noon. Dusk. Summer. Autumn. Winter. Spring. On and on and on. Around and around. We start living in tomorrow, next week, next month and next year, and before we know it, we're old and we find that we're living in yesterday, last month, ten and thirty years ago. But there *are* moments – moments we can't ignore. We become present: all-absorbed, and awake to the now. There are moments that stand out, and when we focus on them, we realise that, like the pavement, life is made up of smaller parts, of pieces put together. These fragments of time, people and places are forever steering us, transporting us, to new and exciting places and sometimes returning us to old ones. Not one of these states of mind is right or wrong; they simply are, as we are. Life and Death and all that fits in-between. Start and end and middle. Point A and point B, and the track that connects them. Every fixed and unfixed mark along the way. Every junction, every passenger, every pedestrian, every other motorist. Every day and every night. Every aspect of the human experience. Little by little. Bit by bit. Step by step. Day by day. Year after year after year. We flourish.

We remember faces: full of joy and wracked with grief, happy and sad, smiling and crying. It comes as no surprise to people who have lived a full life, that in the end, the moments that matter the most are those we shared with the people we love. We cannot remember every detail of the days we spent at a desk, or the time we spent sleeping. Yet life is made up of an infinite series of ordinary, everyday events that are completely and utterly amazing, important and life changing. We wish too many days away, and after a while, we live too much in a past that we can never regain, and a future that may never be. Life ought to be enjoyed while we have it, but it's too easy for a man with a head full of ambition to get caught up in his dreams and to neglect reality. To say there isn't time – that there aren't enough minutes in a day – is folly. Time is *made*. It exists when and how we want it to. It's nothing more than a product of priority and the value placed upon it. Every person determines what they give their time to, whether it be work or family, themselves or others. Time is a currency spent by choice. And yet sometimes we wonder if there really is a point to it all. We watch the world change. We see people go about their lives and we learn that many want to make the most of the time they have, but it seems, for so many, that it gets harder and harder to do so. We fill too much of our day with simply trying to get by. Trying to survive. In the end – the *true* end– we question whether our time here will mean anything at all. And is *that* what we measure purpose against? Do we measure the influence we have? The permanency of what we do? When all is said and done, what difference does any of it make?

In Maria's arms, Arthur drifted through time. He was at peace. Contented. He felt her warmth against his cheek as he was moved by the steady rise and fall of her body . . . breathing. A gentle hand slipped its fingers through his hair to support his head. He thought she may have been humming. But she may have been crying. He breathed her in. It was a familiar, comforting scent. He held it. Exhaled it. Breathed her in again. Held her inside while she held him. And he let her go . . . and breathed her in once more . . . as one last memory filled him . . . one final thought . . . one precious person . . . Jo. It was all Jo. Jo seated upon a bench beneath a sycamore tree, her hair done up, her eyes as blue as the bright summer sky, and she was laughing, and talking. A slight breeze shifted the shade and cast her in golden patches of light, and through it, she was smiling – smiling her kind, loving smile . . .

Epilogue

The evening sun bathed the town in golden light.

Arthur had just finished fitting a pane of glass in a shop front window. He stood back to inspect his work. The glass was glossy and golden as it caught the setting sun.

A bunch of boys ran by as they chased after a bloated old ball. But the glare of the glass made one of them stop. Squinting, the young boy watched as Arthur stowed his tools, grabbed his kit by the handle, and walked away down the street. Slowly, silently, the boy felt something stir inside him – something that bore purpose. He gazed at the glass in awe. His friends and their game were forgotten.

Afterword

Every person has a story that is greater than fiction. After falling ill on the fourth of January, Arthur died at home, in the arms of his second wife and lifetime friend, on the tenth of February 1988. Although I met him, I have no memory of him – I was only six months old. However, the first time *my* father saw Arthur, he was sweeping the floor of the multimillion-dollar company that he had built himself from the ground up. My father's impression was that Arthur was a humble and hardworking man. My Oma, his eldest daughter, always spoke highly of him. I can't say whether or not my portrayals of him and of others are fair or accurate. I admit that much of the truth has been lost and reformed to meet my needs. This is, after all, a work of fiction . . . and more.

Acknowledgments

None of this would have been possible at all, in more ways than one, without my grandparents, Oma and Pa. Without them, the story may have never been told. Likewise, my parents, Kevin and Nicole, and my brothers, Martin and Rhys, for their love and support. Without their encouragement, I may never have found the confidence or motivation to write. My wife, Keisha, for her love and patience. Without her support, I would have never had the time or the belief needed to make this novel possible. Finally, my editors, proof readers and publisher, James, Alex, AJ, Rebecca, and Rommie, for their expert guidance and attention to details. Without their knowledge, I would have been quite lost. So thank you, all of you, for this and so much more.

About the author

Kevin F. Barber grew up in a small town by a littlish lake in rural South Australia. He is kept busy chasing after his children and enjoys a strong cup of tea with a biscuit or three. *ARVAH* is his first novel.

www.ingramcontent.com/pod-product-compliance
Lightning Source LLC
Chambersburg PA
CBHW020336120726
47904CB00002B/424